"Lillard's evocative prose, well-drawn protagonists, and detailed settings result in an inspirational story of romance, faith, and trust."
—*Library Journal* for *Caroline's Secret*

"Lillard is skilled at creating memorable characters with enduring faith, and readers will look forward to the next installment."
—*Publishers Weekly* for *Marrying Jonah*

"There are family and friends, interesting characters, lots of angst and problems, sadness, sorrow, death, anger, insecurity, fear, jail time, reminiscences, tears, disappointments, stubbornness, secrets, laughter, happiness, romance, loving, and love."
—Romancing the Book for *Loving a Lawman*

"This story was so funny and fast-paced, I had a hard time putting it down."
—Coffee Time Romance & More for *Brodie's Bride*

"Amy Lillard never disappoints! Her writing is always fun, fresh, and fabulous!"
—Arial Burnz, *USA Today* bestselling author

"Amy Lillard weaves well-developed characters that create for lovers of romance a rich fabric of love."
—Vonnie Davis, author of A Highlander's Beloved series

"Amy Lillard is one of my go-to authors for a sexy, witty romance."
—Kelly Moran, Readers' Choice finalist

ALSO BY AMY LILLARD

MAIN STREET BOOK CLUB
MYSTERIES
Can't Judge a Book by Its Murder
A Murder between the Pages

AMISH ROMANCE
Saving Gideon
Katie's Choice
Gabriel's Bride
Caroline's Secret
Courting Emily
Lorie's Heart
Just Plain Sadie
Titus Returns
Marrying Jonah
The Quilting Circle
A Wells Landing Christmas
Loving Jenna
Romancing Nadine
A New Love for Charlotte
A Mamm for Christmas, The
Amish Christmas Collection
A Summer Wedding in Paradise,
The Amish Brides Collection
A Home for Hannah
A Love for Leah
A Family for Grace
An Amish Husband for Tillie

HISTORICAL ROMANCE
The Wildflower Bride
The Gingerbread Bride
As Good as Gold, The Oregon
Trail Romance Collection
Not So Pretty Penny
No Greater Treasure

CONTEMPORARY ROMANCE
Brodie's Bride
All You Need Is Love
Can't Buy Me Love
Love Potion Me, Baby
Southern Hospitality
Southern Comfort
Southern Charm
The Trouble with Millionaires
Take Me Back to Texas
Blame It on Texas
Ten Reasons Not to Date a Cop
Loving a Lawman
Healing a Heart

OTHER MYSTERIES
Unsavory Notions
Pattern of Betrayal
O' Little Town of Sugarcreek
Shoo, Fly, Shoo
Strangers Things Have Happened
Kappy King and the Puppy Kaper
Kappy King and the Pickle Kaper
Kappy King and the Pie Kaper

A Murder Like No Author

A Main Street
Book Club
Mystery

Amy Lillard

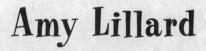

Poisoned Pen
PRESS

Published by Poisoned Pen Press, an imprint of Sourcebooks
P.O. Box 4410, Naperville, Illinois 60567-4410
(630) 961-3900
sourcebooks.com

Library of Congress Cataloging-in-Publication Data

Names: Lillard, Amy, author.
Title: A murder like no author : a Main Street book club mystery / Amy
  Lillard.
Description: Naperville, Illinois : Poisoned Pen Press, [2021] | Series:
  Main street book club mysteries ; book 3
Identifiers: LCCN 2021014764 (print) | LCCN 2021014765 (ebook) |
  (paperback) | (epub)
Subjects: GSAFD: Mystery fiction.
Classification: LCC PS3612.I4 M873 2021 (print) | LCC PS3612.I4 (ebook) |
  DDC 813/.6--dc23
LC record available at https://lccn.loc.gov/2021014764
LC ebook record available at https://lccn.loc.gov/2021014765

Printed and bound in Canada.
MBP 10 9 8 7 6 5 4 3 2 1

To Sarah.
Being brave is hard. Hang in there.

1

HER CELL PHONE STARTED TO RING AS ARLO STANLEY ROUNDED the corner of Main and started toward her bookstore. *Great,* she thought as she shuffled around in her bag trying to locate her phone. Why was it that, every time she needed it, it was always at the bottom of said bag hiding among the empty gum wrappers and random paper clips? Paper clips she never remembered dropping into the tote in the first place.

Truth be known, Arlo and Chloe's Books and More was not simply *her* bookstore; it was so much more than that. Yes, it was a bookstore located on charming Main Street in quaint little Sugar Springs, Mississippi, situated between Memphis, Tennessee, and The Shoals of Alabama. Yes, it bore her name, but also that of her best friend and business partner, Chloe Carter. Chloe was in charge of the *more* part of Books and More, serving up specialty coffee drinks as well as a few baked goods to the locals. Though since her son had moved into her cottage, Chloe baked less and less. Arlo couldn't blame her. Sometimes that's just how things went.

Arlo finally managed to locate her ringing phone and dragged it from the depths of her bag. She checked the screen. Elly. Her nickname for Helen Johnson, the woman who had served as Arlo's guardian when she had needed one—after she had told her nomadic

2

parents that she wanted to make Sugar Springs her forever home. She had been sixteen at the time and desperate for roots. She had moved in with Helen, and the rest, as they say, was history.

"Elly?" she greeted. Thankfully she had picked it up before it had transferred to voice mail. Helen's messages tended to be long and rambling.

"Arlo." The one word was strained. A little choked but firm. It wavered a bit, but sometimes that was expected. Helen was in her eighties, after all.

"What's wrong?" she asked, bracing the phone between her shoulder and her cheek as she shifted everything to one arm so she could get the door. On clear, sunny days like today, when the weather wasn't sweltering hot, she and Chloe kept the doors propped open, but that didn't happen until Arlo came in. Otherwise, Chloe kept them shut tight. This was something that had started last year when Wally Harrison had been found dead on the sidewalk in front of the store.

Arlo used one foot to flip down the doorstop, but the darn thing was stuck. She tried again. "Elly?"

Before Helen could respond, a voice interrupted the quiet street behind Arlo.

"Hold that door." Daisy James-Harrison, widow of Wally Harrison, bustled across Main with a pale pink box in her arms. Since moving to Sugar Springs, Daisy had opened her very own bakery and sweet shop right across from Books and More. Lately, With Sugar on Top had become an unofficial extension of the bookstore, and Daisy's baking skills had nudged Chloe further out of the treats game. Just in the last month or so, Chloe had pretty much stopped baking altogether, and instead Books and More featured a few tasty items from With Sugar on Top.

Okay, so Daisy's muffins were better than Chloe's, though no one said it aloud. And seeing as how Chloe and her son, Jayden, had lived apart for the last couple of years, no one in town begrudged the changes, including Chloe, who came into the store a little later after sending Jayden off to school.

To even things out on the muffin front, Daisy kept only regular coffee and decaf on hand, so if people wanted something more, they had to go see Chloe. So far, the arrangement was working out well.

"Hang on, Elly. I'm just getting to the store." Arlo smiled at Daisy and stood with her back to the door, holding it open as her newfound friend hurried onto the sidewalk.

"Thanks," she called, the words trailing behind her as she passed Arlo and swept inside Books and More.

As usual, Daisy was dressed New York chic in a slinky dress and high heels. Arlo looked down at her own, definitely more comfortable, footwear. Such was life. Though for all her seeming airs and big city ways, Daisy was as down to earth as they came. Looking at her, a person would never know that she had grown up on a mushroom farm in Missouri. But it was the honest-to-God truth. Further proof that truth was stranger than fiction.

Arlo nodded in response to Daisy, having shifted a few things back and once again holding her phone to her ear. "Elly?" she asked, thinking perhaps they had been cut off. Helen had been on the phone for a while and hadn't said a word. Of course, Arlo's attention had been split, as was the way with cell phones.

"I'm here," Helen said, her voice still holding a firm, almost forced note.

"Can I call you back?" she asked. "Things here are—"

"No!" Helen raised her voice. "No," she continued, in a more normal tone. "I'll wait."

Arlo gave a small sigh. She had a busy day ahead of her, and Elly was making her antsy. Plus all the hype that had been going on with the movie premiere. She supposed that all of it was amplified, since despite the hectic feel of this Monday morning, it had been a quiet winter. Arlo and Sam hadn't been on any more dates during these colder months, though from time to time they found themselves at the same party. Sugar Springs wasn't the kind of place you lived if you wanted to keep your dating/love life low-key. But Arlo knew that, despite the dates they had gone on before, Sam couldn't allow his attention to stray too far from his mother these days. After seemingly going into remission, Marjorie Tucker had taken a turn for the worse. Now the whole town waited to see when she would finally succumb.

Mads, of course, was as brooding as ever, but considering the year they had had, the quiet was good for a change. The chief of police had had two murders, which was unheard of in their little town, and he'd had to deal with Arlo's book club thinking that they needed to get involved in the crime solving. But for now, things were back to normal for sleepy little Sugar Springs.

And then there was the book club. Even though they had gone months without a mystery to solve, somehow all the ladies found themselves at the bookstore each day. They were still reading and still arguing over what to read, but these days they found themselves trying to solve the mystery of why Sandy Green, the Realtor, had dyed her hair pink—you know, when her name was green and all.

Arlo shook her head at the memory, flipped the doorstop down—third time's a charm—then she waved to Chloe as she stepped into Books and More behind Daisy.

"Are you ready for today?" Daisy asked Chloe, though she looked back toward Arlo as she said the words.

"Rawk! Big day," Faulkner squawked from his cage. Chloe had left the bird covered when she had come in. Not that Arlo could blame her. She had thought the bird would be a great addition to the bookstore—hypo-allergenic, he could actually "talk" to the customers, and with a name like Faulkner...well, he belonged in a bookstore, didn't he?—but sometimes (okay, more often than not) the Amazon Parrot proved himself to be a pest. He loved attention, loved the people coming into the store all day, and enjoyed his life at the bookstore. Sometimes a little too much.

"Arlo?" Helen asked, her voice timidly seeping through the phone line.

"I'm here." All she heard was silence on the other end. She nodded toward Chloe and Daisy, who had started to talk about the day ahead.

There were two weeks left until the premiere of *Missing Girl*, the movie made from the book written by Wally Harrison, local author, now deceased. And since Wally had died just outside Books and More last year—thank heavens the city finally managed to get the spot on the sidewalk to be the same color as the rest—the event was of great importance to them all. Practically the entire town was on the beautification committee formed to work on restoring the historic Coliseum theater to its near turn-of-the-century (twentieth, not twenty-first) glory.

"Elly? What's going on?" Helen was unusually quiet today, but there was so much happening in the store that maybe she was waiting on a calm moment to continue.

"Just a sec." Her tone was starting to worry Arlo.

"Is everything okay?"

"Gimme a minute." Same quavering voice, same strained note.

Arlo waited for Helen to continue as she made her way through the downstairs section of Books and More and into the tiny office she shared with Chloe. She dumped her bag next to her desk, which was really a table with chairs on both sides, but it served them well.

She slipped out of her light spring jacket and tossed it over the back of her chair. It was that time in Mississippi when the mornings were chilly and a little damp, and then the afternoons turned off warm and humid. Summer was on the way.

"There's a problem," Helen finally said.

Normally Helen wasn't the one for dramatics. Of all the book club members, she was the one with a level head, even more so than Camille, who maintained something of an Aussie-British calm in every situation. Or perhaps that was because she had a mysterious white handbag with heaven only knew what inside. It seemed as if when anyone needed anything, Camille had it at the ready, stored in that mystical white bag of hers. That sort of preparedness would make anyone calm.

No, the hothead of the bunch was Fern Conley, who Arlo was sure must have worked at the FBI or the CIA, or perhaps the KGB. Who knew with Fern? She was as dependable as dirt and as unpredictable as the wind. And like the rest of the ladies in her Friday night book club, Arlo loved her with everything she had.

"What kind of problem?" Arlo asked.

"A problem problem."

Maybe Helen was a little more high-strung today than usual.

"I can't help you if you don't tell me what's going on." She walked back out of the office, pointing to the phone and mouthing *sorry* as Daisy and Chloe looked to her.

"That guy," Helen said. "You know the one."

Arlo bit back a sigh. It seemed the part of Fern would be played by Helen today. "What guy?" she asked as patiently as she could.

Arlo had a full day ahead; she wasn't up for added histrionics. The children from the elementary school were coming over for a mini book fair and book reading, and Arlo had several cases of Wally's book scheduled for delivery today to stock up for the movie premiere. Arlo figured the balance of customers in the area who hadn't read the book yet would surely want a copy now that the movie was out.

"Rwark!" Faulkner screeched. "Let me outta here! Let me outta here. I'm dying over here." The latter was spoken with a New York cabbie accent, though Arlo had no idea where it had come from. The bird was like a finicky sponge absorbing all the bad phrases and habits and leaving the positivity quotes Arlo tried to teach him for the other poor suckers who wandered in.

She gave an apologetic look to Chloe and Daisy, mouthing "Helen" so they would understand, then she made her way over to the bird's free-standing cage. She braced the phone between her cheek and shoulder as she removed the cover and folded it.

"The guy," Helen said again, as if that explained anything at all.

Arlo stuffed the cover in the cubby under the cage and straightened.

"Open the gate! Open the gate!" Faulkner screeched, but Arlo ignored his pleas for freedom. She hadn't seen Sam this morning, but he could be upstairs, which meant Auggie, the orange tabby who lived in his office, could be lurking around. Auggie took every opportunity he could to come down to Books and More and terrorize Faulkner, an activity that had mixed results, seeing as the bird was a good-sized parrot. And this morning, Arlo simply wasn't in the mood for their shenanigans.

"Oh, yeah. Him." Arlo drawled sarcastically.

"Don't get cheeky," Helen said, her voice taking on a hard, nervous edge. "The guy from yesterday."

"Hey, lady," Faulkner called as she moved away from his cage. "Laaaadeeee."

Arlo ignored him once again. "The foreign guy?" As soon as she said the words, she wished she could call them back. She preached to the ladies in her book club constantly about political correctness, and here she went classifying people with terms most might not consider to be respectful.

"Yeah, the one with the accent. He was going around yesterday saying he had proof that Wally didn't write *Missing Girl*."

"I remember." How could she forget?

When she had left Books and More the day before, a crowd had been on its way toward the town square, just a few blocks up Main from the bookstore. It was a typical town square with park benches situated all around, a courthouse with wide concrete steps, and large oaks providing shade on all four corners.

The man, Chenko she believed he said his name was, had been standing on those wide concrete steps that led to the pale brick courthouse, a microphone from a Memphis television station shoved in under his chin. Arlo had recognized several other call letters of stations from Tupelo and Columbus as well as Jackson, Tennessee, and Birmingham, Alabama.

The stranger had claimed he was having a press conference today to tell the world his proof that Wallace J. Harrison had not written *Missing Girl* and that in fact his assistant (and possibly lover) Inna Kolisnychenko had written it.

Gasps had gone up in the crowd from spectators and media alike.

At the time and even now, Arlo wondered what kind of proof he had and, if he did indeed have proof, what it would do the sales of *Missing Girl*. She supposed it could go either way. After all, Helen still owned her cassette tape of Milli Vanilli. She played it and danced around her large boarding house when she thought no one was watching.

As the news reporters tried to get this newcomer to spill his secrets, the man just shook his head. "Tomorrow," he promised in his slight Slavic accent, "I vill show all tomorrow."

"I know him," Helen continued. "He's been staying at the inn."

"Yes." Arlo already knew this as well. Helen had called her right after he checked in to say that he had rented a room for two weeks, obviously planning to stay and make his statement more than once. Perhaps he would even show up and try to ruin the premiere…

"Good morning, all!" Phil from next door sauntered into Books and More for his usual morning coffee. Phil was a good neighbor, even though Arlo wasn't sure how he kept his video rental store open in these times of streaming. Maybe it had something to do with his quarter arcade that drew the younger crowd in after school.

"And he's having a press conference today," she reminded Helen, giving Phil a cursory wave by way of greeting. He waved back, the light glinting off his slick bald head, which was interrupted only by the fringe of dark hair that ran from ear to ear and matched his thick moustache.

"No," she returned. "He's not."

"Good," Arlo replied. They didn't need a bunch of drama to muck up their small-town life. Not with the premiere only a couple of weeks away.

"You don't understand," Helen said. "He's not coming to the press conference because he's dead."

2

ARLO STOPPED DEAD. BAD PHRASING, BUT THAT'S WHAT happened. She was stuck there, rolling the words over in her head as she tried to block out Faulkner's inane chatter and the conversation going on over at the coffee bar. "He's what?" she whispered into the phone. Well, it was more like a hiss, but she did manage to keep it low enough that no one overheard.

"He's dead," Helen said again, this time with a little more confidence.

"And you know this how?" Arlo asked.

"I came to the Coliseum early, you know. I am the Chairman of the Community Restoration Committee." It sounded more important than it truly was. Chairman of the Community Restoration Committee was just a fancy way of saying she got to boss around the citizen volunteers who had promised to help the contractors execute their job in order to get the Coliseum in tip top shape for the upcoming premiere.

"And he's there?" she asked. "At the theater?"

"Yes."

"Not the inn?" Arlo pressed.

Helen ran the Sugar Springs Inn, which had affectionately come to be known as "the inn." It was more than a place to stay serving a supper to guests each night. Her table was always filled mostly with the bachelors and male widowers in their small town who longed for a home-cooked meal.

"No," she said, her voice losing most of its earlier quaver. "He's at the theater."

"I'll be right there," Arlo said.

"Gimme some sugar," Faulkner squawked, making a kissing sound in his throat.

Arlo blew an air kiss in his direction and started for the back room to grab her purse and jacket. "Chloe, I've got to go out for a bit," she said as she made her way through the store.

She grabbed her bag and was back out and heading for the door in less than three heartbeats. She was pulling on her jacket as she aimed her steps toward the front door.

"You just got here," Daisy said with a pretty pout. That was one thing about Daisy, everything she did was pretty, from her hair and nails to the designs she bestowed on the top of her cupcakes and treats.

"I'll be back." Arlo pulled her waist-length, chocolate-colored hair out from under her collar and gave Chloe a pointed look, hoping her friend understood. She couldn't relay what Helen had just told her. Not until she confirmed it to be true. And definitely not with Phil standing there, his watchful brown eyes trained on her. Now was not the time to go spreading rumors.

Arlo and Chloe had been friends long enough that Chloe merely nodded.

"Do you want me to go with you?" Daisy asked, ever conscientious. Maybe she could read Arlo's stressed-out aura. "Oh, shoot. I can't go. I don't have anyone to watch the bakery. And speaking of...I should be heading out."

Chloe thanked Daisy for bringing over the order, though her gaze was on Arlo, concerned, questioning.

As Daisy walked out, Fern Conley strolled in. "Hey, folks."

Arlo wasn't getting out of this one easily, not with the most tenacious member of her book club now in her path.

"Hi, Fern," Chloe said.

Phil was too busy looking at the assortment of treats that Daisy had brought over to pay them much mind.

"Don't touch that bear claw," Fern warned. "It's got my name on it." She started over to the coffee bar but paused midway as if just now noticing that Arlo was on her way out.

"Going somewhere?" she asked, giving a pointed nod toward Arlo's jacket.

Arlo shrugged as if it was no big deal at all. "Just over to the Coliseum to see Elly. Take her some coffee."

Chloe nodded and moved toward the coffee machine to make Helen's usual and one for Arlo to go.

Fern buzzed over to the counter and snatched the bear claw from inside before Phil could decide that he might want it. She took a large bite, then spoke as she chewed. "I'll go with you."

Arlo had seen that coming the minute Fern had stepped inside. And she couldn't very well protest. Any objection she had might start the rumor mill grinding before there was even a rumor to spread.

She nodded at Chloe, who started making Fern a to-go coffee as well.

Phil lingered over the box of treats from the bakery as if the decision he was about to make would affect him for the remainder of his life.

The coffee machine seemed extra slow today, maybe because Arlo was anxious to get over to the theater. What if the man wasn't dead? It wasn't like Helen was an expert in dead bodies. What if he came to and started after Elly?

Well, that might not prove to be any problem. Helen was as statuesque as Jane Russell. Even more so, since Helen had a good four inches on the iconic sex symbol.

What if? What if? What if?

She needed to stop fretting and get going.

Chloe popped the lids on the to-go cups and placed them in a cardboard carrier.

Fern finished off the bear claw and reached for a muffin—cinnamon by the look of it. "Do you think Helen might want something?" She turned to Arlo, then answered herself. "I'll just take her this blueberry one."

Arlo didn't want to say it, but she was fairly certain Helen wouldn't be in the mood to eat anything, especially not in the presence of a dead body…if he really was dead. Maybe she should call Mads first…

"'Kay," Fern said. "Are we walking or driving?"

"Walking," Arlo replied. Immediately realizing it'd be a long walk, she said, "On second thought, let's drive."

Fern palmed the keys to her Lincoln Town Car. "Let's go."

Books and More wasn't far from the theater. Well, in truth nothing in Sugar Springs was far from anything else. Still, walking would have taken fifteen minutes or so, not factoring in having to stop and say hi to anyone they met and running the risk of offending anyone if they cut them off mid-sentence with plans to keep on their way. That was just small-town life. And the drive would take less than five with no chatty pit stops. But after two turns, Arlo was beginning to wonder if maybe she should have insisted that she drive instead of Fern. The woman might be in her eighties, but she maneuvered her car as if she were trying to earn the number-one pole position at Talladega. Six white-knuckled minutes later, Fern parked her car across the street from the Coliseum, the ornate historical theater where the premiere of *Missing Girl* was to be held.

The Coliseum sat on the corner of Main and Johnson. It faced Main, but there were stage entrances on the side street.

"Should we go in the front?" Fern asked.

Arlo had no idea. She hadn't thought to ask Helen where she was in the theater. She had been more concerned about whether or not the man she found was truly dead. "See if it's open." Arlo gestured to one set of the double glass doors that sat on either side of the old-fashioned ticket booth.

Fern pulled opened the first one with ease.

The inside of the theater smelled of new paint and old wood. Arlo wished she had time to check out all the restoration that had been done to the gracious interior of creamy plaster and ornate marble, but she was too concerned about Elly. She hurried across the deep-red carpet toward the large doors that led to the main floor of the theater. Like the doors that led in from the street, there were two sets flanking the concession area, a large extension of the box office. The doors on the left had been propped open, and Arlo directed her steps that way.

"Elly?" she called.

"I'm here," Helen replied.

Midway down the sloped aisle, between the left and the middle rows of wood, iron, and questionably cushioned seats, Helen knelt on the faded burgundy runner that once matched the old-fashioned chairs.

There, between one section of seats and the aisle itself, lay the crumpled body of a man. The same man Arlo had seen yesterday in the town square announcing that Wally hadn't written *Missing Girl*.

Arlo urged her feet to hurry, but they didn't seem to be listening to her brain. Her steps actually slowed the nearer she came to the spot. Fern had no reservations, prodding her from behind to move on.

All her early concerns about the man possibly still being alive were squashed the moment she saw his face. His sharp blue eyes stared at the ceiling, unseeing, unblinking. The worst part was that his head seemed to be turned too far around, his body propped on one side, tilted toward his stomach while his face looked to the heavens.

"Gracious," Fern breathed.

"I guess he fell," Helen said. Her gaze was still trained on the man lying on the worn carpet of the theater. "He fell from the balcony and broke his neck. I came in early to make sure everything was okay for the carpet layers. They're putting in the new carpet today."

As if on cue, a man called from the front of the theater. "Allied Carpet. Anybody home?"

Arlo turned to Fern.

"I'm on it," the other woman said. She paused a moment, then turned on her heel and hustled back toward the theater entrance, still carrying the muffins she had taken from the bookstore. Arlo watched her for a second. The legs of Fern's overalls swished against the ankles of her high-top Chuck Taylors as she made her way to intercept the carpet installers.

Arlo turned back to Helen. "Have you called Mads?"

Helen shook her head.

"I think we should." She reached for her cell phone, averting her gaze so she wouldn't have to look the deceased in the face. It was unnerving, the stare of a dead man.

Helen pushed herself to her feet with surprising grace for one so tall and in their eighth decade on earth. "We only need to call him if this wasn't an accident, right?" She put a hand on Arlo's arm to stop her retrieving her phone.

"I think we should call him regardless of what happened."

"You don't think he could have been murdered?" Helen asked.

"It was the ghosts," Fern said, making her way back down the aisle sans the sack of muffins. She jerked a thumb over her shoulder. "Door's locked now. The carpet people are coming back tomorrow."

"They came all the way from Nashville," Helen lamented.

"And they can come back," Arlo said. Granted, Nashville to Sugar Springs was more than a Sunday drive, but they had more important things to worry about than extra mileage.

"I bribed them with Daisy's muffins." Fern smiled proudly as if she had accomplished a great feat.

"It's the only carpet the historical society would approve for the building," Helen bemoaned. "There are certain specifications, you know." She seemed more than frazzled, as if the prospect of disappointing the carpet installers trumped the dead body at their feet. Arlo was certain it was shock talking.

"And they can come back tomorrow," Arlo repeated.

Fern turned and looked back over her shoulder toward the balcony looming above. "Had to have been the ghosts that did it."

Helen had started to tremble a bit, and Arlo thought it not the time to get into a discussion concerning the supernatural with Fern. "They trusted me," Helen said. She glared down at the man at her feet. "Now this."

She was quickly running through the stages of shock, and Arlo hoped she would be back to herself by lunch, if not sooner. She was a strong woman.

Still, it wasn't every day that you found a dead body.

"Look at those bruises." Fern gave a low whistle.

Arlo had been so concerned about the unnatural angle of the man's head and the unblinking stare of his eyes that she hadn't noticed the dark-purple streaks marring his arms. He was wearing a deep-blue T-shirt, so different than the shirt he had been wearing yesterday. That one was long-sleeved, Western-style with flap pockets and pearl snap buttons. Perhaps she had only noticed because it was so out of place in Sugar Springs. She was sure that a few men around might have a shirt like that, but his was a deep pink with ornate flowers and skulls embroidered on it. His jeans were new and starched, and his cowboy boots were long and pointed. Roach killers, she had heard them called, because when you wore them, you could kill a roach in a tight corner. The outfit would have been perfect...in Texas. But in Sugar Springs it appeared as a caricature of what the man with the Slavic name and strong accent thought Americans would wear.

He still wore the same jeans and boots, and Arlo figured the elaborate pink shirt must be at the inn with the remainder of his things.

"Ghosts don't leave bruises," Helen said firmly.

"We should call Mads." Arlo reached for her phone.

"And tell him what?" Fern asked. "This man is dead. You need to call the coroner."

"Let Mads call the coroner," Arlo said.

Once again Helen reached out and blocked Arlo from using her phone. "I found the body," she said, each word succinct, near staccato.

"Yes, I know."

"But then he'll think I had something to do with it," Helen said, her voice sounding a little desperate.

Arlo almost laughed. Almost. The serious look in Helen's eyes kept the chuckles at bay. "Why would he think that?"

Helen shook her head, her red-tipped braid slipping over her shoulder. "Last night, at the inn, he came downstairs and was really upset about something in his room. He said there were bugs and mice droppings and all sorts of problems with the room I had put him in."

"That's ridiculous," Fern scoffed. "You don't have bugs or mice, and what could be wrong with the room?"

"And?" Arlo prompted, ignoring Fern's interjection. They all knew those accusations weren't true.

"He threatened to leave me a bad Yelp review if I didn't comp him immediately."

"I sure hope you didn't," Fern said.

Arlo looked down at the dead man then quickly away. Like a comped room would matter now. "What did you do?" she asked instead.

Helen took a deep breath before answering. "I asked him to show me what he was talking about in his room, but he said he had already cleaned it up and then threatened me with a bad review again."

"So he just wanted a free room." It seemed to be the entire reasoning behind the complaints.

"But he was down on the main floor," Helen said. "At supper," she added. "I mean, if word gets around—false or not—that the inn is not a clean or friendly place to stay—"

"—then it could ruin the business you'll do during the premiere," Arlo finished.

"And even afterward as well," Helen said. "Who wants to eat at a restaurant that has bugs?"

Fern gave a little shrug. "There is that place over close to the Tennessee state line," she started.

Arlo shot her a *Please be quiet* look that could have easily been read as *Shut up now!*

Fern raised her hands as if in surrender. "Just sayin.'"

"Mads isn't going to think that you're capable of murder," Arlo said.

"I found the body," Helen reiterated.

"We know," Fern replied.

Then something Mads said came back to her. It could have been from years ago, or he could have said it to her last week. She had no way of remembering, but his voice rang strong and true in her memory all the same. "Everyone's capable of murder," Arlo murmured.

Helen sadly shook her head. "I've heard him say that more times than I care to remember."

"He wasn't talking about you," Arlo said gently.

"Everybody means everybody," Fern added.

"You are not helping." Arlo did her best not to yell, but the acoustics in the Coliseum amplified her voice, bouncing her words back at her from several different directions. She supposed that standing over a dead body discussing the murder could have a trying effect on anyone.

"It was suppertime," she said again. "When he was down making all those accusations and demanding his room be free. Everyone heard. Everyone knows he was there and what he was saying."

"Just the people who were there," Fern said. At least she seemed to be trying to make Helen feel better now.

But this was Sugar Springs they were talking about. If two people knew, the entire town was privy.

"Mads is not going to arrest you for murder without evidence."

"He arrested Chloe."

"Fern, please." Arlo looked to the ornate vaulted ceiling as if the answer to keep the woman quiet was hidden there in the shadows.

"He found evidence against Chloe," Helen said.

"Planted evidence," Arlo reminded them.

But worry still puckered Helen's brow, wrinkling it even more than usual.

"We need to call him," Arlo said. They needed Mads on the scene, the dead body cleared away, and a maybe a shot of whiskey for Arlo's nerves. Was it too early in the day to drink? Did the rules fall by the wayside when dead bodies were involved? That would give Emily Post something new to talk about.

"We have to call Mads," Arlo said giving each of them a pointed look before finally reaching into her bag and retrieving her phone. She thumbed it open and found his number, dialing it with a flick of one finger.

"Mads is in your favorites, huh?" Fern said with a grin in her voice.

"Fern, please," Arlo said.

"Interesting," Helen agreed.

Arlo rolled her eyes and waited for Mads to pick up.

"Arlo?" His voice came through the line, strong and confident with just a slight question in his tone. It seemed they talked less and less these days. She wasn't sure what that was about, but they had been friends since she had first moved to Sugar Springs as a teenager, though he had left a couple of years later to go to college, and then went on to pursue his NFL dreams. One blown-out knee and one not-so-successful commentator career later, and he was back enforcing the law and keeping the peace in the tiny Southern town. Like so many, he had tried to escape and was dragged back in. And like those who were just like him, he didn't always understand Arlo's connection to the town or the motives of those who stayed by choice.

"I'm at the theater," she said, trying to figure out the best way to say the rest. "You need to come here."

"Any hint as to why?" he asked, his tone as dry as ever. For a man who was explosive on the football field and diligent when it came to keeping the peace, he was remarkably laid back.

"Uhh…" Arlo bit her lip and decided telling someone about a murder—even if that someone was chief law enforcement officer—was sort of like ripping off a bandage. Best to get it over with quick. "There's a dead body."

3

FERN WENT TO UNLOCK THE DOOR AND WAIT FOR MADS. ARLO moved a little farther up toward the double doors under the pretense of waiting for Sugar Springs's chief of police, but really she wanted to put a little more real estate between her and the deceased. It was those eyes, just staring upward, that unnerved her. As if he were Lot's wife, looking back over his shoulder at...

What? She didn't know. And she was fairly certain that he hadn't fallen as a punishment from God. And she was almost as certain that the ghosts that reportedly haunted the old theater hadn't had a hand in it either. Because...well, they were ghosts.

It was said that a person could come into the theater around midnight, and they could find the ghost of Mary Marie Anderson, a young woman who fell to her death from the balcony back in the thirties. Others claimed to have saw a man in a top hat and coattails wandering up and down the aisles just before a big show was about to start. There were other stories Arlo had heard over the years and forgotten, but it seemed that most everyone over the age of forty had a ghost story of their own centered on the historic building. But no one had said any of the spirits were vengeful or angry.

"I saw it on *The First 48*," Helen said in a quiet voice. "A body doesn't bruise when it's dead."

As far as Arlo knew, that was one hundred percent correct. But she didn't tell Helen that. Instead she said, "His arm could have hit the seats before he landed." Which was also true, but the lines of bruises that mimicked the grip of fingers told another story. And they both knew it. This man had been pushed. Grabbed forcefully and tossed to his death.

The thought was staggering, and Arlo had to lock it away while they waited.

Thankfully Mads arrived a short time later, though it felt as if an eternity had passed.

"Stand back there," instructed Jason Rogers, Mads's second in command, who strode into the theater, camera in hand.

Behind him, Fern rolled her eyes.

Okay, so Jason was a little overzealous and acted as if he was reading for a revival episode of *Hill Street Blues*, but they all knew he meant well. Which is why Mads bit back a sigh as he approached the body. Arlo could tell. He always got this look on his face when he was annoyed but trying not to show it—a little exasperated and hiding that too. She called it his *Please, no* look. But only to herself.

Jason began to snap pictures of the dead man, the flash of the bulb on the camera somehow obscene in the dim theater lights. Those bursts of white made it all too real. A man was dead. A man that no one knew. A man who had come to town to ruin the movie premiere.

That left the suspects list open, from Phil next door to the mayor. Anyone of them could have done this to protect the town, but there were two people who stood to lose a great deal on a more personal level: Chloe and Daisy.

When Wally had died, he had left a third of everything to Daisy. Jayden, his son, had inherited the rest, cared for of course by Chloe. Their relationship might have been over before it even began, but in the end, Wally had stepped up and taken care of his family. Plus he had made enough from *Missing Girl* that Chloe and Jayden were looking for a house; they wouldn't have to worry over much for a long,

long time—maybe not ever, if their investments held out. Meanwhile, Daisy had returned to Sugar Springs and bought the building across the street from the bookstore and opened her bakery. Neither woman was hurting for money, but both still deserved more than Wally gave them. In life and in death.

But was it enough to commit murder?

What was wrong with her? She knew better. Chloe was a kind and loving person. And all she knew, Daisy was the same. Neither one was capable of killing more than a mosquito—and only then if in danger of contracting malaria. They wouldn't be capable of tossing a man to his death. And certainly not for something as vulgar as money. No matter how much they deserved those proceeds.

But still, they could be viewed as suspects.

Mads stood from a crouch where he had been examining the body and pocketed his phone. Arlo had been so deep in her own thoughts that she had watched him pull on rubber gloves, kneel down, and study the dead man as if she were in a dream. But as he removed the gloves and came toward her, reality came crashing back.

"And you didn't move the body any?" he asked her.

"Elly found him," Arlo replied, only then realizing that she hadn't truly answered the question. "I didn't touch him."

He turned to Helen, who shook her head.

"What about Fern?" he asked.

Arlo shook her head. "We were with him the entire time since we called you. No one has touched anything." She said, suddenly aware that Fern was nowhere around.

Please don't let her be snooping up on the balcony.

But even as she thought the small prayer, she knew it to be futile.

Where else would Fern be besides the balcony? And what else could she be doing except mucking up the crime scene?

At least she wasn't down here, frisking the dead body.

Nope, that seemed to be Jason's job. He had stopped taking pictures and was now pilfering through the dead man's pockets.

"Where is Fern?" Mads asked.

"I'm right here." She appeared from behind the last row of seats as if she had been there, hidden by those chairs, the entire time, though Arlo knew for certain that she hadn't been.

"Did you touch the body before we got here?" Mads asked.

Fern shuddered. "Not hardly." Even to Arlo, her reaction seemed a little forced. But that was typical Fern when she was hiding something. What she could be keeping a secret was anybody's guess. As far as Arlo knew, Fern hadn't been left alone with him any time since they had found him. So there had to be something else she was keeping from everyone.

But Arlo knew better to call her out in front of Mads. With Fern, there was no telling what was going on. Best reveal that kind of stuff in private. Or at the very least in the bookstore after Mads had gone back to his office.

"Can we go?" Arlo asked. What more was there to say?

Mads looked at his notes, then nodded. "If I have any more questions, I'll find you at the bookstore."

Arlo nodded, grateful to be released from the scene. Half an hour with a dead body was half an hour too long. But before she could move away, toward the door of the theater, Jason sauntered up the aisle to where they stood.

"Interesting thing," he said, in that cocky way that he had. "This fella is from the same place that Inna was from."

Inna Kolisnychenko. Wally Harrison's assistant, his possible one-time lover, and the Ukrainian beauty responsible for his untimely demise.

"Ukraine?" Arlo asked.

"New York." Jason held up a New York State–issued driver's license bearing the man's picture. Arlo couldn't read it from the distance where they were, but it was definitely the man lying on the theater floor. Dead.

"Of course they are connected," Fern said. "How else would he have this so-called proof that Inna was the author of *Missing Girl*? Maybe they are kin or something."

"Says his name is Petro Chenko. Not the same last name as Inna, but it sounds close. But everyone knows close only counts in horseshoes and hand grenades."

Fern frowned. "Like gas?" she asked. "Don't the Brits call gasoline 'petro'?"

"That's petrol," Mads said. "With an l on the end." Then he shook his head at himself for getting caught up in the drama that was Arlo's whenever-they-wanted-to-meet book club.

Sure, they had started out as a Friday night book club, but seeing as how only the three of them had shown up, they decided they could meet whenever they wanted. Since all were pretty much free to do as they chose—Helen being the exception since she ran the Sugar Springs Bed & Breakfast—they met whenever they felt like it, a.k.a. every day.

And they somehow managed to drag everyone into their shenanigans.

Arlo used the defense of watching out for them, which was the truth, but others, like Mads, wanted her to curb them—okay, outright *stop* them—but the three ladies were cunning and crafty. It took all Arlo had to make sure that her store was taken care of and that they weren't out causing mischief of one kind or another. So from time to time, they did manage to get away from her. Such was life.

"Kolisnychenko," Jason said slowly. "That was Inna's name. Inna Kolisnychenko." His pronunciation was a slightly off, a little more Mississippi than Ukraine, but she knew what he was saying. "So even if he's not kin to Inna..." Jason turned back to the spot where the man lay. "What's he doing here?"

"My thoughts exactly," Fern said. "'Pretty suspicious, if you ask me."

"We didn't," Mads said.

Arlo said, "If it's so suspicious, how come he's the one who ended up dead?" Great. Now she was the one getting dragged into the drama.

"That's right," Helen added. "And I didn't do it because he came into the inn and started complaining about his room last night." The words came out in a fluster as she shook her head so vigorously that her braid swished like it was caught in a hurricane.

"He's staying at the inn?" Mads asked.

"Yes, but I'm okay with whatever he wanted to post on Yelp."

Mads frowned.

Arlo couldn't tell if he was thinking about the case or trying to figure out what the heck Helen was talking about.

"I'll need into his room," Mads told her.

Helen nodded. "Of course," she said. "I can take you there now. As long as you know that I don't mind people making complaints; it's all part of the service business."

Arlo inwardly groaned and did her best to send Elly a telepathic message to shut the heck up!

Mads nodded. "I know. I just need to check his room for any clues to see who might have wanted him dead."

"So he *was* pushed." Fern held up a triumphant hand. "I still say it was one of the ghosts."

Jason scoffed. "Everybody knows that ghosts don't leave physical marks. If they had wanted him dead, they could have used their mind powers to push him off the balcony. A human did this." He gestured behind him.

Mads sighed as someone knocked on the front door of the theater. They turned to find Garrison Smith standing there, coroner for Alcorn County, Mississippi. Mads gestured as if to say, *Be right there.* "As much as I to admit it, Jason's right. This wasn't done by a spirit. We have a human suspect to find."

And only two weeks to find him before Hollywood descended upon Sugar Springs.

....

"Come with me," Helen implored as they walked from the theater.

"Back to the inn?" Arlo asked.

Helen nodded and looped her arm through Arlo's. "I need your support."

Her one-time guardian was a tough nut, competent and strong, but finding a dead body seemed to have thrown her a bit. It was understandable and all, but it worried Arlo all the same. Helen hadn't acted this flustered when they had watched Haley Adams fall down the staircase at Lillyfield just last year, but they had all been together then. Helen had been alone in a reportedly haunted, historic theater. Alone. Wait, she had already mentioned that. But as far as Arlo was concerned, that ratcheted up the creepy factor a hundred percent.

"Of course," Arlo murmured.

"And I'll be right behind you," Fern promised. She looped arms on Helen's other side, and together the three of them crossed the street to where their cars were parked.

"See you there," Fern said and slid into her tank of a car.

Arlo nodded and gingerly climbed into Helen's Smart Car. Arlo wasn't sure how Helen managed to get inside the micro vehicle with such grace given her height, but she did while Arlo felt a little like Gulliver among the Lilliputians.

Helen drove just under the speed limit all the way back to the inn. Mainly because Jason and Mads were in Jason's police cruiser and following closely behind them with Fern hot on their tail.

On the way, Arlo texted Chloe and let her know that she would be a bit longer. She left out all the pertinent details like a dead body and a police investigation, but Arlo knew that, if she said anything, she would have to tell everything, and she didn't have that kind of time at the moment.

"You'll show me his room?" Mads said as they climbed the stairs to the large porch. It wasn't a question, but he had softened his normal stoic, chief-of-police tone so the words didn't sound quite so demanding.

Helen nodded and let them into the inn.

Stepping inside was like coming home for Arlo. No, it was coming home. No *like* about it. She had moved in here at age sixteen and moved out when she was twenty-five, when she bought her own house. Those nine wonderful, stable years—even with all her time away at college—made it the longest she had ever stayed anywhere. Yes, it was home.

Silently Helen led the way to the second floor. She stopped at the first door on the left, sucked in a fortifying breath, then opened it.

Arlo stood next to her in the hallway, Fern slightly behind, as Mads pulled on a pair of rubber gloves and covered his shoes with what looked like paper shower caps. Then he ducked into the room.

Jason started taping yellow police caution tape across the door frame.

Mads stopped, the man's suitcase in hand, and looked back to Jason. "Maybe you want to do that after we search the room."

Jason froze and nodded importantly. "Yeah, sure," he said.

Mads waited a heartbeat. "You want to come join me?"

"Oh, yeah. Sure." Jason patted his pockets, pulled out his own protective gear and put it on, then he looked to the caution tape he had strung across the door. Like a poacher trying to squeeze through a barbed wire fence, he lifted the top band and pushed the lower one down while squeezing through them and into the room.

Arlo supposed that, if the moment hadn't been so tense for her, Fern, and Helen, they would have laughed. Jason tried. He really did, but Arlo was certain he wouldn't make it on a police force outside of Sugar Springs.

So badly she wanted to wriggle in behind him and see what the man had left. Perhaps a clue. Maybe a suicide note. It could have been a suicide, she thought. He could have sustained the bruises even days before he fell to his death. But the theory was flimsy at best. Perhaps she just didn't want another murder in her adopted hometown.

So a suicide is better? she asked herself. Fern must be rubbing off on her.

Something had. Why else would she want to go in behind the police and search a dead man's room?

"And these are all his things?" Mads asked a time later. Arlo and Helen had been hovering in the hallway waiting for the men to finish. Arlo supposed they could have gone downstairs, but Helen seemed glued to the spot.

Helen nodded.

Mads nodded in return. He looked down at the pink shirt he held in his hands. It was the same shirt the man had been wearing at the press conference announcement he had made the day before. Ornate stitching, pearl buttons, bright raspberry pink.

"That is one ugly shirt," Fern said.

Arlo couldn't argue with that. The shirt was definitely—or maybe hopefully—one of a kind, leaving no doubt that the man had been here and changed clothes before going back out to the theater.

"Did he have any strange habits?" Mads asked, leading the conversation back to the investigation at hand.

"He was only here for one night," Helen told him. "He didn't come for supper yesterday, and he never showed up this morning for breakfast." She slowed with each word she spoke, and Arlo knew what she was thinking. Maybe he hadn't come for breakfast because he was already dead.

"What about visitors?"

Helen started to shake her head, then stopped. "He had a visitor," she finally said. "A woman wearing a red dress, but I didn't get a good look at her."

"Hair color, height?"

Helen thought about it moment. "She was slight but curvy. Long, dark hair, but I didn't see her face."

To Arlo it seemed as if she had just described Inna, but that was impossible. So it had to be someone else.

But was it impossible?

It had to be. Murder One wasn't easy to wiggle out of. Even for someone as crafty as Inna Kolisnychenko.

At any rate she decided to keep her deduction to herself. Any claim she made might muddy the waters. Best to leave this investigation to the professionals.

"That sounds like Inna," Fern said. "Dark hair, slight curves." She nodded as if she had just discovered the cure for the common cold. "And since they're from the same place, you know, New York. It's probably her."

"Or maybe not," Mads said, But Arlo could tell he immediately regretted even addressing the thought.

"Right," Fern said. "And just how many Ukrainian immigrants who aren't related could possibly show up in Sugar Springs, Mississippi, population one thousand?"

"Nine hundred and fifty-two," Jason corrected her.

"Fifty-three," Helen murmured. "Susan Atkins had her baby yesterday afternoon."

Fern raised an eyebrow and waited for Mads to answer the rhetorical question. Whatever the population, her point had been made. This man who had fallen to his death, who had claimed he could prove Inna wrote *Missing Girl*, had to have known Inna in some way.

There was no way they were strangers. So just how well did Petro know Inna? And since he was dead and she was in prison, how would they ever find out?

"What are the odds?" Jason murmured.

Arlo shook her head. "C'mon, Elly, let's go get some cake."

"Agreed," Fern said. "All this investigating is making me hungry. You know," she said as they made their way down the stairs. "Someone should call Camille."

Helen shot her a look.

"You know what?" Fern said. "I'll do it." She thumbed her cell phone awake and placed the call just as they got into the foyer of the inn.

"Would you like some cake?" Helen asked Mads and Jason.

"Sure," Jason said enthusiastically.

"No. Thank you," Mads said over him. "We need to head over to the coroner's office. See what else we can find out about this guy."

Jason didn't bother to hide his disappointment.

"Okay," Helen said. "But you know you're always welcome."

Mads smiled. And Arlo realized that was the first smile she had seen from him the entire time that they had been together this morning. Was he getting more solemn, or was his "cop mode" keeping him so stern?

"Thanks, Helen." He nodded toward Arlo and Fern, then herded the cake-less Jason out onto the porch.

"We'll be back this afternoon," Mads warned them. "We'll need to talk to the guests. Make sure they're here if at all possible."

Helen nodded, but Arlo could tell that corralling her guests was the last thing she wanted to do.

4

"WHAT IN THE WORLD IS GOING ON?" CAMILLE ASKED IN HER lilting Aussie accent. She might have lived in America longer than Arlo had been alive, but she still carried the inflections of her home country.

Arlo figured she must have been close by, seeing as how as they walked Mads and Jason out. She pulled her silver Mercedes into the drive at the inn. She got out of the car and hooked her large white handbag over one arm. If Arlo believed in magic, she would have said that the bag had been charmed. It seemed that whatever Camille needed she could pull from the bag at will. This theory was extended as Camille never let it go. She sat with it in her lap even when among friends.

Helen waited for Mads and Jason to pull away before answering. "There's been a murder."

"What?" Her steps quickened until she was almost skipping. "When? Who? What happened?"

Fern hooked one arm over her shoulder. "Come on inside and we'll tell you all about it."

Once the ladies were all nestled around the large center island in Helen's kitchen, Arlo decided it was time to take her leave. Helen had been pretty shaken up earlier, but she seemed to have gotten her bearings back. Now she was dishing out cake, percolating coffee, and filling Camille in on all the details, with Fern's occasional interjection of course. Now was the time Arlo could go back to work and tell Chloe what had happened.

"None for me," she said, holding up a hand as Helen tried to slide a piece of lemon poppyseed and lavender cake onto a plate for her.

"Why not?" Helen asked.

Arlo gave her one-time guardian a gentle smile. "I've got to get back to work."

Helen stopped, thought about it a second, then nodded. "You'll come back though." It wasn't a question. Helen was strong and surrounded by friends, but of course she wanted Arlo there as well. They were close, she and her Elly.

"I promise," Arlo said. "Just call me when Mads comes back, and I'll buzz right over."

That seemed to satisfy Helen. She nodded, and Arlo said her goodbyes.

"Wait," Helen said. "How are you going to get back to the bookstore? You don't have your car."

She was right. Arlo had ridden over to the theater with Fern. She supposed she could walk, but that would take long enough to make it not worth the trip.

"Take my car," Fern said, her mouth full of cake. She dug in the pocket of her overalls and pulled out a set of keys.

"Your car?" Arlo asked. Fern's car was a barge on wheels. There was no way she was maneuvering it on the tiny streets of Sugar Springs.

"She doesn't want to drive that tank," Camille said. She daintily wiped the corners of her mouth and reached into her magical purse and brought out the keys to her vintage Mercedes.

As much as she didn't want to drive Fern's car, she didn't want to drive Camille's twice as much. It was in mint condition and older than she was. And if it got so much as a scratch on it...well, she knew that Camille would just have it repaired, but that wasn't something

Arlo could live with. She was a good driver with a good safety record, but Sugar Springs had more than its fair share of reckless drivers with large, rambling trucks who acted like they owned the road. It wasn't a risk Arlo wanted to take.

"Take mine," Helen said, swiping her keys from the counter where she had tossed them when they had come inside. "You can bring it back when you come over this afternoon."

She would still have to find a way back to Books and More in order to get her own car later, but they could work that out then.

"Thanks, Elly." Arlo took the keys, then kissed Helen's wrinkled cheek. She waited a heartbeat, then wrapped her arms around Helen and hugged her close. "Everything's going to turn out just fine," she said where only Helen could hear. "You'll see."

"I hope you're right," Helen whispered in return, and her eyes swam with tears.

"See ya in a bit," Arlo said.

"Hey!" Fern complained. "No whispering, you two."

Arlo smiled, squeezed Elly's hand, and waved farewell to the other two ladies in the book club.

Driving Elly's Smart Car was a little like driving a tin can. No, that was too big. It was more like driving a ring box with a windshield. But it beat trying to handle Fern's town car or keep Camille's Mercedes pristine.

"Finally," Chloe said when Arlo made her way back into Books and More.

"Hi, Bestie," Arlo said, her tone cheeky. "I missed you, too."

"Welcome back," Faulkner squawked. "Good to see you again."

But Chloe wasn't falling for a guilt trip. "You going to tell me what happened?"

"Only if you'll make me a coffee." Arlo slid onto one of the barstools that sat on one side of the dogleg counter that surrounded the coffee makings.

"Deal." But instead of starting Arlo's favorite mochaccino, she reached for her phone and started sending a text.

"What are you doing?"

"Letting Sam know you're back. He's been down three times to see you. I think he was starting to get worried."

"He's in his office today?" These days it was hit or miss as to whether he came into the third-floor office that Arlo rented to him for his private detective business or whether he worked from home. With his mother's turn for the worse, he stayed close to her as much as possible. After all, she was the reason that he came back to Sugar Springs. Arlo briefly wondered what he would do once she passed. And not to be a pessimist, but that passing looked to be soon. The thought saddened her, and she pushed it away. Her entire day had been like that. One draining emotion after another.

Before Chloe could even answer, Arlo heard Sam's quick, thundering footsteps on the stairs that led to the third floor.

"Arlo," he greeted her as he made his way through the bookstore. He slid onto the stool next to her and breathed a sigh. Of relief, she supposed. Or maybe he was winded from his supersonic trip down the stairs.

"Hey, Sam."

He reached one arm around her and gave her a quick squeeze. The hug was warm and sweet and over too soon, but Arlo wasn't complaining. Every time she got near Sam, her emotions went into hyperdrive. They had a lot of history, she and Sam. And Mads too, but now was not the time to work it out. Not with Sam's mother's health worsening, a movie premiere mere weeks away, and a dead body in the theater.

"So tell us what happened." Chloe slid the specialty coffee in front of Arlo, then presented Sam with one of his own. Then she stood back and sipped her tea, a preference she had picked up when studying in Paris and spending all her spare time in England.

Arlo looked around to make sure none of the customers were listening or lingering too close or needing help with a book, then she turned back to her friends. "There's a dead body in the theater."

"What?" Chloe screeched, drawing the attention of a couple of patrons browsing the shelves.

She closed her eyes and shook her head. "What?" she asked again.

"Well, I suppose he's not there any longer," Arlo corrected. "The coroner came to get him."

"Tell us what happened," she repeated. Chloe's voice rose a little but not enough for the customers to hear.

They weren't so lucky with Faulkner. "Spill it," he called. "Snitches get stitches."

"Where does he hear these things?" Arlo asked.

"Who knows?" Chloe said. "Now focus."

"You know the man, the one who was saying that he had proof Wally didn't write *Missing Girl*? It was him."

"The guy in the ugly pink shirt?" Sam asked.

"I thought it was pretty," Chloe said.

"Now who needs to focus?" Arlo countered.

"How'd he die?" Sam asked.

Arlo drew in a breath. "Well, he either fell or was pushed over the balcony railing."

"And this happened sometime last night?" Sam asked.

"Or this morning," Arlo replied. "Why?"

"I came into the office about ten last night. Mama was sleeping, and I needed to check on Auggie." He gave a small shrug. The cat had taken to office living, and since Sam's mother was sick and allergic to cats, Sam opted to leave the furball in his space above the store.

"And?" Arlo prompted.

"I saw a woman go into the theater," he replied. "I didn't think anything of it. I mean, people are coming and going all the time these days."

True. With all the renovations, there was always someone going in and out doing one chore or another. And there were a lot of new faces in Sugar Springs. Faces that would disappear once the premiere was over and done.

"You don't suppose…" Chloe trailed off.

Arlo shrugged. "Maybe." She thought of the bands of bruises on the man's arms. Such marks would take great strength to make. Could a woman have such a grasp? But it was a little suspicious all the same, her being there. "What did she look like?" Arlo asked. "This woman you saw going into the theater."

"It was dark," Sam said. "I didn't get a real good look at her face or anything. But she had long, dark hair, and she was wearing a red dress. You know, the slinky kind that hugs all the curves."

"It was too dark to see her face, but he managed to check out her figure. Such a man." Chloe rolled her eyes.

But for Arlo, it was too much of a coincidence. The dark hair, the slinky red dress. It sounded considerably like Inna. But it couldn't be. It had to be someone else. But who?

"Have you ever seen her around?" Arlo asked. But she knew the answer.

Sam shrugged. "I'm spending all the time I can with Mama." And that was something Arlo already knew. "And there are so many new people bustling around."

"You should tell Mads," Chloe said.

Arlo agreed.

"I will, but it'll only matter when they figure out the time of death," he explained. "If he died early in the morning, then perhaps there was someone else in the theater. Or before ten, when I saw the woman."

"Fern thinks it was the ghosts," Arlo said.

Sam and Chloe both laughed.

"It was no ghost," Arlo continued. "I can guarantee you that."

"How do they do that?" Chloe asked. "Determine when a person died?"

Sam launched into an explanation that included words like "lividity" and "livor mortis" and "the four stages of death."

It was all a little over Arlo's head. Or maybe she had just had too much to absorb in one day.

"Four stages of death?" Chloe asked. "How that can be?"

Arlo was saved the explanation as the delivery driver arrived with all the extra copies of *Missing Girl* she had ordered. She was taking a small chance that the movie premiere would cause an uptick in demand.

"Gotta work now." She smiled at Sam and slid off the stool.

He smiled back, and she carried her confusion with her to the newly stacked boxes. There had been a time...but that time had long passed. And then last year, she had thought for a moment that Sam might want to rekindle their high school romance, and then his mother's health declined and his attention was centered elsewhere.

And...well, she didn't know how she felt about it anymore than she knew how he did.

She sighed and grabbed a box knife.

"See ya later," Sam said and headed up to his office.

Arlo waved farewell and sliced open the box.

She pulled out a copy of *Missing Girl* and turned it over. Wally's New York black-and-white picture stared back at her. In an instant, she remembered the stack of books she had to mark out of stock because someone had drawn a big black X across the back-cover photo. She had never figured out who vandalized the books, though looking back she supposed it was Inna, his assistant. Inna with the dark hair who liked slinky dresses and said she was the one who actually wrote the book. But that had never been proven, and the man who said he could do it was now lying on an exam table at the coroner's office.

The woman in the red dress had to be somewhere. Though by now she could be halfway to Aruba.

Then again, didn't the experts say the killer usually hung around after the murder, watching the drama and heartbreak they had caused?

She shook her head at herself. She was getting way too involved in something that didn't concern her. But what if it did concern her? Or at least, the people she cared for...

Mads would be able to see that Helen hadn't harmed the man over

a bad Yelp review. So who else would be hurt if the man had proven
that Wally hadn't written *Missing Girl*? As far as financial hurt went,
the list was short, and it included two of the people she loved most in
this world: Chloe and Daisy.

....

The following day, the media descended on Sugar Springs. There
were news crews from as far away as Jackson, Mississippi, strolling
about the town, ready to pounce on anyone who might have news
about the murder. Soon the whole world would know about the dead
man in the haunted theater. Who knew what would happen then?

Arlo stayed at Books and More until Andy came in, then made her
escape to the inn. Andy Baker, Sam's nephew, had been working at
Books and More for several months now. Arlo had hired him last year
to fill in when needed. After struggling at Auburn, Andy came home
to Sugar Springs and now, like the rest of the family, was waiting to see
when his grandmother would give up her fight. And despite all the
trials in his life, Andy was a hard worker. And he had managed to take
a few online courses through a local community college. More than
that, he had been a big help to Arlo, allowing her a little more freedom.
She loved her bookstore. It'd been a long dream of hers. But even the
realization of a dream deserved a little time off. And Andy was a good
addition to the crew—strong, young, and a little nerdy in a hipster
sort of way. Arlo was glad that she had his help during times like these.

Mads had set up downstairs in the common room of the inn. It
was a large room just off the foyer with pocket doors and a vaulted
ceiling. It boasted a long table that could seat ten, twelve in a pinch,
and was usually where the guests of the inn enjoyed their breakfast:
muffins, quiche, cinnamon rolls, or whatever Helen decided to make
that day. It was also where the many non-cooks of Sugar Springs came
to eat a home-cooked meal they couldn't get at home. Now it seemed
to be headquarters for the investigation into Petro's death.

Jason of course was in the room with Mads, but the chief of police had made the ladies in the book club gather elsewhere. So they did the best they could, hovering in the kitchen as close to the door that led from the common room as they could be and still manage to look like they had a purpose. None of that surprised Arlo. But what did give her shock was that Veronica Tisdale was seated around the big kitchen island, drinking coffee and ignoring the piece of cake that sat in front of her.

Veronica was Wally's agent. She was beautiful, African American, tall, and willowy, with her head shaved nearly down to the skin. On Veronica, the style was elegant, sophisticated even, but Arlo knew that, if she ever did that, she would look like she'd lost a bet. She couldn't imagine. She'd had no more than two inches cut off her hair at any one time her entire life.

"What are you doing here?" Arlo asked. The moment the words left her lips, she wished she could call them back. She hadn't meant to be so demanding. What was wrong with her today? For heaven's sake, she hadn't even asked the woman how she was doing.

But as beautiful as Veronica Tisdale was, she was just as abrupt. She had that New York get-things-done attitude, not a common mindset in sleepy little Sugar Springs.

"Ms. Tisdale is staying at the inn through the release," Helen said pointedly.

Arlo knew that. She had just forgotten, what with dead bodies and all. Veronica had arrived a couple of days ago, just ahead of the Hollywood crowd that would soon be flocking to Sugar Springs.

"But right now, I'm waiting to be questioned by the police."

Arlo nodded. "Of course."

Veronica pressed her ruby-colored lips together, and Arlo wondered how she felt about all this murder business. She had a lot at stake with this movie premiere. So many of them did. Practically the whole town of Sugar Springs.

"Coffee?" Helen asked, even as she slipped off her own stool and made her way to the electric pot.

"Not for me," Arlo said before her one-time guardian could pour her a cup of the brew. She was jittery enough as it was.

Helen stopped and turned around. "You sure?"

"Positive." Arlo made her way around the side of the island and sat down next to Camille.

As usual, the tiny Aussie was perched on the stool, back straight, mysterious white handbag nestled in her lap, as she ate cake that Helen had served earlier.

"What's that smell?" Arlo asked.

Helen eyes grew wide. "Oh, I almost forgot." She hustled over to the oven, hot pad in hand, then pulled out a tray of beautiful-looking rolls. Beautiful and tasty.

But as delicious as they appeared, Arlo knew what was behind them. Helen was nervous, and when she got nervous, she went on a baking spree. It was therapeutic for her and terrible for Arlo's waist. She'd have to spend more time on the treadmill if Helen remained this nervous until the movie premiere.

"Surely he'll get this thing solved before the movie," Fern said, echoing Arlo's own thoughts. Solving it ASAP. That was key. How could they have Hollywood come to Sugar Springs if there was a murderer on the loose?

"He's working on it," Camille said, as trusting as ever. "Mads is a good cop, and he'll find out who killed that man."

But even as she said the words, Arlo saw the wheels spinning behind those innocent blue eyes.

Helen turned from where she was buttering the top of the rolls, making them appear even more delicious than Arlo already knew they would be. "There's only so many people in Sugar Springs. How many people did the man know anyhow? And we all know that everything he said about the inn was a lie. So why would I do anything to him? Who else did he know in town?"

"Well, if we knew that," Fern started. She didn't finish the sentence; there was no need.

"Maybe it wasn't someone he knew from town," Camille mused.

Arlo looked from one woman to the other, like she was monitoring a tennis match. But she said nothing as the ladies continued their discussion.

"Are you saying there's a stranger in town?" Helen asked. "Someone we don't know and don't even know is in town? I mean, we know who's staying at the inn."

"Maybe this person is staying at the motel," Camille said.

There were only two places to stay if you came to Sugar Springs and didn't have the option of staying in a family member's home—the Sugar Springs Inn and the motel off the highway. And since so many people had been coming in and out of Sugar Springs over the last few weeks—hadn't Helen told her that the carpet people came all the way from Nashville?—how were they supposed to keep up with the strangers in the area?

"It's possible," Camille added. "But that leaves any number of people. Then you have to ask yourself, why would any of them want to kill a Ukrainian immigrant?"

Camille had a point. Whoever killed Petro had either known him or needed the man to stop the news conference he was going to hold the next day.

Again her thoughts went back to the fact that whoever might have killed him had to have a purpose. Which led right to Chloe and Daisy. Both of them stood to make a great deal of money on the movie that was about to be released. But if it was proven that Wally didn't write *Missing Girl*, she supposed someone in Inna's family could sue for the proceeds to go back to them.

Daisy was left a third of Wally's estate and a third of potential revenue coming in under Wally's name, which was motive enough to keep Wally as the rightful author. But the real problem was that Chloe, or rather Jayden, had inherited the remainder of Wally's estate. Considering the fact that Wally signed away all his rights to Jayden before the child was even born and hightailed it to New York in order to make it big, the distribution of assets seemed fair enough to Arlo. And though Chloe and Jayden had enough money now to keep them comfortable for the rest of their lives, Arlo knew that people could do strange things, out-of-character things, when enough money was involved. Or at least that's what the police would think. And rightly so, but this was Chloe they were talking about. Arlo didn't believe that Chloe was guilty for a minute.

Still the motive was stacking up. And that was worrisome for her friend, guilty or not.

"I think I'm a suspect." It was the first thing Veronica had said in a great while, and all the ladies turned to look at her.

She picked up her fork and used it to push the cake to the other side of the plate, then one by one, she scraped the crumbs over as well.

"You're a suspect?" Fern asked. "How?"

"I came here to talk to Daisy about Wally's next book."

Fern clapped her hands together sharply. "I knew it! I knew Wally had another book. What's it about?"

Veronica shook her head, pressed her lips together. "I can't discuss that right now, but I will tell you that it's pretty amazing." She smiled, a secretive smile, sort of like a large cat with a mouse tail hanging out of his mouth, caught in the act but not remorseful. "Completely different from *Missing Girl*."

"Can we read it?" Fern asked.

The ladies all nodded in unison.

Now they want to read books.

Veronica shook her head. "It's just a manuscript really. Not at all ready for publication."

"And how does that make you a suspect?" Camille asked. She finished her cake and was sitting primly back, handbag still in her lap as she waited for Veronica's answer.

"Location. If they can prove that Wally didn't write *Missing Girl*, then the family could sue for everything that he made off of it—fifteen percent of which went to me as his agent. They could sue me for not investigating further into the actual origins of the book."

Fern shook her head. "What a shame."

Helen had finished buttering the rolls and was now standing with her back to the counter facing the island, arms folded across her chest. "I'll tell you what is a real shame. Inna could sue for the money, and then the prison might get all of it."

"What?" Fern screeched.

"It's true." Helen nodded. "I saw it on TV. This man in prison wrote a book, and the prison system sued him for the money in order to pay for the cost of his incarceration."

"That's the craziest thing I've ever heard," Fern said. "And I've heard some crazy things."

"It's true," Arlo said in back up to her guardian. "Not all prisons do, but some prisons can ask for money to help offset the cost of prisoner care." She had read it online. This prisoner had received a low six-figure advance and standard royalties, of which the state in which he was imprisoned petitioned him to turn over to them to pay for his care. The state had demanded ninety percent of the money. As far as Arlo was concerned, she would rather the money pay for Jayden's braces and college than to keep Inna stocked with commissary Twizzlers.

"Well, kiss a pig," Fern said. "I've heard it all now."

Camille circled back to Veronica. "And you'll be ruined," she said.

Veronica turned the saucer around so the cake was closer to her once again. She began to push it with her fork as she gave a small shrug. "I suppose it's a possibility."

"That's not going to happen," Helen said with certainty. Arlo could tell she had been practicing positive thinking, possibly to help bolster her spirits concerning the Yelp review and her own motive—as weak as it was—to kill Petro.

Veronica had managed to push the cake on way to the other side of the saucer without missing a crumb. Then as if she realized what she was doing, she dropped the fork and straightened her spine.

"I wonder how much longer Mads is going to be in there interviewing everyone." Helen took up her coffee cup and refilled it from the pot. Arlo suspected she only did it to have something to do with her hands. She didn't even take a drink of the brew after pouring it.

"I heard him say that he wanted to know more about the woman in the red dress," Camille said.

Fern shook her head. "Every woman in town has a red dress, even Connor Smallwood."

"Don't start on him again," Camille said. "He's a nice man."

"I didn't say he wasn't nice," Fern said. "I just said he has a red dress."

"What he does in his own time is his own business," Camille said.

"Amen," Helen echoed.

"You miss my point," Fern continued.

Camille shook her head. "I get it. Trying to find a woman in a red dress is like trying to find a toothpick in a haystack."

"I think the expression is a needle in a haystack," Veronica corrected gently. Arlo supposed she thought that, with Camille being from another country originally, she didn't quite know all the American idioms.

Camille shook her head. "Needles are shiny. And shiny would be easier to find. But a toothpick in a haystack? That would be nearly impossible."

5

FOR HOURS IT SEEMED MADS AND JASON QUESTIONED THE GUESTS, and the more time that passed, the more Arlo began to worry about Chloe. Not that she thought her friend was guilty, but that Chloe stood so much to lose in this situation. Arlo just had to trust that Mads would do all he could to get to the truth.

How ironic though, she thought, that all the suspects were women. The chief suspects, anyway. Chloe, Daisy, and Veronica all stood to lose a great deal of money, and perhaps even more in Veronica's case, and then there was this mysterious dark-haired woman in the red dress.

Again, Arlo thought about those deep-blue marks on the arms of their victim. Was a woman strong enough to do that?

To Arlo it looked as if someone had grabbed the man by his arms and tossed him over the railing of the balcony. She supposed a woman could be strong enough to do that. A woman in very good physical shape, or maybe one who was angry, or one who had a running start. But she could more see a woman planting her hands flat against the man's chest and toppling him over the railing to the floor below. It made much more sense, but there were no male suspects so far as she could see.

Of course Mads and Jason hadn't said a word. That was odd for

Jason, so Arlo figured Mads had threatened him with unpaid time off if he spouted off anything about the case while they were working it.

Once they had questioned everyone at the inn, they came into the kitchen where the ladies still gathered. Arlo could tell Fern was waiting for any juicy tidbit. Camille was probably feeling the same, but she was too elegant to let it show.

"We're going now," Mads said. "We searched his room for evidence, but we would prefer that you leave it that way for as long as possible. Do not let anyone in or out. Can you do that?" he asked.

Helen nodded slowly. "But I have guests coming."

"He rented a room for two weeks, did he not? That's what I'm hearing from everyone."

Helen nodded. "But he didn't pay."

"I understand," Mads said. "Just give us a couple more days, then I'll release the room. But until that time, leave it as is. Okay?"

"Okay," Helen said.

"Excuse me." An unfamiliar male voice spoke up from the doorway of the kitchen.

They all turned to the newcomer. Arlo had never seen the man before. He was slim with dark hair, and when he spoke, his Slavic accent was so thick you could cut it with a knife. "I come for Petro," he said. He lowered his head as if realizing the English phrase he just used was incorrect. "I come for Petro's items, suitcase."

Helen took a step forward, the innkeeper in her coming out instinctively. "His things? You want Petro's things?"

"*Da*." The man nodded.

"And you are?" Helen asked.

"A friend," the man said.

"Do—you—have—a—name?" Jason spoke in a near shout as if the man would be able to understand English better if it was hollered at him.

"Lord, Jason," Fern said. "He's Ukrainian. Not deaf."

"I am Aleksandr Gorky. I am Russian. Not from Ukraine."

Mads took that time to come forward. "I'm very sorry, Mr. Gorky, but Petro's things are still part of a police investigation. I can't release anything to you. And even when the investigation is over, I would have to have some sort of proof that you're entitled to them."

Gorky frowned. "Entitled?"

Mads shook his head. "Your right. I would need to know why you have a right to pick up his things and take them."

Gorky nodded, though Arlo wasn't sure if it was in understanding or just some sort of knee-jerk reaction to it being his turn in the conversation. "He has no one. Not in America. Not at home."

"What brings you to Sugar Springs, Mr. Gorky?" Mads asked. Even for Mads, the question had a conversational tone, but Arlo could see the interrogation had begun.

"I come for movie."

"You came here for the premiere of *Missing Girl*?" Fern asked.

Mads shot her a look.

Fern shrugged. "Tell me you weren't going to ask that next."

Mads said nothing and turned his attention back to Gorky. "Is that why you're here? The premiere of *Missing Girl*?"

Gorky nodded. "*Da*," he said. "Inna's movie." So this man knew Inna, too.

"The movie premiere is two weeks away," Mads told the man.

Arlo was thankful that he didn't also tell the man that there was no proof that it was Inna's movie, and as far as everyone in Sugar Springs was concerned, it was Wally's.

Still she could see the writing on the wall. His referral to *Missing Girl* as Inna's movie showed where his allegiance lay. Perhaps he was truly a good friend of Petro Chenko.

Gorky nodded as if two weeks in Sugar Springs was no big deal. "I come for the movie."

"Mr. Gorky," Mads started. "I hate to bother you with something such as this, but could you come identify Petro's body?"

The man's English might be stilted—but, Arlo conceded, much

better than her Russian—yet he understood what Mads was asking. She supposed he understood more than he could speak. His already-fair complexion blanched. And that old song "A Whiter Shade of Pale" came to mind. She had never seen anyone lose color so fast. Especially not when they didn't have much to lose.

"If that may help."

"It would help very much."

"Then I will do."

Arlo had to give him points for bravery. Or maybe it was points for friendship. It was hard to know for certain.

"If you'll come with me," Mads said, gesturing toward the front door of the inn even though it wasn't visible from their spot in the kitchen.

Gorky hesitated just a moment before giving a nod and allowing Mads to lead him from the kitchen. Jason and Helen followed behind.

For a moment Arlo wondered about this Aleksandr Gorky. What was it like to be in a country where you spoke so little of the language, perhaps even had no friends? What made a man pick up and move halfway around the world with so little knowledge or support?

She shook her head. She was being fanciful, for sure. So much of the world felt that a better life waited in America. And for so much of the world, a better life could be had if they could only get here. So many never made it.

"And now it's time for this." Fern opened the tiny pouch she carried cross-body and pulled out a piece of paper, smacking it on the island counter as she did so.

Helen returned to the kitchen just in time to witness the display. "And what is this?"

"Well," Fern drawled out, obviously enjoying the attention being centered on her for the moment. "I found this in the balcony at the theater."

"You what?" Arlo tried to keep her voice at a normal tone. "If you found that in the theater, then it's most likely evidence and should be turned over to Mads immediately."

Fern scoffed. "It's not most likely evidence. It is *definitely* evidence. It's a love letter."

Camille daintily sipped her tea and cast a disparaging look at the paper Fern had placed before her. "It looks like *half* a love letter to me."

"Whatever," Fern sniffed. "Half a love letter, a whole love letter. It's still a love letter."

Veronica peered over at the paper. "How do you know it's a love letter? It's written in Russian."

"Or maybe Ukrainian?" Helen added. "Petro was Ukrainian. Right?" She looked to the others for agreement.

Fern and Camille nodded.

Veronica waved a hand in the air as if dismissing the argument before them. "Ukrainian or Russian, whichever it is, I don't suppose you know how to read either language?" Arlo was sure she didn't mean to sound snotty, but between her strong New York accent and her genius demeanor, as well as her superior posture, the words came across a little intimidating.

Not to Fern of course. "I don't need to speak either language to know it's a love letter. Look here, hearts all over it."

That part was definitely true. It seemed as if every line had a heart somewhere on it, and that was just half the letter they had. Arlo supposed there would be double the hearts if they'd had the whole thing.

"Too bad there's no signature," Camille said.

Only the letter S graced the bottom. But with the way the paper had been torn, there was no discerning if there had been a signature or if the single letter was all there ever was. And without the other half, they would never know.

"Too bad," Fern repeated.

"Hearts mean love, right?" Helen mused.

"As far as I know," Fern replied.

"And love can mean passion," she paused for a moment. "What happened today looked to be a crime of passion."

"Just what I was thinking," Fern said.

"The woman in the red dress," Camille added, not one to be left out of a mystery investigation.

And that investigation by these three ladies was something Arlo needed to put a stop to and quick. "That letter is evidence and should go to the police."

"So whoever wrote that letter to Petro was very much in love with him." Helen stated.

"Or Petro wrote the letter himself," Fern said. "To someone else."

"To the woman in the red dress." Helen snapped her fingers.

Camille shook her head. "That doesn't look like a man's handwriting. Men don't write so swirly. And all those hearts."

Arlo supposed Camille had a point. Though all these ideas were ones that Mads needed to come up with for himself. Or Jason. Whoever was running the show. "That letter needs to go to Mads," she said again. She didn't know why she was repeating herself. Maybe with the hope that Fern would step up, do the right thing, and promise to deliver the letter to the police station as soon as possible.

Arlo almost snorted at the thought. Yeah, right.

"So the woman in red wrote that letter to Petro and then pushed him off of the balcony to his death," Helen said. "That just doesn't seem right."

"Maybe it was a Dear John letter," Camille said. "Maybe she was breaking up with him, and he didn't like it. They got into a tussle, and he fell off the balcony."

Fern shook her head. "You didn't see those bruises on his arms."

She didn't think anyone else noticed, but Arlo saw Helen give a small shudder.

"Somebody forcibly pushed him from the balcony," Fern added. "Maybe even picked him up and tossed him over the rail."

Helen shuddered again. But Arlo knew that what Fern said was correct. It didn't take a coroner to figure that part out.

"Wait a minute," Veronica interjected. "Do you have a signature on that letter?"

Fern flipped it over. "Just an S. The rest is torn off."

"One letter really doesn't tell us anything," Veronica said.

"It tells us that the lady in red's first name begins with an S," Helen said.

"If it is her first name," Veronica said. "Could be a nickname. Or a last name. A pet name, even. Without a signature, a translator, or even a handwriting analyst. We don't even know if the letter belongs to either of them, Petro or the woman in red," Veronica continued.

Once again Veronica was spot on.

"It stands to reason, though," Helen said. "How many people speak Russian or Ukrainian in Sugar Springs?"

She had a point, Arlo conceded. It seemed as though chances were that the letter belonged to either the woman in red or Petro or possibly even Aleksandr, and that it had been written for him or by him. But in the big scheme of things, she supposed it could belong to anyone.

"Technically, I suppose, it could belong to anyone," said Fern. "But my money is on Petro."

Arlo nodded. "But I know one thing for certain," she said. "I know who's going to get it next."

....

"You don't have to walk down here with me, you know," Fern grumbled as Arlo marched her down to the police station the following morning.

"Uh-huh," Arlo replied as they continued along.

"Seriously."

"Uh-huh," Arlo replied again. She didn't have to say it out loud. Fern understood. She didn't trust her as far she could throw her when it came to coming down and handing that piece of paper to Mads. Fern and the rest of the book club ladies had gotten a little too accustomed to doing things their own way (i.e., trying to solve mysteries and murder cases when they were supposed to be discussing the latest bestseller). It wasn't like they didn't trust Mads or even Jason to use their skills and protect the town; Arlo figured they were just bored. Their meddling was a natural consequence of sharp minds forced into retirement.

Fern continued to grumble all the way to the police station.

Arlo continued to ignore her.

She opened one of the glass doors of the police station and swept an arm across as if to welcome Fern inside.

"You don't have to open the door and everything," Fern grumbled some more "I'm not going to make a run for it."

"Of course not," Arlo smiled. "Don't say 'and everything.'"

"Made a photocopy of the letter last night. Scanned it into my computer and everything." She marched saucily into the police station.

Arlo rolled her eyes and followed behind.

There was no one in the lobby save Frances Jacobs, longtime receptionist for the Sugar Springs Police Department and star shortstop on city's softball team. Frances was sharp as a tack, but somehow the electronic age had left her behind. She was totally incompetent when it came to the monster computer sitting on top of her desk. She had an old-fashioned manual about size of the Memphis, Jackson, and Nashville phone books combined. She was flipping through pages as they entered. The chain that held her reading glasses around her neck sparkled as she looked up. Frances didn't bother to stand. "Arlo," she greeted. "Fern."

Fern nodded but didn't say anything.

"We need to see Mads," Arlo said.

Frances waved a hand in the direction of the door that led to Mads's office. "Go on in. He's not busy."

Arlo had a feeling that Mads would feel differently about such a statement, but she'd come this far with Fern and she wasn't leaving until he had that half a love letter in his hands.

She rapped lightly on the door and received a gruff "Yeah?" in response.

"It's Arlo."

The door swung open and Mads stood there, almost expectantly. "And Fern."

"That's right." Fern marched past him and into the office. "I have something for you." She said the words as if the whole transaction was her idea.

Mads nodded, though his gaze never left Arlo. "Come in." He stood back and waited as she stepped inside, then he walked around to the other side of the desk.

Arlo couldn't decide whether to stand next to Fern or block the door in case she decided to make a run for it. Arlo had no idea whether Fern actually scanned the half a letter into her computer or not. If she hadn't, it was quite possible that she would make a run for it. That was just Fern's style.

"You have something for me?" Mads asked.

Fern reached into that little pouch of a bag she carried and pulled out the half a letter.

"Only this." She said it as if *this* wasn't anything remotely important and definitely not connected to a potential murder in their town.

Mads's normally stoic, all-business expression changed. His eyes widened and his chin dropped open for a moment before he recovered himself. As fast as it happened, he went back to looking like Mads once again. "And where did you get that?"

Fern shrugged. "I found it upstairs in the Coliseum."

Mads reached into his desk drawer and pulled out a pair of latex gloves. He slipped them on quickly, with practiced ease, then took the letter from Fern. "And you've had this how long?"

Fern shrugged. "Just since day before yesterday."

Mads closed his eyes. Arlo imagined he was counting to ten in order to keep his temper. Not that he was normally an angry man; he just had that cop demeanor, that law-abiding citizen structure and belief system, and when someone trampled on that the way Fern had just done, it didn't set well with him. That was just Mads.

Mads opened his eyes and looked back at the paper he held in his hand, the blue ink almost like marker, the hearts, the unfamiliar language. "All right," he finally said. "Fern, I need to talk to Arlo for a moment."

The woman nodded.

"Alone," he emphasized.

Fern appeared unabashed. She started for the door of the office, pausing once she got there. "And you're welcome." On that note she went back out into the lobby while Arlo faced Mads alone.

"You have got to get control of them." His tone was emphatic, hard, frustrated.

"Why are they my responsibility?" she demanded.

"You started this insane book club," Mads said.

"That doesn't mean I'm their babysitter." She was not going to get mad. She was not going to get angry. She was not going to agree with Mads. Maybe if she told herself that one more time… But she knew in her heart he was just aggravated. There was a lot of stress in the town, what with the premiere just around the corner and now a dead body. She could forgive him this frustration.

Mads took a deep breath, and the inhalation seem to bring him a bit of calm. "I would really appreciate your help. We need to get this murder solved ASAP, and I can't do that if your book club is pilfering clues from the murder scene."

Arlo decided it best not to point out that it was one member of the book club, and it technically wasn't the murder scene itself, she supposed, since the body was found on the first floor and the letter was found on the second floor. And the only two things that tied the victim and the letter together was the fact that it was written in an Eastern European language and the man was Eastern European.

But even in her thoughts her excuses sounded lame.

"Just please," he said. "I know they want to help, but they need to leave this to the professionals."

Arlo nodded. "I understand." And she did. She tried to keep the book club focused on books and only books, and not murders from books and the like, but they were three very stubborn ladies with a lot of time on their hands. And Arlo had a store to run.

"I appreciate it." Mads sounded tired. He actually sounded old and tired and not like Mads at all.

She wanted to ask him if he was okay. If he was sleeping well or if his dog was keeping him awake or if something else was wrong and was making him so stressed. But she decided it best not to delve into his personal life. It wasn't her business anymore. She'd lost that right when she threw Mads over for Sam on prom night all those years ago. And even though, at the time, she felt she'd made a mistake, especially when Sam told her he was leaving town as well, that didn't mean she didn't care about Mads. She always had.

He nodded toward his door as if dismissing her. Typical Mads.

"I'll see you later," she said.

She stepped back out into the lobby to find Fern behind Frances's desk, showing her something on the computer.

"Now what is this again?" Frances asked.

Fern pointed to the screen. "This is where Petro, the victim was from. And this"—she made a wide circle with one finger—"is where Gorky says he's from."

Frances shook her head. "It's been a blur to me since it stopped being the USSR."

"I guess I didn't realize there were so many different little countries in here," Fern said. "Estonia, Kazakhstan, Turkmenistan, Tajikistan."

"Lots of 'stans,'" Frances said.

"*Stan* means *place of* or *where you stand*," Arlo said.

"Where'd you pick up something like that?" Fern asked.

Arlo smiled. "A book. You should join a book club and read one someday," she quipped.

"Hardee har-har," Fern said, then she waved goodbye to Frances and followed Arlo out of the police station, leaving the "stans" and the half a love letter behind.

6

When Arlo and Fern arrived back at Books and More, Helen and Camille were waiting there patiently.

"We promised to go help touch up the paint today," Helen explained. She pulled up the clipboard she had taken to carrying since she had become committee chair and had to organize the volunteers to ensure everything got done before the premiere. "I have you down to help today." She smiled expectantly.

Arlo sighed. She had said that she would help. And she would do her part. It was just that, between murders and trips to the police station, she was getting a little tired. It had nothing to do with the fact that there would be a big circle of caution tape around the spot where Petro's body was found. More than likely the balcony would be taped off as well. It had nothing to do with that at all.

Okay, maybe a little. But she promised to help.

She turned to Chloe. "Andy should be here in about an hour," she said.

"Go on," Chloe said with a flip of her hand. "I got this."

After a not so quick discussion on who was driving and who was riding with whom, they all set off—the book club in Fern's town car and Arlo in her own vintage Rabbit. She wanted her car at hand just in case. Besides, she might not want to stay the entire time. She did have a business to run. Volunteer or not.

As suspected, both wide marble staircases that led to the balcony were taped off with yellow police caution tape.

"Here." Helen handed Arlo a white jumpsuit already splattered with paint. "This will keep your clothes from getting messed up. And for your shoes." She gave Arlo a pair of shoe covers so very much like the ones Mads had used to go into Petro's room at the inn. She quickly slipped into the jumpsuit, pulled her hair out the back, and used the scrunchy she usually kept around her wrist to pull it out of the way. If she had known that she was going to be painting today… Well, that wasn't right. She had known that she was painting today; she had just forgotten. So if she hadn't forgotten that she was painting today, she would've probably braided her hair just to keep it out of the way. As it was, a ponytail would have to suffice.

Helen distributed jumpsuits and shoe covers to the rest of the volunteers, including Camille and Fern. Then everyone was instructed to take one of the small jars of paint and a paintbrush and go through the downstairs, touching up any space that needed a little bit of attention. Cover those spots where someone had scuffed the paint on the wall or maybe even nicked it a bit. The Coliseum was nearly a hundred years old, after all.

Once everyone had their paint, a brush, and instructions, they set to work.

Arlo immediately wished she had brought her earbuds so she could listen to music while she worked. Or better yet an audiobook. She preferred paper, but there was nothing like reading, even when she was doing something else.

Carefully she dipped her brush into the paint. She pushed against the side of the container to keep any excess from dripping, then began on the section she had been assigned. There were a couple of marks where she was, and she went down to get the low ones. Once that task was complete, she stood and leaned back to admire her handiwork. But it didn't look quite right.

Maybe it's the light in here, she thought. It wasn't like the Coliseum was the best lit building in the area. After all, the lights over the chairs didn't need to be well lit. Add in the high and ornate vaulted ceilings and the lights pointing up toward the stage, it made for shadows—plenty of shadows. Yet the shadows seemed to be only where she touched up the paint.

"Elly," she called. Maybe it would dry the same color. But as of right now what she was putting on the wall was close, but not quite the color they needed.

Helen was staring at her own paint as if trying to figure out the same thing running through Arlo's head.

"Something's wrong." As she said the words, the rest of the volunteers stopped painting and started examining the work they had just done.

"It's not right," someone said.

And it wasn't right; it was off by a shade, maybe two, but enough that the paint they had put on the walls created a bigger mess than what they had with the tiny marks and scuffs.

Helen closed her eyes. "The entire theater will have to be painted now."

And she was right. They even had scaffolds with people painting up high. How damage occurred so high in the theater Arlo had no idea, but there it was. One of the scaffold painters climbed down from his perch and came over, shaking his head. "I mixed the paint exactly by the color code you gave me. Are you sure we bought the right brand of paint?"

Helen's brows raised. "That can make a difference?"

The man wiped his hands on the rag he had tucked in his back pocket, then replaced it when he was satisfied with a small amount paint still on his hands. Arlo figured he was the professional of the volunteers. "Yeah," he said. "It can make a big difference. Enough, anyway." And with this he made a sweeping gesture.

Helen shook her head. "I ordered the brand of paint the historical society said I needed to use. I did what I was supposed to do and..." She trailed off.

"Now what?" Arlo asked even though she knew the answer.

"We have to paint the entire theater with the new paint," the man said.

Like they had time for that.

"What about the historical society?" Camille asked. "Will they be okay with the new color?"

"Technically it's not a new color," The painter said.

Helen sighed. "I suppose we can deal with that when the time comes."

"It's the ghosts," Fern said emphatically.

"I got a call from the specialty paint shop in Memphis," the painter continued. "The gold leaf won't be here for another week to ten days."

That was pushing it way too close.

Helen closed her eyes in obvious frustration and anxiety.

"Ghost," Fern said in a singsong voice.

Helen opened her eyes. To Arlo she seemed a little more composed than she had just moments before. "That's not a ghost," Helen said. "That's pure bad luck." She turned to the painter. "Is there any place else where you could get the gold leaf? Maybe Nashville, even Jackson. Mississippi? Not Tennessee."

"I'll see what I can do. It's just that you need such a large amount."

The walls of the theater were framed with cornices and other ornate detailing. And those had, per the original builder, been rubbed with gold leaf to stand out. Winston Benjamin Franks, the genius designer behind the Coliseum, wanted it to be a premiere place for movies and other events. For the time it was elegant in its design, and that design had stood the test of time and survived for nearly a century. Hopefully, with a few good connections, it would be returned to its original glory in time for the showing of *Missing Girl*.

"There aren't really ghosts in here, are there?" a young volunteer asked. She looked to be high-school age, and Arlo figured she was getting some type of theater credit or community service kudos for helping today. But at the mention of ghosts, it looked as if she was rethinking her decision.

"No," Arlo said in what she hoped was a reassuring voice. It didn't help that Fern gave an emphatic "Yes!" on top of Arlo's response.

"Lots of them," Fern continued. "And then the man that just died. It's probably him trying to keep us from showing the movie before his murder is solved."

"Fern, hush," Helen said, echoing Arlo's own thoughts.

"I'm just saying." Fern's tone was defensive.

"It's just a little bad luck," Helen said.

Arlo nodded in agreement.

"None of these problems started until after he was killed," Fern reminded them.

"Bad luck," Helen said. Once again, she briefly closed her eyes, then opened them once more. "Bad timing."

"I'll say," Fern said.

"We're going to need more paint as well, aren't we?" Helen turned to the painter, the professional.

"Looks that way." He turned and gazed up at the balcony. The railing was composed of thick balusters all painted the same color as the walls.

"If you're really careful, you might not have to paint the balustrade and still have enough to get by for the event."

"But it's too close to call?" Helen asked.

The painter nodded.

"What about that man?" Fern asked.

Helen turned from the painter. "What man?"

"The one who came by the inn. The one who wanted Petro's things from his room. Has anybody seen him around?"

Everyone shook their heads. Arlo knew that he wasn't staying at the inn, so he was most likely at the motel. Or perhaps he was driving in from one of the larger surrounding cities, like Corinth or even Memphis.

"What does he have to do with anything?" Helen asked. Her stress was starting to show once more.

"It just seemed like maybe he wasn't too happy about the movie premiere."

"What gave you that idea?" Arlo asked.

"I don't know." Fern gave one of her one-armed shrugs. "Just a feeling I got. He could be shaking up things all over."

Helen shook her head. "He's not responsible for the paint color or the fact that the gold leaf was back-ordered or that we might not get it in time and we have to find another vendor." She looked to the painter for verification, Arlo thought perhaps in hopes that he *could* find another vendor for the gold leaf.

The painter picked at his fingernails.

A sudden crash sounded somewhere off to the left.

The scaffolding that held a large bucket of paint crashed down, sending a wave of not-quite-right beige-colored paint over the last five rows of seats at stage left. Maybe six. The paint dripped down the tops of the chairs covering the upholstery, metal, and wood. It sludged down the slanted floor, covering concrete and carpet alike. The brand-new carpet that had just been laid that very morning. All except for a small strip they had left, sectioned off with caution tape. The strip where Petro Chenko had died.

But the paint had no qualms about running under that tape into the actual crime scene. Any clues that remained there were now most likely lost in a beige wave.

"Ghost," Fern said again.

And this time no one corrected her.

7

THAT EVENING FOUND ALL THE LADIES GATHERED BACK AT THE inn. "I don't understand," Daisy said. "The paint just fell?"

"It wasn't just the paint," Helen explained. "It was the scaffolding. That place where you stand. Something came loose, and it came undone on one side."

"A five-gallon bucket of Beige Delight." Fern nodded.

"I believe the color is called Milquetoast," Helen said.

Like it mattered. There was new upholstery to be found and prayers to be said that they could find something that matched what was already in the theater. And that would take time. Yet time was something they really didn't have.

"And it got all over the new carpet," Camille added.

"That's a shame," Chloe said. Jayden was spending the night with his grandparents, and Chloe was enjoying a night off from motherhood.

Arlo knew there'd been some large adjustments to having Jayden move in with Chloe. They were all trying to get used to the differences. Including Arlo herself. Since Jayden had moved in, there had been no more Sunday morning breakfasts, and Chloe's time was devoted now to homework and walking Manny, Jayden's white bichon frise. The little dog's real name was He-Man, which is what happens when you allow a four-year-old to name the family pet. Personally, Arlo thought it was funny—unique and oh-so-Jayden.

"You don't seriously believe that the theater is haunted?" Veronica asked. Still sequestered at the inn, she was spending quite a bit of time around Helen's kitchen table.

"Of course we do," Fern said. "Everyone knows about the ghosts that live in the theater. And now we have a new one since Petro was killed there."

"This is not a Shirley Jackson novel," Helen said emphatically. "There are no ghosts."

Camille adjusted her handbag in her lap and gave a slight shake of her head. "I'm not so sure anymore. I've never seen anything like that."

"It was a loose screw," Helen said. "And that's all there is to it."

The ladies fell silent for a moment as they each mulled over the events of the day. Well, everyone was silent except for Fern, who was using the edge of her fork to scrape the crumbs of her coffee cake into a pile. She pressed them between the tines of her fork, then licked them off, looking up innocently at everyone who was staring at her. "What?" she asked.

Helen shook her head. "Nothing."

"I want to know about that letter," Veronica said. She was staring into her teacup as she spoke.

"It's with Mads now," Arlo said.

Fern smiled and pulled a copy of it from her pouchy purse.

So she *had* scanned it into her computer. Arlo should have known that she wasn't bluffing, but with Fern one could never be sure.

"Do you honestly think it's a love letter? And whoever wrote it tossed Petro over the balcony railing?" Veronica finally looked up at each one of them, her brown eyes questioning. It was obvious she had never expected such violence in tiny Sugar Springs.

"I could only see that happening if the killer was a man," Daisy said.

It seemed logical with the bruises on the man's arms.

"But it's a love letter," Camille said.

"We think," Arlo said. "We don't know for certain. It hasn't been translated yet."

"Hearts and hearts and hearts," Fern said. "This letter is covered with hearts."

"But that would mean..." Helen started.

"Petro was gay." Camille finished it for her.

Oh no, Arlo thought. *Here we go again.* She was getting weary of being the "PC police" when it came to the book club. They were two decades into a new millennium, and yet these ladies had trouble understanding and evaluating all the changes in the world.

"That shirt," Fern said. "That pink shirt. But I already said this."

"That's a big assumption," Chloe said.

Arlo nodded in agreement.

"It's possible, though," Helen said. "I mean, it's not like any of us knew him at all."

And that was true as well.

Camille braced her arms on the counter in front of her, the metal clasp of her handbag clinking against its edge. "I saw a show on television about gay people in Russia. Well, not all of Russia, but this one place. Chechnya, I think the name was."

"I think I saw this," Veronica said. "Some of the gay people were actually killed if they were discovered, and the government does nothing about it."

"That's tragic," Daisy said.

"Very," Veronica said.

"Petro was Ukrainian," Camille said. "And the man who came to the inn wasn't. He was Russian."

"Very interesting," Veronica said. "The two men know each other."

"Apparently," Helen said. "Especially if he wants to pick up Petro's things."

"I suppose there's no one else to pick them up if Inna is still in prison," Fern added.

But was she? Arlo thought of the woman with the dark hair, the one in the red dress. And she stomped down the thought of contacting the jail to make sure Inna was still there. Would they even tell her? Was it like a hotel and you had to know the room number in order to find out information?

Who knew?

But the description of the woman and the similarities to Inna were hard to ignore. Then add in the fact that Petro came to Sugar Springs to ruin the movie premiere by producing proof that Wally didn't write *Missing Girl*…

"Here," Helen said, grabbing up her phone. "That's easy enough to find out. It's a matter of public record."

"What are you doing?" Camille asked.

"I'm finding out if Inna is still in jail." Helen typed the name carefully into her phone.

"Look at you go." Fern clapped her hands.

"And bingo." Helen turned the phone where they could see Inna's name and the fact that she was still in the Alcorn County Jail.

"Now what?" Camille asked.

Helen shrugged and shoved her phone back into her pocket. "Now we know Inna isn't the woman in red."

For what good it did.

"You know, the letter couldn't be from Aleksandr," Helen said. "It was signed with an S."

"Maybe it was a nickname." Daisy looked from one of them to the other as if for confirmation.

"Possibly," Camille said.

"And we don't know for a fact that he was gay," Veronica said. "Or that he and Petro were involved. It's all speculation."

And it was, Arlo conceded. But that's what these ladies did best.

....

Arlo was in the middle of rearranging the Civil War shelves in the history section when Fern called the next day.

"I found him," she said in a husky whisper as if she were in a closet or under a bed in a room where she wasn't supposed to be. Which, with Fern, either one could possibly be the case.

"Where are you?"

"I'm at the motel. Out on the highway. I talked to the manager here—"

"I'm not really the manager," Arlo heard someone say in the background, "I just fill in on Thursdays."

"Okay. I talked to the guy who fills in on Thursdays," Fern corrected herself. "And guess who's staying here."

"I have no idea," Arlo said.

"Of course you do," Fern said. "You didn't even try to guess."

"Is all this necessary, Fern? Can't you just tell me, please?"

"None other than Aleksandr Gorky."

Fern sounded so satisfied with herself that Arlo hated what came out of her mouth next. "Didn't we already figure out that he was staying there?"

"Not completely," Fern said. "We suspected it. Now I know for certain. He staying here in room 8-B."

"Well, that's good," Arlo said. "Now we know. Thanks for calling."

"You should come out here."

"Why is that?"

"It seems Camille has something on this kid," she said. "The one who runs the front desk."

"Camille is there, too?" Heaven help them all! Hopefully Helen was at the inn and not running around with these two, terrorizing desk clerks and investigating something they shouldn't be investigating.

"He's going to let us into Gorky's room."

"No, he is not," Arlo said.

"He's not?"

"He's not. Because you are coming back here."

"Why would we do that if we can look in this guy's room?"

"Because I'll send Mads out there if you don't."

"Arlo," Fern's voice came across as half-beseeching, half-demanding. "This is a great opportunity."

"Book. Club." It was something Arlo had to remind them of often.

"We decided not to meet today," Fern said. As if that made all the difference.

"Why is that?" They had been meeting practically every day since that first Friday night.

Fern hesitated. Arlo waited. Then finally she said, "Helen's a little wigged out right now."

Wigged out?

"Would you like to define 'wigged out' for me, please?"

"You know how she's been lately. Always worried."

That was true. This movie premiere had everyone on edge. Helen especially, considering she was the one who had discovered Petro's body at the theater.

Arlo smiled as a customer walked into Books and More. She gave him a quick wave, then she nodded toward Chloe in a silent request for her to see to the customer if they needed anything. Hopefully she would just be on the phone for a minute more. With any luck, anyway.

"I know," she replied to Fern.

"So she decided to stay home today and clean. She wants to make sure she gets good reviews."

"And as one of her best friends, why aren't you over there helping her?" Arlo asked.

"Because I'm at the motel finding out about Aleksandr Gorky." Then she stopped. She must have thought about it for a moment. "Oh…" Arlo could almost hear the nod in her voice. "You think Camille and I should be there helping her clean."

Got it in one. "That's right. So get in your car and head to the inn. I'll meet you there in fifteen minutes, and if you're not there in fifteen minutes—"

"I know. I know," Fern said, desperation coloring her voice. "You'll send Mads after us."

"Worse than that," Arlo said. "I'll send Jason."

Thankfully no call was made, and Arlo met Fern and Camille at the inn a short time later.

Just as Arlo was leaving, a woman swept in, willowy with blond hair that just brushed her shoulders. But her face. Right smack in her face she looked just like Alayna Adams, female lead in the upcoming movie made from Wally's book *Missing Girl*.

She was dressed as elegantly as Daisy, too much for a weekday afternoon in Sugar Springs, but with Daisy it was just her style. This woman seemed to have something to prove.

Arlo had done a double take, noting that the characteristic beauty mark, one of Alayna's hallmark features, was a fake. But she still had to look twice, and the woman had noticed.

"No," she said kindly, as if she had been asked many times before. "I'm not her." Her words were practiced and a little condescending as she arrogantly assumed Arlo had mistaken her for someone famous. "I'm Missy Severs."

Arlo didn't miss the emphasis on that first word. As if she might not be the famous actress, but she was someone important just the same.

"I heard you have autographed copies of *Missing Girl* for sale," Missy said.

Arlo nodded. "There are only a few left." Even as they were selling well above cover price, Wally wouldn't be signing any more, that was for certain.

"I'd like a copy, please."

"Of course." Arlo went to the glass case where she kept the few rare books she had in the shop. Not that she was so worried about theft. She was more concerned with coffee stains and dog ears. In the digital age, paper was certainly not as prized any longer. "Is that all?" Arlo asked. "Or would you like to look around a bit more?"

"That's all." Missy didn't bat an eye at her total, simply pulled out her credit card and inserted it into the reader.

Arlo placed the book in the sack and handed it to Missy along with her receipt.

"They're changing the cover, you know." Missy smiled sweetly, and somehow Arlo got the feeling that the young woman felt as if she had pulled off a great heist. "The new one's supposed to have the movie poster on the front instead. That means the old ones will be even more valuable."

Alrighty, then. "I suppose so," Arlo murmured and thanked the woman for coming in, though in all honesty she hoped she didn't run into her again while she was in Sugar Springs.

"Tah," Missy said with a small wave and sashayed out the door.

Out-of-towners, Arlo thought. They were already descending on Sugar Springs, an explosion of famous, almost famous, and ones who wished they were. She just hoped her little hamlet could survive the blast.

Fern and Camille actually made it to the inn before Arlo got there. And she found the three of them in the common room chatting away as if they hadn't almost just broken into a man's room or deserted their friend in a time of need. "I thought we came here to clean," Arlo said as she eyed the coffee cups and dessert plates in front of everyone.

"'Course we did," Camille said.

"You don't have to do this," Helen said. "The inn is my responsibility."

"Oh, but a friend in need," Fern said with a big smile.

They all pushed up from the table, gathered their dishes, and took them to the kitchen. As quick as a wink, they divided up all the chores and set to work. Arlo was a little interested to see what Camille did with her handbag when she was cleaning, but alas the magical, bottomless bag was nowhere around. Chalk that up for another oddity of the day.

Arlo's first chore was washing a few dishes, and the second was to vacuum upstairs. As far as she could tell, everything looked spotless, but Helen had been so frazzled lately, so concerned about reviews and this movie premiere, that Arlo just played along. Though she was a little concerned for her.

She finished up the dishes, then went in search of Helen. She found her seated on the stairs themselves as she ran a polishing rag between the rails of the staircase. Arlo sat down two steps below her.

"Hey," Helen said, but she didn't stop working. It was as if her hands were in a frenzy of their own, separate from the rest of her.

"Are you okay?" Arlo asked.

"Of course." But once again she didn't look up from her task, didn't decrease the speed at which she was rubbing and polishing.

"You don't seem okay."

"I don't?" Wipe. Wipe. Wipe. Polish. Polish. Polish.

Arlo reached out a hand to still Helen's. "No," she said quietly. "You don't."

Helen sighed. She dropped her hand into her lap, and her shoulders drooped as if the tension that was holding them up suddenly drained away.

"Are you going to tell me what's going on?"

They were about a third of the way up the staircase, and Helen looked back over her shoulder toward the second-floor landing, then she turned back to Arlo. "Do you think Veronica is still on the suspect list?"

So that was what this was about. "I suppose," Arlo answered as truthfully as she could. "As far as I know, we all might be." It wasn't something that Mads would discuss with her or anyone. She just knew what she and others had deduced from what they knew of the case. Veronica, like Daisy and Chloe, stood to lose a great deal of money if the movie flopped or if the next book for some reason couldn't be published.

"But Veronica?" Helen asked again.

"Yeah, probably."

"That's what I was afraid of," Helen said.

"Are you worried about the guests or—" Arlo couldn't finish the statement.

"It's just that we don't know much, if anything, about her," Helen said. "I mean, she doesn't look like the type, but—"

"Everyone's capable of murder," Arlo quoted Mads.

"Exactly," Helen returned. "What if it gets around that she stayed here or that Petro stayed here?"

"First of all, I don't believe for a moment that Veronica is guilty. And second of all, for every person who would be turned off by the prospect of staying in the dead man's room, there's probably twice as many others who would think that was fantastic. Plus by the time Mads releases the room, any stigma of the whole thing may have already worn off."

"You don't think Veronica could be guilty?" Helen asked. Leave it to Elly to get hung up on that one thing.

"I don't." But as she said the words, she felt the doubts creeping in. They knew next to nothing about Veronica, only what little there was on the agency website. And a three-paragraph bio was not the door to a man's heart. Or a woman's heart, in this case. It didn't outline her dreams or her passions, her drive, or the lengths she could go to in order to achieve what she considered to be success.

"You do," Helen breathed, the words a bit shaky as she exhaled them.

"Don't go borrowing trouble, Elly."

"I know, I know," she said, then she sucked in a deep breath as if trying to calm her nerves. "It's just at night, sometimes, I lay in bed and think about him and how he looked. Just lying there. And I think about all the people he was going to hurt if he did have proof that Wally didn't write *Missing Girl*. And I think about the town and how it could affect Sugar Springs if proof got out."

"Maybe you should go see the doctor," Arlo suggested. "Maybe get something for your nerves."

Helen looked horrified. "My nerves are just fine," she said. "I'm just a little concerned."

Arlo held up both hands as if in surrender. "All right, all right. But if you need to talk—"

"I know." Helen turned back to the wood railing and begin polishing it once more.

Arlo supposed finding Petro's dead body was a little more shocking to Helen than anyone had realized. Add to that movie premiere and Yelp reviews, and it was no wonder Helen was a little frazzled Arlo stood and started up to the second floor.

"There's a vacuum in the hallway closet upstairs."

Arlo stopped halfway up the staircase. "I know." She may have only lived at the inn part of her life, but she knew it like the back of her hand.

Helen waved her away without looking up from her task. "Well if you know, then get to it."

....

Vacuuming was one of those chores that allowed too much time for the mind to wander. Or maybe it was the constant drone of the vacuum motor. Whatever it was, Arlo kept mulling over everything they knew about Petro and wondering why someone wanted him dead.

Well, she supposed, to the outsider, that the "why" was pretty obvious, that he was going to blow the whistle on *Missing Girl*, and it would affect a lot of money for several people. But she knew those people. Well, most of them—Veronica was the exception. But Veronica was smart, savvy, and so New York. Was she the type that would dirty her hands with something like murder?

But what did she really know about her? Not much. Not like she knew Chloe and Daisy... Neither one could do something so horrendous, despite Mads's theory on murder. She had known Chloe since they were sixteen, and though she hadn't known Daisy near as long, Wally's widow had become a steady, integral part of their community. And a good friend to boot. That left just Veronica.

Arlo vacuumed the empty room at the end of the hall, bypassing the room across from it, which Helen had told her had already been cleaned for a new guest.

The next room was Veronica's. How easy it was to rap lightly on the door, even though she knew Veronica had gone out earlier. Helen had told her that she had seen her leave. The vacuum cleaner still roared out its song as Arlo pushed it into the room.

She had been in the space too many times to count over the last few years (ahem, decade plus) since she had come to live with Elly in Sugar Springs. And the inn looked no different today than it ever had before. Veronica had settled in nicely.

Arlo left the vacuum running while she opened the doors to the chifforobe.

Veronica's New York style stared back at her—elegant slacks, beautifully pressed shirts. A rainbow of scarves bloomed on a plastic tie hanger, holding everything together. And down below, a straight and even row of shoes. All designer labels; nothing suspicious.

"What are you doing?"

Arlo pressed a hand to her heart and whirled around. "Elly, you scared me."

Helen switched off the vacuum and waited for Arlo to answer.

"I'm cleaning," she finally said, lifting her chin in defense.

"Uh-huh." Helen didn't have time to say more as the sound of someone running up the stairs thundered in and around them. It was Fern.

"What's going on?" Fern asked. She was out of breath. She bent in half and braced her hands on her knees as if somehow that would help her get her air back.

"We heard shouting." Camille was right behind.

"We weren't shouting," Arlo groused. "We were just talking over the vacuum cleaner noise."

Fern straightened and looked around in awe. "This is Veronica's room."

"Oh, it is," Camille said in apparent glee.

"What are you doing in Veronica's room?" Fern's bright gaze pinned Arlo in place.

No, not Elly. Just Arlo. She supposed because snooping was so not her thing.

"Did you find anything interesting?" Camille asked.

Helen raised her brows and waited for Arlo to answer.

"Nothing," Arlo said. She closed the door to the chifforobe and pretended to herself that she had never opened it. "Now if you'll excuse me, I have vacuuming to do."

"Would you look-a-here." Fern stood near the nightstand next to the bed. She held up a book for all of them to see.

Under the Buttonwood Tree by Wallace J. Harrison.

"Oh, my," Camille gasped.

"She said it was only a manuscript," Helen recalled.

"It's an advanced reading copy," Fern said. "It says so right here."

"Publishers send those out to books stores and reviewers before the book's release. To get interest up before the publication date."

"Then she lied," Fern said.

Arlo nodded. "She lied."

....

It took all that she had to get the ladies out of Veronica's room and back to their chores.

Fern had to be forced to leave the book behind. "For all we know, she could have a whole case of those hidden in there," she protested.

Arlo knew it was true, but they had already surpassed their ethical boundaries for the day. It was time to shore up and behave a bit.

It wasn't that she didn't want to read the book or look a bit longer to see if she could find any evidence against Veronica. More than anything she wanted to find something that would ease Elly's nerves about Veronica staying there at the inn. But all she had done was make it worse. Veronica had lied about Wally's new book. What else had she not been honest about?

Yellow caution tape still crisscrossed in front of the white door of Petro's room, and as badly as Arlo wanted to go inside, she resisted the temptation. One unsolicited entry a day was enough.

She must've been hanging around with her book club a little too much if she was willing to start solving mysteries on her own. She shook her head at herself and continued her chore, wondering when Helen might decide to get some new carpet for the hallway. It was better to think about that than *Under the Buttonwood Tree*. As a book-seller, heck even as just reader, the book called to her, like the sirens to Jason. But she ignored it and continued her chores.

The rooms all had hardwood with thick rugs tossed about to keep down the noise. Helen had had carpet installed a few years back. Long enough that it was a little shaggier than carpet usually was these days. As far as Arlo was concerned, the short shag carpet was a lot easier on the feet than something like berber. Flat berber had a clean, smooth look that represented the current design aesthetic in a way the shag could never pull off.

Carpet. Yeah. That's what she needed to be thinking about. Not murder suspects. Not advanced reader copies of Wally's book. Carpet. Though it was hard when she was standing right outside Petro's door.

A small clunk sounded as something hidden in the strands of the shag was sucked up into the vacuum. It rattled around for a second then quit. Arlo supposed the vacuum had spit it back out instead of pulling it all the way into the cannister. She returned the handle to the upright position and switched off the machine. Getting down on her hands and knees, she felt around the carpet until she found the offending piece. Probably a rock, she thought as she dug it out of the fibers. But it wasn't a rock; it was an oddly shaped piece of red-colored plastic studded with rhinestones. Somewhat familiar, but she couldn't place it. It was just a little bigger than the head of the pencil with an indention on one side and worn lines on the other. It resembled a slanted rectangle. What was that? A parallelogram? Who outside of fifth grade would know? She shook her head. It was probably something off a toy one of the younger guests had dropped. Some little Lego or a piece of a Transformer. Or maybe even something for Barbie. She really didn't know. But it had a familiar look, though somehow, something about it wasn't quite right. She turned it over in her fingers. It had marks on it like little cuts from its trip into the vacuum or from some other trauma…

What was she doing? She stood and shoved the little piece of plastic into her pocket. What had the world come to if she was evaluating trash? She turned the vacuum back on and finished the hallway, reminding herself to throw the little plastic piece when she was done.

8

ARLO STORED THE VACUUM CLEANER BACK IN THE HALL CLOSET and made her way downstairs. As expected, the ladies had made short work of the cleaning and were now all seated around the kitchen island, coffee cups and dessert saucers in front of them once again. She supposed once you hit eighty, cake every chance you got was a good idea.

"Are y'all eating again?" Arlo shook her head.

"Housework is hungry work," Camille said.

Arlo supposed she couldn't argue with that.

"You want some quiche?" Helen asked. "It's a new recipe. It's got double the cheese, and the crust is made out of Parmesan and cauliflower. I'm trying it out for my low-carb guests."

"You had me at double cheese, then you lost me a cauliflower," Arlo said. She would have been happier with cake. Much happier.

"Come on and try it." Fern patted the stool next to her. "Where's your sense of adventure?"

Arlo didn't have a sense of adventure, not like her family, who seemed to roam around the country taking jobs when they needed money, quitting when they thought they had enough, then moving on to the next town. If that was adventure, leave her out of it. She would rather get her thrills from reading any day. And when cauliflower was involved...

"Come on," Fern said again, patting the stool next to her once more.

Arlo washed her hands and reluctantly took up her place on the stool next to Fern.

Helen cut her a slice of the experimental quiche and slid it over to her.

"We were just talking about Petro," Camille said. Surprise surprise. The magic handbag had turned up and was sitting primly in Camille's lap at that very moment. "And the m-u-r-d-e-r."

Fern scoffed. "Camille, you're a jewel. Why are you spelling it when we're all adults here?"

Camille shrugged and sniffed lightly. "It's just such a harsh word."

"It was just such a harsh action." Fern added.

"Hear, hear," Helen said.

Arlo forked up a bite of quiche then hesitantly put it into her mouth. She supposed it wasn't horrible, but at the sound of the word *murder*, she shuddered.

"Oh, it's not all that bad," Fern said.

Arlo managed to swallow. She had grown up eating new foods, but she found that she preferred more traditional dishes. Like a quiche with the crust made from…crust. But the shudder wasn't for Helen's efforts. "Oh, no," she said. "It's just Petro."

Fern leaned in so that only Arlo could hear. "Nice save."

Maybe if she just ate the top part of the quiche and left the crust. Yeah, maybe that would work.

"Why do you want to talk about his murder so badly?" Arlo asked. "Wouldn't it be better to talk about the murder from a book?" Any book.

"Speaking of," Helen started, "I think we should ask Veronica about Wally's new book. You know, I'd be a good beta reader."

The other two women erupted with their own qualifications to read for Veronica.

"Do not ask her about that book," Arlo told them.

A chorus of protests went up all around.

"If you ask her, then she might suspect that you've been in her room."

Helen cleared her throat.

"*We've* been in her room,"' Arlo corrected.

Helen smiled and gave her a little nod.

"So we'll have to figure out some other way to get her to share it with us," Fern mused.

Good luck with that.

Arlo didn't think Veronica was going to let them anywhere near Wally's new book.

"Do you think Wally really wrote this new book?" Fern asked.

She didn't ask if they thought Wally had written the first book. None of them did. Though none of them were talking about that. What's done is done, they had decided. And for that, Arlo was glad. With the majority of the profits from book sales going to Jayden, he could go to college where he wanted and not have to worry about grants, scholarships, or student loans like the rest of the world. He could concentrate on his studies, make something good of himself, and maybe even write a book of his own.

"I think he always wanted to write something," Camille said. Arlo had somehow pushed the fact that Camille had taught Wally to the back of her mind, which was strange because Camille had pretty much taught or tutored everyone over the age of thirty in Sugar Springs.

"He had a contract, you know," Daisy stood at the entrance to the inn's kitchen.

The chorus of greetings went up all around.

"What are you doing out here?" Helen asked as Daisy smiled and somehow managed to wiggle out of trying the cauliflower crust quiche.

"I came to check on Arlo." She shot Arlo an apologetic look. "Chloe was worried. She tried to call you three or four times, but you never answered."

"I didn't hear my phone." She reached toward her back pocket, but her phone wasn't there. Then she remembered taking it out of her pocket while she was vacuuming and setting it on the table in the hallway. It was probably still there.

"Just a sec." She slid from her stool and wondered if there was a way she could covertly dump the quiche in the trash without Helen seeing but decided to forgo that action instead. She loped up the stairs, and there was her phone, on the table, just where she had left it. She slipped it into her back pocket and then remembered the little piece of plastic. She should throw it away when she got back downstairs. She pulled it out of her pocket once again, rolling it between her fingers as she walked back into the kitchen.

"What's that you got there?" Fern asked.

Arlo shook her head. "I don't know." But before she could show the tiny piece of plastic to the others and see what they thought about it, the front door to the inn slammed shut.

They all turned toward the noise as an unknown young man brushed in. He was smartly dressed in that sort of big-city casual way that screamed he wasn't from Sugar Springs. Lightweight sweater, creased chinos, and loafers. His medium brown hair looked designer styled, and his teeth were perfectly straight and perfectly white. Arlo had never seen him before.

"Are you on the committee?" He looked to Helen.

She nodded.

"You gotta come quick; there's been an accident."

....

Come to find out the man with the light sweater and white teeth worked as an assistant to the publicist. It was him, the publicist from the movie company, who had been knocked unconscious. He had come in from LA to check out the theater and get some shots for social media. Now he was in the hospital, knocked out cold by a wayward bag of sand, the kind used to weight the stage curtains.

"I don't understand," Fern said the following day. "Did the bag of sand fall on purpose or not?"

It was Friday, midmorning, and the ladies had already been to the beauty parlor for their weekly set. Well everyone but Fern. She claimed she didn't have the money to have her hair done every week, though Arlo knew that she just didn't feel like paying someone to do something for her that she could do for herself. That was just Fern. Still not wanting to miss out on all the gossip, she went and listened as the women talked, pretending to have to wait on Helen and Camille so she could take them home. Or in this case, back to the theater under the guise of "helping" with the restoration.

"No one knows." Helen gave a shrug. She might be a little frazzled, might be a little anxious or even "wigged out," as Fern had said, but her hair looked good. Helen was one in a million. Her long, thick hair reached the middle of her back, and she normally wore it in a braid. On the top, it was iron gray. Right at about her shoulders it was dyed a deep Valentine red. Arlo supposed it was her way of saying *Yes, I belong here in this small town, but I can fit in anywhere I want*. Or maybe she was just being fanciful.

"You're in charge of the volunteers," Fern protested. "I would think you would know before anyone else."

"I'm the wife," Helen quipped. "Always the last to know."

Arlo laughed and shook her head. She had spent the morning helping sand down the new wrong-tinted paint so that, when the new right-tinted paint arrived, they would be ready to slap it on the walls. But for now, it was time for her to be getting back to her store.

"How would you know?" Camille asked before Arlo could make her exit. Camille made her way from the audience seats up onto the stage. "He was standing up here, right?" She craned her neck back to look at the darkened ceiling above.

"I guess," Helen answered.

Camille tilted her head back right. "He would have had to have been if the sandbag was attached to one of the curtain pulls."

"Yup." Fern followed Camille onto the stage. "Someone could have cut it."

Helen crossed her arms. "Like one of the ghosts?"

"Don't make fun." Fern pointed a stern finger at her friend. "Ghosts are real."

"But I don't believe ghosts care one way or another about Hollywood premieres," Helen retorted.

Time for her to make her escape. "I think I'll just—"

"You know what we need?" Fern said. "A ladder. So we can climb up there and see if the rope was cut."

"Oh, no, you don't," Arlo said. "None of you will be climbing a ladder." Not at their age. It was simply too dangerous.

Fern smiled at her sweetly. "How kind of you to offer to do it for us."

This really wasn't part of her plans, but maybe she could use it to her advantage. "If I climb the ladder, then the three of you have to come back to Books and More and stay out of everyone's way."

"Everyone's?" Helen asked.

"Mads's," Arlo specified. "He may need to get in here himself."

Camille shook her head. "Mads isn't coming here. He thinks it was an accident."

And that should tell them something, but truth be known, it was hard to tell these ladies anything.

"Do you agree?" Arlo asked. She looked at the ladies each in turn. They all nodded. "Fine," she nodded. "Get me the ladder."

....

Aside from it being really high and really dark and really dusty, her trip up the ladder was really scary. She climbed ladders constantly at work and thought nothing of climbing another, but at Books and More, she never had to climb into the rafters.

"Are you sure this is where it fell from?" Arlo asked.

"That's what the guy said. The one who came to the inn."

"Dustin," she reminded them. "Dustin Ackerman." But how did he know? Arlo wondered. He was here when the sandbag fell, but how was he able to tell where it fell from?

She shook her head at herself and took one more step up on the ladder. Her legs wobbled, and she used the top rung for balance. "This is as high as I'm going," she called down to them.

"Chicken," Fern taunted.

"Not falling for it." Arlo settled her attention on the tangle of ropes and pulleys that made up the ancient curtain system at the theater. How was she supposed to know if the rope had been cut or just accidentally ripped free of its moorings? It wasn't like—

There it was. The rope she was looking for. Cut. It was obvious that the rope had been cut part of the way through, then allowed to fray. But with a setup like that, anyone could have been under the sandbag when it fell. Any one of them at all.

"What do you see?" Helen called up to her.

Arlo started down the ladder, as quickly as she dared. "Somebody go get Mads."

....

After being run through the ringer by Mads about just why she was up on the ladder in the theater in the spot where the publicist from the movie company had been purposely bludgeoned by a wayward sandbag, Arlo herded the book club back to the bookstore.

"But—" Fern protested as Arlo shooed them out of the theater.

"No buts," Arlo said. "You promised." *And I have work to do.*

Traffic had picked up in Books and More these last couple of days. Ever since Missy Severs had come in, it seemed there were so many more unfamiliar faces around Sugar Springs. Hollywood had come to town, and it would be so much easier for her—and for Mads—if the book club was occupied at the store rather than running amuck in the theater.

Like a den mother with a wayward scout troop, Arlo marched them back to Books and More.

Chloe fixed everyone a coffee, and the ladies settled down in the reading area while Arlo went back to the work in the Civil War section that she never managed to finish the day before. Cut ropes and new clues aside, she was bound and determined to get a little bit of work done today.

Faulkner bobbed on top of his cage at the ladies, and Arlo could only hope that, in the next few minutes, or at least within the next hour, they would stop talking about the cut rope and start discussing what book to read next.

A girl could dream, anyway.

"Do you think he'll come down and tell us what he finds out about the rope?" Camille asked.

"No," Fern scoffed. "We'll have to pry it out of him."

"How?" Camille asked.

"Heineken and cake." Helen said with a firm nod. "Those are the two things he likes best."

"What about Arlo?" Fern asked.

She stuck her head out of the aisle. "Don't even think about it. You cannot prostitute me out for clues."

"Who said anything about that?" Fern innocently asked. "Perhaps your mind is someplace it oughtn't be?"

With a low growl, Arlo ducked back between the shelves. "Book club," she called to them. "Read a book!"

"Read a book!" Faulkner squawked in return. "Read a book!"

From her place in the coffee bar, Chloe chuckled.

Okay, so it would take more than reading a book to keep those three out of trouble. Aside from the fact that this new clue was perplexing, more often than not, the ladies would start a book, then stop reading it only after a chapter or two. They quit reading two of Neil Gaiman's. The last one they ditched was Kurt Vonnegut's *Cat's Cradle*. Arlo had suggested that they read a more mainstream offering, like something by John Grisham or even Sherryl Woods or J. K. Rowling. Harry Potter, anyone? But they were still talking about other things. Like Wally's new book, *Under the Buttonwood Tree*, and whether or not they could convince Veronica to let them read the advance copy. That would be a trick, seeing as they weren't supposed to know that there were any physical copies of the book.

"I for one think he really wrote this new book." Camille gave a certain nod.

"How can you say that?" Fern protested. "No one other than Veronica has seen it or read it."

Camille sniffed delicately. "It's just a feeling I have."

"Feeling, schmeeling," Fern said. "I bet Veronica has tons of copies just under the bed waiting to be read."

"We'd have better luck getting an electronic copy," Camille said.

Both Camille and Fern turned to look at Helen.

"What?" she asked.

"She doesn't happen to leave her computer lying about, does she?" Fern asked.

"I know you're not about to break into Veronica's computer," Arlo said. She had abandoned the Civil War shelves for now. It seemed her attention was more needed elsewhere. Like trying to keep her book club from going to jail.

"Is it really breaking in if she leaves it open, say, on the dining room table?"

Arlo closed her eyes, just briefly. She opened them again and tried to smile. She failed miserably. "I'm not even going to answer that."

"Well, I for one would love to take a look at it," Camille said. "I mean, I'm dying for something new to read."

Arlo resisted the urge to sweep her arms around as if displaying the two-story bookstore that they currently sat in. Camille might be in her mideighties, and she might be a voracious reader, but there was still plenty out there for her to read, and that plenty didn't necessarily need to include Wally Harrison's new book.

Chloe coughed. Or maybe she choked trying to keep her laughter at bay. Whatever the sound was, it wasn't helping Arlo keep the ladies from their tangents.

The bell over the door to the bookstore rang, and Veronica stepped inside.

"Speak of the devil," Fern said. The words slipped from the side of her mouth, and thankfully, Veronica was too far away to hear. At least Arlo hoped she was.

"There you are," Veronica said as she caught sight of Arlo.

She bustled over to where Arlo stood. "I just wanted to tell you that they think the publicist is going to be okay. He's got a concussion and will have to stay in the hospital for couple of days. I guess it was a pretty bad blow to the head. They think he'll be completely fine. When he regains his memory, that is."

"What?" Arlo was beyond stunned.

"He lost his memory?" Chloe added.

Veronica delicately shrugged one shoulder as she looked from one of them to the other. "They think it's temporary. And they're bringing in a new publicist from LA. The show must go on." She gave a trembling smile.

"Why are you telling me all this?" Arlo asked. Not that she didn't appreciate the information. Or rather the book club appreciated her getting the information where they could hear.

"I don't know. I guess I figured, since you and that policeman seemed pretty thick, that you would want to know."

Thick?

Behind Veronica, Fern mouthed *I told you so.*

Chloe coughed again. Or maybe she choked. Whatever.

Arlo ignored her, ignored them both. "Well, thanks." She managed not to tack *I think* onto the end of that sentence.

"One more thing," Veronica said. "Is there a shoe repairman in town?"

"Yeah, just off Main. Why?"

"I popped the heel cap off my favorite shoes." She raised one foot so Arlo could see the damage. "That rock path leading to the inn is tough on shoes."

Helen winced. "Yeah, sorry about that."

Veronica turned and smiled at her. "It happens."

Yes, it did. It most certainly happened.

But now Arlo knew what the little plastic piece she had found in the hallway was. A heel tap off someone's shoes. She had just never seen one in red or studded with stones. Only black and sometimes a tan color. And never in such an unusual shape. Still there was no denying what it was.

"Hang on a sec." Arlo moved out of the aisle and back to the office. She grabbed the little plastic piece from her purse. She wasn't sure why she had dropped it into her bag, but for some reason, she couldn't see throwing it away. Which was absolutely ridiculous, but there you have it. She held it out to Veronica. "This is one of yours?"

Veronica shook her head. "No. Not mine."

The book club ladies were on their feet and in seconds all gathered around to see what Arlo held. Even Chloe came over to get a better look.

"What is it?" Fern asked. Seeing as how she mostly wore Chuck Taylors these days and Arlo had no idea what she had worn back in the day, it was very possible that Fern had never seen one in her life.

"It's a heel cap." Helen turned to Fern. "It goes on the bottom of dress shoes to protect them."

"Well, it's not one of mine. But thanks. Just off Main?" Veronica asked.

"Down at Second."

Veronica nodded once again. "Thanks." And on that one word, she clipped from the bookstore.

"We shouldn't let her get away," Fern said.

"She's not a fish," Arlo said.

"Yeah, but she's got Wally's book." Fern stared wistfully at the front door.

"There are millions of books you haven't read yet," Arlo patiently explained. "Choose one today, start it, and leave that poor woman alone."

"Or we could aggravate her until she lets us have the one we want," Camille said.

Fern grinned. "I like the way you think."

"I don't." Arlo frowned at the two women.

Behind them Helen laughed and Faulkner mimicked the sound. "Gimme a kiss," he squawked at Helen. Arlo's one-time guardian obliged.

"I'm just teasing," Camille said. Though Arlo could tell that, if given half a chance, all three women would jump on it.

Once again the book club ladies settled around in the reading nook, and Arlo almost breathed a sigh of relief.

"Do you really think that, if it comes out that Wally didn't write *Missing Girl*, it would ruin Veronica's career?" Fern asked.

Helen shrugged. "It's an ethics matter, isn't it? If she didn't check her clients' credentials."

"And money," Camille added. "There's a lot of misplaced money if he didn't."

"I was looking online last night," Helen started.

"Good for you," Fern said with a clap of her hands. Helen wasn't the most tech savvy of the group, though in the last few months, she had been trying harder.

"I saw this article about one author who stole another author's work. That's basically what we're talking about here. If what we're talking about is even right." Helen looked from Fern to Camille.

Arlo took that moment to settle herself back in the history section. At least from there she could still see the book club. Lord, sometimes she felt like a babysitter.

"Her reputation would be damaged," Camille said. "And to me that's more telling than just losing some money over the deal."

All that Daisy and Chloe stood to lose was money. Though it was quite a bit of money, to be certain. Arlo looked to her best friend, who had once again stationed herself behind the coffee bar. Chloe was a lot of things, none of them perfect, but she would never harm another for money.

"And if the new book is so different than the old book..." Fern said.

Arlo had forgotten that Veronica had mentioned the books being so different. Not that it was unheard of. Writers changed, their voices grew, their views slid sometimes from one topic to the next. Who was to say where creativity came from and that it should all be the same?

"One author can write in two different styles. Look at ghost-writers," Camille said. "They have to write in someone else's voice entirely. Just because *Missing Girl* and *Under the Buttonwood Tree* have different styles doesn't mean that Wally didn't write both of them."

Helen nodded.

"True," Fern said.

"Why, didn't I read that Dean Koontz used to write romance eons ago?"

Arlo took that moment to step from between shelves. "Koontz. Now there's a good author to read. He's got some new ones out, if y'all are interested."

"I love Koontz," Chloe added. *Now* she wanted to help.

"Put that on our list," Helen said.

"Got it." Camille had already written it down in her stenographer notebook. Arlo had no idea how long their *Gonna Read* list had become but it increased by at least one more today.

"If we could just find out whether or not Petro really had proof that Wally didn't write *Missing Girl*..." Fern trailed off.

"Mads will never let that out," Arlo said.

"Absolutely not," a male voice sounded from the other side of the bookstore.

"Sam!" The ladies stood to greet him as he came down the stairs. As if her day wasn't confusing enough.

Sam Tucker, her one-time high school boyfriend, the one that she had thought was "the one," only to find out he was leaving town with his own big plans in pocket.

"We've known Mads our entire lives." Sam said. "Well, I have, anyway." They had both been born in Sugar Springs, unlike her. She had come in at sixteen and decided it was home. "Mads won't let out anything that he's not supposed to."

Fern's eyes brightened with an idea. "Jason," she breathed.

"No." Arlo knew that her words would fall on deaf ears, but she had to try. Hadn't she promised Mads?

"What harm would it do?" Fern asked.

Once again Arlo closed her eyes just for a moment. Then she opened them again. "It could do a lot." But she knew she was fighting an uphill battle.

Camille's eyes grew wide. "What if he's translating the love letter?"

"Half a letter," Arlo reminded them.

"Frances is in charge of that," Helen said.

"How do you know that?" Arlo asked.

Helen gave her a smug grin. "Beauty shop. You really should go sometime."

"Frances." Fern snapped her fingers as if in great success. "She's our ticket in." And before Arlo knew what had happened, the three ladies had linked arms and buzzed out of Books and More, no doubt on their way to the police station to pin someone down and try to extort clues from them. What was a girl to do?

She turned to Sam. "I didn't expect to see you today."

According to him, Sam's work as a PI could practically be done anywhere, especially when he was working on cases that involved lots of research. But he had rented her third floor; she supposed to get some privacy and to take his business out of the home. But now that his mother had taken such a turn, Sam rarely came into the office. Usually it was because he needed supplies—letterhead or other office necessities. And of course to check on Auggie.

Auggie! "Where's your cat?" she asked, checking the immediate area to make sure the beast wasn't lurking around.

"My cat," Chloe called.

Arlo didn't think Chloe would ever give up the beast entirely. And with as ornery as the orange tabby could be, Arlo would cut him loose in a second. Not really, but she liked to tease Chloe about it. Seemed that the feline wasn't as testy with either Sam or Chloe. Just Arlo.

"Upstairs in the window as usual. Why? You want me to bring him down?"

"So he and Faulkner can chase each other around the bookstore? No, thank you."

"I probably won't be in the office for a while." He didn't elaborate, but Arlo knew his mother had most likely asked him to stay near. Or maybe he just knew the time was coming. She didn't pry.

"If you could check in on him," Sam said. "Maybe bring him down and let him wander around the bookstore some. He seems perfectly content to make his entire world the couch in the corner and wherever his food and water are, but I worry about him."

"Of course," Arlo said.

"Do you want me to bring him back to my house?" Chloe asked. "If it's just for short time, we can take Manny to my mom and dad's."

They both knew Jayden would hate it, but Auggie had originally been Chloe's cat and had only come to live with Sam, or rather in Sam's office, when Jayden had moved in with Chloe, bringing Manny with him.

"I don't think that's necessary," Sam said. "He seems to have settled into being a loner."

Chloe nodded, her blond curls bouncing. "Just let me know if you change your mind."

Sam nodded. "Will do." Then he turned back to Arlo. "They've been gone"—he checked his watch—"ten minutes. I'm not sure if I'm surprised or impressed that you haven't already followed behind them."

Arlo sighed. "I'm not sure myself."

"I'd go down with you, but…" He trailed off, but the words weren't necessary for him to say.

"No problem. But like Chloe said, just let me know if you need anything. Worse comes to worst, Auggie could come to my house." Though the orange striped cat seemed to think Arlo was more predator or prey than housemate.

"Thanks, Arlo." Sam gave her a sad smile. He waved to Chloe and headed out the door.

Arlo watched him leave. She hated to see her friend hurting so, but his mother's illness was the exact reason why he had come back to Sugar Springs. She should be grateful he was here to spend time with her during her last days.

Yeah, you just keep telling yourself that.

"I can't believe you haven't left already," Chloe said.

"I guess I should." She turned back to her best friend. "Say a little prayer that Mads isn't there. Cross your fingers. Maybe light a candle."

"You got it," Chloe said. "But I draw the line at blood sacrifice and reading chicken entrails."

Arlo chuckled. "Good to see you still have standards in place." She even managed not to sigh as she started out the door.

It wasn't far to the police station from Books and More, and it was a nice day for a walk, but there was a damper on her movements—why she was walking and where she was walking to and why she was walking there, or something like that. Anyway, somehow her life had turned to this: bookstore owner and chaser-downer of little old ladies who wanted to solve murders.

Maybe she should get them all a set of Encyclopedia Brown books. There might not be murders in the books, but there was always a case to be solved. The answer was in the story, hidden in the clues, but it was also in the back of the book. Arlo had adored those stories when she was little. She must've read them all two or three times, if not more. The thought brought a smile to her face. And it was a joy that she definitely needed. Because she saw Mads's large SUV parked at the police station.

Oh great.

Walking into Mads's office was a little like walking backstage just before a performance. Or at least, it was like that when Helen, Fern, and Camille had decided to come down together. They were all three chattering at Mads at the same time. He sat patiently behind his desk, apparently listening, though his arms were crossed and his nostrils flared just a bit. He must have heard at least part of what they said because Arlo knew that look. He was on the edge for sure.

There was one more person in Mads's office. Someone she hadn't expected to see. Petro's friend, Aleksandr Gorky.

9

WHEN HE CAUGHT SIGHT OF HER, MADS STOOD. "A LITTLE HELP," he said.

Arlo nodded. "Okay," she said. "Fun's over. Let's go."

"But surely Frances is done with that letter by now," Fern protested.

"Half a letter," Arlo reminded them.

Camille nodded. "I'm dying to know what it says."

"Even if it was translated, I would not share that information with you," Mads explained almost patiently. "This is an open investigation, and it cannot be discussed with anyone not directly involved."

"I found the dead body," Helen pointed out to him.

"That's not what I mean." Mads pressed his lips together. Arlo saw a muscle in his jaw jump. She almost felt sorry for him. Murder in a small town was never easy, or so she figured. But it certainly wasn't easy with three amateur sleuths trying to help out at every turn.

"I only wanting Petro's things," Gorky said. "Why I cannot have?"

Mads leveled his gaze to the other man in the room. "At this point, all of his possessions are still considered to be evidence. Clues," he added. "I can't release anything until we wrap up our investigation."

"How long in time?" Gorky asked.

"It's hard to say," Mads replied. "Two or three more days. Maybe four. Maybe longer than that. I don't know."

"It is too long."

"I'm sorry can't help you," Mads said.

"Just let me look at what she's got so far," Fern said.

"Fern," Arlo nearly screeched. "Seriously, take it back to Books and More."

"He was friend," Gorky said.

"I understand that," Mads said patiently. Though Arlo could tell his patience was nearing an end. And with Mads, that was saying a lot. "We're still looking for next of kin. Until I find them, I can't release anything to you. Even if we have the investigation wrapped up. You understand?"

Gorky shook his head. "No, why you not give me his things? He was friend. There is no kin."

Mads sighed, but Arlo knew it was to disguise a groan. Or maybe even a growl. "I can't do my job like this."

"Book club, to the bookstore," Arlo called as if she was a drill sergeant. But the ladies weren't having any of it.

"You say you want clues, but his things are things. No clues."

"They can be, and that's why I'm keeping them until the investigation is closed. We are trying to uncover who might have killed him." Mads said each word slowly and succinctly, as if perhaps that would help Aleksandr Gorky understand more about what was happening in American crime solving.

"What clues?" Gorky said. "Why clues?"

"That's what I want to know." Fern picked that time to chime in. "What clues are you talking about here, Mads?"

Mads had had enough. He pointed toward the door. "Everybody—out."

Arlo had to hand it to Camille. She at least knew when Mads was at his breaking point. She looped arms with Fern and tried to lead her from the room.

"Mr. Gorky," Fern said. "Why don't you come to Books and More with us? Get a cup of coffee."

"I think that's a fine idea," Mads said, though Arlo wasn't sure how true the statement really was.

"Coffee." Gorky nodded. "I like American coffee."

"What about specialty coffee?" Helen asked. "Cappuccino? Mochaccino? Something with a little hazelnut syrup and some whipped cream on top?"

Gorky allowed Helen to steer him toward the door. "I don't know these words, but I do American coffee. *Da*."

And just like that, Arlo was alone with Mads. He shot her a pointed look. "You too."

She saluted him, then clicked her heels together and left his office.

Arlo was only a few feet behind the book club ladies and Aleksandr Gorky as they all walked back to Books and More. Every so often, she caught a part of a sentence. She heard the words "book club" and "reading" and "find," and he responded with nods and a look that was almost fearful. That was something she could definitely understand. The book club ladies were nothing if not intimidating.

But surely he knew he was free to go. Surely…

Everyone was standing around the coffee bar when Arlo came in. Phil was first in line, getting his afternoon refill with the book club and Gorky close behind.

Thankfully the ladies were back at the bookstore and not out causing trouble for Mads or Jason or any of the other officers involved in the investigation of Petro's untimely death, which meant Arlo just might have an afternoon to get some work done.

She shot Chloe an apologetic smile as she ducked back into the history section and continued to alphabetize the books on the Civil War. It was a large section, of course, since there were so many history buffs who lived in the area. But honestly, it was hard not to be, considering the heritage of the people. And their proximity to Corinth. Corinth had been an integral part of the War Between the States, part of the Battle of Shiloh and the push to gain control of both river and railroads. The area was rich in the history of such a tumultuous time in America. Why, they even had their very own reenactment of the Skirmish of Sugar Springs, though at that time the town had only been called The Springs. No one knew for sure when *sugar* got added. As far as anyone knew, it just started being called that over time.

"Now you can sit here, Aleksandr," Arlo heard Camille say. She was just across from the reading nook where the book club was settling in with their newest addition, who didn't look as if he knew whether or not he should be there. He had something of a stunned expression on his face as the ladies tried to explain what their club was about. "We read books, and then we talk about them," Camille said. "It's all fairly simple."

Arlo swallowed back a snort. If there was one word she would not use to describe her book club, "simple" would definitely make the short list.

"Do you like to read, Aleksandr?" Fern asked.

"*Da*," he said. Arlo looked over just in time to see him nod in reinforcement. "Yes. I like reading. But I no like Aleksandr."

"Tell me anyone who likes their name," Helen said.

"I like my name," Chloe chirped from her place behind the coffee bar.

Score one for Team Chloe, Arlo thought with a small laugh.

"I'm just saying," Helen said. "Most people don't like their name."

"Well, everybody has to be called something," Fern said.

"Sasha," Gorky said. "My name Sasha."

Arlo looked over as Fern drew back, an extra wrinkle in the center of her forehead. "That's a girl's name," she said. "Is that your girlfriend?"

Gorky shook his head. "It is not girl's name. It is for both."

"So unisex," Helen said.

"Like Arlo," she said from her place in the history section.

"You're the only girl I know named Arlo," Helen tossed back.

"Yeah well not everybody can be named after '60s folksingers. That's all I'm saying." Of course she was grateful that she had gotten saddled with Arlo and her brother with Woody. The other way around might be even harder for her to explain how she got the name she had.

"In Russia," Gorky started, "Sasha is name for boys and girls."

Fern shook her head. "I don't know, that sounds awfully feminine to me."

"I suppose it only seems that way if that's how you perceive it," Camille said. "Look at all the men's names that have become women's names over the years. Like Whitney and Ashley and Lindsay and Leslie." She counted the names on her fingers. "And that's just a few."

"And Arlo," Arlo called from where she stood in the history section.

"We already covered this," Helen tossed back.

Faulkner squawked. "Don't cover me. Don't cover me." He squawked again. "I'm going in. Cover me! Cover me!"

"But with a name like Aleksandr," Fern started. "You could be Alexi or Alex or Xander even—"

"Sasha," Gorky said. "I always been Sasha. We can't change now."

"Well, Sasha," Fern said. "It's your funeral. And good luck picking up girls with a name like that."

....

On Saturday the bookstore was beyond busy. There was less than a week until the opening premiere of the movie, and it seemed as if anyone in town who hadn't read *Missing Girl* was coming in to get their copy. Of course, everyone wanted to read it so they could come out of the theater saying, "The movie was good, but the book was so much better"—the cry of readers everywhere.

The book club sans Gorky, a.k.a. Aleksandr, a.k.a. Sasha, was doing its thing in the reading nook. You know, pretending to be discussing one book while trying to figure out how to get their hands on a copy of *Under the Buttonwood Tree*.

No lie, Arlo wouldn't mind reading it herself. *Missing Girl* was a little literary for her tastes, and with a name like *Under the Buttonwood Tree*, she figured it would be fairly literary as well. But she still wanted to read it. Like everyone else in the book club, she wanted to compare the two books, if not for content then definitely for style. Perhaps the differences would show if someone different wrote each one.

They all suspected that Inna had truly written *Missing Girl*. She had claimed to, anyway, but since Wally was dead, there was nobody to refute her claim. Daisy had stayed out of his business, or rather, the business side of his business, and had no clue as to the origins of the book. So a chapter or two of *Under the Buttonwood Tree* might truly give a clue.

"What if it has a clue concerning the mystery we're trying to solve right now?" Fern mused.

Arlo steps faltered as she walked past the reading nook. She got the Civil War section reorganized yesterday, just in time for the rush of outsiders. It seemed that, whenever someone who didn't live in the South came out this way, they wanted to know more and more about the war that divided the nation and almost brought it down.

But this…

"Whoever wrote it, whether it was Inna or Wally, was gone long before this man was killed," Helen pointed out.

"I know," Fern said. "But hear me out. You know writers like to experiment and research. What if it was research?"

"You're saying that whoever killed Petro did so because they wrote *Under the Buttonwood Tree* and were using it for research for a murder that we don't know is even in the book?" Arlo was surprised when the question shot from her. She wasn't going to say a word. She was going to walk right by, but sometimes these ladies and their cockamamie ideas had to be stopped as quickly as possible. "That's craziness."

"It's possible," Fern said defensively.

"But not probable," Arlo pointed out, doing her best to nip this in the bud. Whatever *this* was.

"But the author of *Under the Buttonwood Tree* is either Inna, who's in prison, or Wally, who is dead. So, who killed Petro?" Helen asked.

"That's what I'm trying to figure out," Fern said.

"The lady in red." Camille nodded in a self-assured way.

"I had almost forgotten about her," Helen breathed.

"I hadn't." Camille adjusted her handbag on her lap and looked to the other two book club members for their thoughts.

"Sam saw her, right?" Helen asked.

"Maybe she's a ghost," Fern put in. "Didn't he see her at the theater?"

"But I saw her, too. At the inn."

"That's who we need to be looking for," Fern stated.

"Fine," Arlo said. They had already determined that practically every woman and even a couple of the men in town owned red dresses. It was the perfect wild goose chase to keep them busy and out of Mads's way. "You can discuss this all you want right here, but no one bothers Mads or Jason or Frances or Dan. No one."

"What about Henry?" Camille asked, referring to the newest member of the Sugar Springs police force, Henry Franklin.

Fern elbowed her. "Hush."

Camille shot her a look.

"Not Henry, either. No one," she repeated. "Got it?"

"Got it," the ladies said in unison, nodding as well.

That should last all of fifteen minutes, but that was fifteen minutes that Arlo could give to the bookstore before she had to chase down her crazy book club. Again.

"Arlo, that woman is here to see you again." Chloe came up behind her, then nodded toward the coffee bar.

A Hollywood beauty with long, dark hair sat at the flat edge of the dogleg, her back to the reading nook.

"That woman?" Arlo asked. Her stomach dropped, and the tips of her fingers started to tingle. It was like being on the roller coaster at Six Flags. "She wants to see me? That's Alayna Adams."

Chloe shook her head. "Look again."

Arlo started toward the coffee bar peering at the woman as she walked over. She only had a side view, but the closer she got, the more she seemed to look like Alayna Adams. Then she saw it. The fake beauty mark just to the right side of her mouth. And Arlo remembered seeing this woman before, when she was headed out to the inn to help Elly clean. That day, the woman had been a blond with hair that barely reached her shoulders. Today's long mane had to be a wig or professional extensions. And good ones, it seemed. If Arlo hadn't seen her as a blond, she would have never thought they were one and the same.

"Are you Arlo Stanley?" she asked as Arlo came near. She thrust out a perfectly manicured hand. "I'm Missy Severs, president of the Alayna Adams Fan Club and reigning Alayna Adams lookalike."

"Right," Arlo said. "We met once before."

"Of course," Missy Severs murmured in what had to be her signature "Alayna Adams murmur."

Arlo shook her hand. She had expected her to have a wimpy shake, like Arlo was supposed to kiss the back of her hand instead, but her grip was sure and firm. The handshake of a woman who knew what she wanted and went after it.

"Yes," she said, noting Arlo's surprise. "I have a strong handshake. I work out and do Krav Maga and jujutsu."

"Wow," Arlo said. Beautiful and deadly. "What can I do for you today?"

Missy handed her a pink piece of paper. A flyer for this year's Alayna Adams Lookalike Contest. "We were scheduled to have this in the theater. On the stage, but since all of the delays in getting it ready for the premiere, well, we're going to have to move it. What better place to have the contest other than right here in the bookstore?" Her tone rose on the end, and her eyes sparkled with excitement. She was really into this, Arlo thought. Wholly committed to the cause.

"I don't know," Arlo said, looking at the flyer then turning her attention to Chloe. "What do you think?"

"It's short notice," Chloe said. "But it might be good for business."

"Here's what I'm thinking," Missy said. "It'll be no bother, I'm sure. We'll have this next Friday, before the premiere on Sunday. That way we can announce the winner at the premiere. All the contestants will be here in the bookstore walking around and talking to customers. At noon each contestant will perform a short scene from one of Alayna's movies." She turned on her stool and pointed toward the reading nook where the book club had stopped talking about *Under the Buttonwood Tree* and how they could get a copy and instead were concentrating on Missy the Alayna lookalike. "We could have it there. You could just move the couches out of the way, and there will be plenty of room."

Yeah, just move those huge couches out of the way. No problem.

"Set up a ballot box by the door, and people can vote for their favorite when they leave the store."

It sounded simple enough. And as far as Arlo could tell, it wouldn't require anything on her part other than moving couches and putting up some kind of ballot box. But these things never turned out the way you expected them to. Never.

"It would bring a lot more traffic into the store," Chloe said. "If people actually decide to come." Like everyone else, Chloe was a bit concerned that, with an unsolved murder in town, folks might decide to stay at home instead of taking their chances with the killer in Sugar Springs.

"Are you talking about the murder?" She shook her head with a confidence that Arlo had rarely seen. "I for one am not worried. This town is safe, and I've told all my girls in the contest as well as my Instagram followers. This is the place to be."

"I'm sure that will help immensely," Chloe murmured.

"So you'll do it?" Missy's voice rose on the end.

Arlo gave a half-hearted shrug. She hoped the amount of work on her part was going to be as expected, otherwise she may need some extensions herself—after she pulled her hair out. "I suppose."

"Oh, goodie!" Missy clapped her hands and snatched up her phone. "I'll let everyone know right now. This is going to be great!"

....

"Arlo," Daisy's voice sounded from the next aisle over. "Can I talk to you?"

Arlo had been so intent on her work, mulling over the prospects for hosting this Alayna Adams Lookalike Contest and making sure the book club stayed put, that she hadn't noticed Daisy had come into the bookstore. Of course on a Saturday, the bell seemed to ring continuously. At some point Arlo just stopped hearing it at all. Was it any wonder she hadn't known Daisy had come up behind her?

"Of course," Arlo said. She had never seen Daisy look this upset.

"I just got back from talking with Mads," Daisy said.

"Let's sit down," Arlo motioned toward the far side of the coffee bar, the farthest seats from the reading nook where she and Daisy might possibly talk about whatever was on her mind without everyone in the book club hanging onto every word.

It was a nice thought, anyway.

Chloe automatically started them coffees as they sat down. Arlo smiled gratefully at her friend. Besides a good friend, she was a fantastic mind reader.

"I just—" Daisy stopped and tried to gather her thoughts. "I think he's going to arrest me for murder."

"What?" The book club screeched.

She should have taken Daisy into the office. But then again, with the amount of concern that wrinkled her brow, she might need the support of more than just Arlo.

Chloe slid their coffees in front of them as Helen, Fern, and Camille waved them over to the reading book.

"Sorry," Arlo said. "Are you up for that?"

"They really are lovely," Daisy said.

Lovely. Not quite the word Arlo would've chosen. At least not on a Saturday afternoon, when the store was busy and they wanted to talk murder to everyone. It would've been different if it was the *Hounds of the Baskervilles*, but no. They wanted to talk real murder with them. Maybe she should have put up a sign: NO TRUE CRIME STORIES TO BE DISCUSSED, like those music stores with signs that said NO STAIRWAY TO HEAVEN near the guitars. But she figured it would probably get about as much obedience from her book club as that sign did from the guitar players of the world.

Truth be known, when she thought about the ladies and the times when they weren't trying to solve a mystery and worm themselves madly into everyone's business, the word *lovely* might've come to mind now and again. But now… "If you're sure."

With a smile, Daisy picked up her coffee and made her way over to the reading nook. Camille and Fern scooted to one side so she could sit on the couch while Arlo settled on the tiny love seat across from them.

"Why in the world would you think Mads is going to arrest you for murder?" Camille asked.

"I don't know. Just something in how he acts. I don't think he likes me very much."

"Mads doesn't like anybody very much," Fern said.

"Except for Arlo," Helen tossed in.

"Elly," Arlo said with a roll of her eyes. "We're talking about Daisy here."

But Daisy seemed more interested in Arlo's love life than her own chances of going to jail. "You and Mads? I mean, I heard something about prom like years and years ago, but I didn't think anything was happening now."

"It's not," Arlo said emphatically. Just like with Sam, that ship had sailed, and it was not going back to the shore.

"Did he say he was going to arrest you, love?" Camille asked. Arlo wanted to stand and give the woman a hug of thanks for changing the subject back to murder, which was odd. She normally didn't want to talk about murder, but it sure did beat talking about her love life or, rather, her nonexistent love life.

"He didn't, but… You know how he can be. He's so intimidating and big and dark and…" She shook her head. "I don't know. He scares me."

"He scares a lot of people, dear." Fern patted her on the leg.

"I just feel like he needs someone in jail for this murder, and I'm the most likely suspect." Daisy's voice rose at the end until it almost sounded like a wail.

"No," Helen chimed in. "That's Veronica."

Arlo really couldn't argue with that. Veronica did seem like the most likely suspect. Chloe and Daisy had built businesses for themselves. They had made lives outside of Wally. But it seemed as if Veronica's entire career hinged on one man and the two books he possibly wrote. But if it was proven that he didn't write them…

Well, no one knew for sure what would happen. There had been no precedent of such actions. At least not that Arlo had ever heard. So it was anybody's guess. But when faced with the possibility of career failure to the degree of "you will never work in this town again"…well, who wanted to take a chance on that?

"I'm not worried about Veronica," Daisy said. "Veronica has an alibi."

"She does?" Helen asked. "Who?"

"You," Daisy said. "You told Mads that Veronica was at the inn the night Petro was murdered."

"She was…" Helen murmured. "I suppose she was."

"So unless she's working with the lady in red…" Camille said.

"What if she is the lady in red?" Fern asked.

"I thought that woman had long hair," Arlo added, once again sucked into the vortex that was her book club.

"It could have been a wig," Daisy said. "Which is why I'm on the list, too. And I don't have an alibi for that night. I was home alone."

"And you own a dark wig?" Fern asked.

Daisy shrugged. "Sometimes Wally liked to play dress-up. I don't know why I kept it."

Fern whistled low and under her breath.

"That's why I'm worried." She bit her lip. "I really think he's going to arrest me for killing Inna's brother."

10

Wait. What?

The book club erupted all at once.

"Inna and Petro are brother and sister?"

"I knew something was up with them."

"No wonder he said he had proof."

Fern was on her feet in a second. "Petro is Inna's brother. How about that."

Daisy nodded dumbly. "I thought you knew."

"No," Arlo said. "This is the first we're hearing of it."

Which just went to show how close-mouthed Mads could be. She wondered how he found out.

"They don't have the same last name," Arlo said.

Daisy shrugged. "I guess he changed it when he came to America."

"Or to Mississippi," Fern said. "So no one would know how he got the information about Inna and *Missing Girl*."

"Was he ever going to tell everyone who he really was?" Camille mused.

Helen shrugged. "Who knows?"

No one, and there was no one now who could tell them.

"Hot dog!!" Fern danced a little jig in place, the hardware on her overalls tinkling with the motion. "I told you something was up between those two. This changes everything!"

"It changes nothing," Arlo countered. She hoped it changed nothing.

"And this proves what?" Helen asked.

Well, it didn't prove anything, though Fern didn't answer. She simply sat, wriggled a bit in place, but was still smiling as if she'd won the lottery. One thing was certain. Fern loved to be right.

But as Helen pointed out, what did it matter? Petro could be Inna's brother all he wanted, but Inna was still in jail and Petro still dead.

"So who's the woman in the red dress?" Camille asked.

That was something Arlo didn't know. And something she might not ever find out. But it bugged her that the woman fit Inna's description, and now that they knew that Petro was truly Inna's brother… The thought of Inna somehow getting out on bail and coming to Sugar Springs to ruin the premiere for the town… Well, Arlo couldn't stand by and let that happen. But she had no proof that it was going to happen, either.

Daisy shrugged. "I just thought that, maybe since you guys know Mads better than I do, maybe one of you would step in and tell him—"

"No one steps in and tells Mads anything," Fern said. Her voice was serious, but the smile on her face was still triumphant.

"Except for maybe Arlo," Helen added.

"Would you stop?" Arlo asked directing the question at Helen.

"So you really did have a thing?" Daisy asked.

"It was over a long time ago," Arlo said. "Really not worth talking about."

Daisy shook her head. "Let's hear about it. I've got nothing but time, since hopefully I'm not getting arrested."

"It's really a boring story." Arlo tried to keep her voice light and airy.

"Okay, it goes like this," Helen said.

"Helen, no," Arlo begged. But once Elly got in gear, she was in gear.

"So Arlo and Mads were dating. But he had this big scholarship to go play football in Oklahoma. And everyone knew that he would turn pro after. Arlo's family is a bunch of hippies, and they like to move around a lot. But when Arlo got here, she wanted to stay. So she stayed with me and vowed never to leave Sugar Springs."

"But she did leave," Daisy said. "To college, right?"

Arlo nodded. "It's really not an interesting story. And it's really not worth telling again."

"Well, Arlo was heartbroken that Mads was going to leave and she would be left behind. So she decided on—of all nights—prom night to break up with Mads and take up with Sam," Helen continued.

Daisy sat back her eyes wide in surprise. "Sam?" She pointed toward the ceiling, and Arlo supposed she was gesturing toward the third floor where Sam's office was located. "*Sam* Sam?" she asked.

Arlo sighed. "Sam Sam."

"Well," Helen continued, dragging the word out until it had four or five syllables. "It seems that Sam had plans bigger than Sugar Springs and he was on his way out, too."

"But they both came back."

Fern nodded, taking up the story. "Mads blew out his knee in the NFL. Played for the 49ers for a while." She wrinkled her nose to show her distaste for the franchise. "He should have been a Cowboy."

"And Sam?" Daisy asked.

"He came home for his mom," Arlo supplied. At least that's how much she was willing to share.

Daisy nodded. She, like everyone else in town, knew that Sam's mother was ill.

Chloe came out from behind the coffee bar at that time and stood by the love seat. "Speaking of Sam, has anyone seen him today?"

"Sam! Sam!" Faulkner cried. "Has anyone seen Sam?" He squawked a couple of times, then whistled and started in with his "Kitty, kitty, kitty." Arlo supposed, to the bird, Sam and Auggie were inseparable.

The ladies all shook their heads. Arlo did the same. "I don't think he was coming in this weekend," Arlo said. "He asked me to check on the cat, remember?"

"Yeah," Chloe said. "I'm just worried about him."

The words no sooner left her mouth than Arlo's phone rang. She slipped it from her pocket and checked the screen. It was Sam.

Dread filled her, made her fingers numb and cold. But she was just being silly because just moments ago they were talking about Sam. It didn't mean that he was calling with bad news. He was simply calling. Maybe to even ask if she had checked on Auggie upstairs. That was all. Nothing more. She swiped the phone on to accept his call and held the receiver to her ear.

"Hi, Sam." She tried to make her voice as neutral as possible, not too happy, completely without dread, not sad, just somewhere in the middle of nothing.

"Arlo," the one word said it all. And her heart broke for him. "I just didn't want you to find out from anyone else. Mom passed this morning."

....

Arlo couldn't think of anything worse to do on a Sunday than help Sam plan his mother's funeral. But it seemed Sam's sister was not up for the task. She had never been one accused of having a backbone, one of those women who a hundred years ago would get the vapors for certain and faint from the smallest inconvenience. She was a nice enough person, just...fragile. But Sam needed someone on his side right now. And since it couldn't be his sister, Arlo supposed it was only logical that it was her. Though picking out caskets, music, flowers, the clothes that she would wear, the trinkets that Sam wanted in her final resting place—doing all that was about the last thing she wanted to do. But she did it for Sam.

And when it was over, she went home, to her empty house, and wondered what it was all about. It being life. She owned the bookstore. She had friends. She had a life, albeit small-town life, but a life. Even if it did include chasing three geriatric wannabe sleuths. She had everything, except someone to care for her. But was that what *it* was all about? Falling in love?

She just didn't know.

She supposed no one did.

And yet...

She picked up her cell phone, rubbed her eyes, and dialed the number. She waited as it rang, crossing her fingers that the number wasn't changed—again.

"Arlo, honey, is that you?" The familiar, husky sound of her mother's voice crossed the phone line.

Arlo closed her eyes and let it wash over her. "Hey, Mom."

She could almost hear the smile in Henny Stanley's voice, and Arlo supposed she didn't call home often enough. Mainly because home didn't exist. She never knew when she placed the call if her mother would have cell service or if she had changed her cell phone number for some reason or another and forgotten to let Arlo know that there was a new number where she could reach her. Such things were trivial in the big scope of life. Especially when there was a pipeline to protest, a rain forest to protect, or just an awesome sit-in at Burning Man.

And all these were the very reasons that Arlo had decided so long ago to make her home in Sugar Springs.

"How have you been?" Arlo asked.

She could almost hear her mother wave a hand around at nothing. "Oh you know, just the same." Which told her nothing and everything in an instant.

Chances were her mother was too thin, her dad was out of poison oak cream and somehow managed to come in contact with the stuff yet again, and her brother Woody's beard was probably too long, though it would be a cold day in July before he would shave it off completely.

She loved them, she missed them, and she couldn't live with them. Every year it seemed the gulf between them grew even wider.

"Everyone is doing okay?"

That was the truth of her call. Having spent the day helping Sam prepare his mother's final resting place forced her to realize how long it had been since she talked to her own mother. It wasn't lack of love, just lack of commonality. Arlo couldn't decide which scenario was sadder. She supposed it didn't really matter. Her mom was a free spirit, and Arlo herself wanted roots. It was something Henny had never understood, often accusing Arlo of bending to "the man." Arlo never figured out who the man actually was and why it was such a sin to bend to him, but most of the time she let the accusations go. Different strokes and all that.

And then there were times like these, when she wished more than ever that she and her mom were close, that they had a connection, more than just a last name in common.

"I didn't need anything," Arlo said. "I just wanted to hear your voice."

Her mother grew quiet. Silence filled the air between them until Arlo thought perhaps they had gotten disconnected. "Are you okay, honey?" Henny finally asked. "Did you have a dream or a premonition or something you need to tell me about?"

Arlo almost chuckled. Almost. "Nothing like that. I just realized it had been a long time since I talked to you."

"Too long," her mother agreed. "You should find some help at that bookstore of yours so you can join us out here for a while."

"Where exactly is here?" Arlo asked, even though she had no intentions of leaving Sugar Springs anytime soon. They had a movie premiere to get ready for.

Her mother's voice grew distant as she called to someone. "BiBi? It's Arlo. She wants to know where we are." A slight pause. "Ohio? I thought we were in Kentucky."

Behind her there seem to be much debate over which state they were actually in. Pennsylvania was tossed into the hat as well as West Virginia. Considering there were three people and four states had been mentioned… Well, that was her family.

"Let's go with in the Appalachian Mountains," her mother chirped cheerfully.

Arlo didn't miss the *like it mattered* tone of her voice either.

"Great," Arlo said. "Well, I won't keep you…" She trailed off. This was the exact reason why she didn't call, and somehow, it was also one of the reasons she missed them.

"Okay," her mother said, obviously distracted. "See ya. Call again." Then Arlo heard her mother say, "BiBi, not there!"

And then her mother was gone.

"Bye, Mom," Arlo said to no one.

Arlo kicked off her shoes and sighed again. Calling her mother was supposed to make her feel a little less melancholy, but that hadn't worked. It was still early, and somehow, she felt at loose ends. She could call Chloe and see if she and Jayden wanted to watch a movie, but it was a school night; Arlo figured supermom Chloe would have Jayden in bed early.

She was thrilled that her friend had found whatever solution she needed to keeping Jayden close—in all honesty, Arlo figured it was just a matter of standing up to her parents, something Chloe had never been very good at. But Arlo still missed the times they shared together. She supposed things couldn't always stay the same.

She made her way into her bedroom and changed out of her funeral-planning clothes and into something more comfortable: a soft T-shirt and a matching pair of elastic-band pants. Loungewear that could double as pajamas if she so chose. Then she made her way back into the kitchen. She opened the refrigerator, checking out the contents before shutting it again. Sam had bought her a quick bite to eat at the diner less than an hour ago. She wasn't hungry. Dinnertime was over. And then she opened the refrigerator again.

She closed it once more and wandered over to the kitchen sink and looked out the window to her small backyard. Small was actually being kind. Arlo's tiny cottage sat amid bigger houses, and she often wondered if her house had been a mother-in-law situation attached to one of the larger dwellings in the area. Nothing like where Chloe lived, but definitely smaller than those around. She didn't care. It was her little yellow house that she had bought with her own money. It was the first home she truly could ever call her own. She was proud of it. And it anchored her to Sugar Springs. Right where she wanted to be.

She pushed back from the kitchen sink and wandered into the living room. She turned on the TV, looked to a couple of stations, and turned it off again. She wasn't in the mood for someone else's drama. At the moment she felt like she had enough of her own. Dead body at the theater, movie premiere just around the corner, Sam.

Sam shouldn't be listed in with the drama, and yet he was. The entire day, as she helped him, in the back of her mind, the question hovered. His mother was the reason he had come back to Sugar Springs, and now she was gone. Sam hadn't found his own place to live. He had been staying in the family house. He had rented the office on the third floor of her building where Books and More was located on Main. But it was a lease. He could fulfill that and head back out. Truth be told, he was going month-to-month as it was. But now that Marjorie Tucker had gone to her reward, what would Sam do next?

And in the big scheme of things, what difference did it make to her?

She had no idea. She plopped down on the couch, picked up her phone, and thumbed through her contacts. She really didn't look at them as they scrolled past on her screen. There was only one person she was thinking of calling, and that person was Mads. Sometimes that was the worst part of living in a small town—all the past baggage just hung around like the lost and found at the airport.

Arlo tossed her phone onto the coffee table and laid down on the couch. She turned on her side, tucked the pillow under her head, and stared at the painting across the room. It was a Reginald Pollock, not nearly as costly as one from the unrelated Jackson, but beautiful and soothing all the same. She loved the painting, even though when she had bought it, she hadn't had $700 to plop down on a piece of art. But she'd had to have it all the same. Other than dishes, it was the first thing she bought for her house. The original oil painting consisted primarily of half swirls of pale blue that covered the entire canvas with intermittent squiggles in other primary colors. Abstract, yes. But ever-changing, ever-moving. Yet it remained the same. At different times she just saw different things, different values, different colors, different perspectives hidden there in the paint. It was amazing to her, marvelous, that something could be stationary and change all in the same moment.

Much like Sugar Springs. It had been her constant, her steady, and would remain to be so most likely for the rest of her life. And yet it was changing, ever-changing. Some changes were big, some were small. The question was how to accept those changes as they came.

11

"THAT POOR BOY," CAMILLE SAID THE FOLLOWING DAY. EVERYONE
had gathered at the Coliseum once again to work on the historic
building and ready it for the upcoming movie premiere.

Word of Marjorie Tucker's death spread quickly through the
community. So no one asked her what boy Camille was talking
about—of course, they knew. Arlo managed to resist the urge to
point out that he hadn't been a boy in a very long time. If she said
something like that, she was certain that one of them would twist it
around so that it seemed something romantic was going on between
the two of them again. She had barely managed to keep it from them
that she had helped Sam plan the funeral. Not that she had done
anything truly in the way of decisions. She had figuratively, and occa-
sionally literally, held his hand as he decided these last things for his
mother.

"I know." Fern sat back on her rear end and folded her legs,
crisscross-applesauce. "What I don't know is why we have to polish
this stage when there's going to be a movie screen in front of it."

"Hear, hear," Helen said, even though she was the one who had
doled out the task. "I mean, why do the Hollywooders need to have
a tour of behind the scenes?" Helen asked. She slung her braid over
her other shoulder and moved to a new section on the wooden floor.

"Hollywooders." That was the title that they had given anyone associated with the movie. When they weren't in earshot, of course.

The Coliseum had been set up with a beautiful wooden stage that had seen countless performances over the years. The last decade or so—probably closer to five of them, if you wanted to get down to brass tacks—had given this stage a worn-out appearance. And since the Hollywooders were coming in and touring this charming icon of the American South (the historical society's words, not hers) the committee wanted every detail perfect. And the stage floor spotless. And polished.

What Arlo couldn't figure out is why the oldest three people on the committee were the ones on their hands and knees with skate pads and those foam mats used in gymnastics, crawling around on the stage floor and doing their best to return it to its "former glory."

"Do you suppose he'll stay?" Camille asked.

"In Sugar Springs?" Helen asked in return.

"Of course in Sugar Springs. He's here now. He couldn't very well stay in Jackson, now could he?" Fern grumped. The chore seemed to have made her grumpy. Like it took much out of her.

Arlo crawled over to get a clean buffing cloth. "And who exactly said that electric buffer would be too harsh for this floor?"

Helen rolled her eyes. "Patty Holmes." Patty was president of the Sugar Springs Historical Society. Actually she was pretty much all there was to it, and she took great pride in all things Sugar Springs.

"The one woman with nothing better to do." Fern braced herself back on her hands and knees and started polishing once again. "I'm not going to be able to move tomorrow."

What Fern said was correct. Now that Patty had turned fifty and had turned up with an empty nest, she needed other things to occupy her time. So when her youngest daughter headed to Ole Miss, Patty had decided that Sugar Springs needed its very own historical society and broke off from the Alcorn County Historical Society to form the club as it was today.

"Pretty much if it has to be done, it's because Patty said," Helen grumbled.

Though Patty was barely five foot and might have weighed a hundred pounds on a bloated day, she was a force to be reckoned with. Arlo supposed that's what happened when you raised four boys enamored by Alabama football and a daughter determined to go to college on a full pageant scholarship. As her children gained lives of their own, they had left Patty without one for herself. So basically, even though some sort of electric buffer would have done the job just as easily, if they could manage to keep the changeup from Patty, no one would know the difference, but no one was willing to take the chance that she might find out. It was too easy in a town the size of Sugar Springs for word to get out.

"I heard that Mads and Jason didn't find any fingerprints other than Petro's in Petro's room at the inn, Helen." Fern looked to Helen for confirmation.

"If you're going to chat," Camille started, "for heaven's sake, at least keep working."

"Hear, hear," Helen said. "And talk a little louder. So we can all hear."

Arlo bit back her laughter.

"I am working," Fern grumbled.

"Working those lips," Helen said.

Honestly, Arlo did her best to stifle the chuckles that demanded release, but this time she couldn't keep them at bay.

"I don't know what's so funny," Fern said. She started polishing the floor once again.

"You" was surely not the best answer at this time, so Arlo gave a quick shrug and stuffed her laughter back down.

"It's tragic. Without any fingerprints, they don't know who visited Petro at the inn. So nobody still knows who this lady in red is."

"What if she's just a figment of everyone's imagination?" Camille asked.

"We're not writing the story, Camille. We're trying to figure out what it is," Helen said.

"Hear, hear," Fern said sarcastically. "Too many people have seen this lady in red for her to be anything other than real."

"But she's only been seen twice and not again," Arlo pointed out. Then she shook her head at herself for getting dragged into their conversation and amateur mystery-solving. At least when they were polishing the floor and going over all this at the theater, they weren't underneath Mads's feet. That was a bonus.

"How do you know they didn't find any fingerprints?" Helen said. "They didn't say anything to me about it."

"Of course not," Fern scoffed. "Mads is too professional to go around letting things like that slip."

Camille sat back on her heels and daintily dabbed her brow. "So how do you know?"

Fern gave a cat-eating-canary grin. "Jason. Seems he was out at the honky-tonk last night and had a couple too many. He let it slip that they didn't have any different suspects than before."

And those three suspects were Daisy, Chloe, and Veronica.

"Do you think Veronica is capable of something like that?" Camille asked. No one mentioned the fact that Chloe and Daisy were on that list, mainly because no one believed that Daisy or Chloe could have murdered Petro.

"Have you heard that woman on the phone?" Fern asked. "She's a shark."

Arlo couldn't argue with that. Veronica had a certain demeanor, something Arlo would consider her "big city ways," and they hung around her like an aura. Composed, in control, unruffled, flexible, and yet unmoving. She walked around Sugar Springs in designer clothes, with designer shoes and jewelry that, if hocked at the right place, could probably feed half of Sugar Springs for a year. But Arlo knew those items were her armor. That's how she survived in the world she lived in. And it wasn't like she would buy new clothes to come to Sugar Springs for only a couple of weeks. She came with what she had; what she had was just a lot more than what most in Sugar Springs had. But then she had heard the woman on the phone, and her collected demeanor became dark and dangerous. Veronica was one person that Arlo would not want to cross.

"She's a shark," Fern said. "And sharks are killers."

Camille and Helen seemed to mull over what she had said.

"I'm not sure that's a fair assessment," another voice said.

The words, or something very much like them, had been in Arlo's thoughts. Yet she had not been the one to speak them. All four ladies turned to find Veronica standing at the stairs at the edge of the stage. Arms were crossed, manicured fingers drumming against rail-thin arms, lips pressed together, and one dark brow arched upward as if silently asking for an explanation.

"Watch out!" Helen yelled.

Some unnamed intuition called Arlo to look up. Perhaps a miracle, especially when the perceived danger was at stage right. But look up she did as a beam from the catwalk high overhead crashed downward.

She moved without thinking into almost a home-plate slide. It was an instinctive motion meant to scoot Fern out of harm's way. Or perhaps she thought she would throw her body over the other woman. It was just that, on some level, she knew that Fern needed her protection. The sound of the beam hitting the stage was like a sonic boom. Complete with delay. It was this great noise, a beat of silence, then red-hot pain.

Nausea crept up somewhere in Arlo's middle leaving a salty taste in her mouth. It took another heartbeat to realize what had happened. She had indeed pushed Fern out of harm's way, only to land herself right smack dab in the middle of it.

12

"YOU WERE SERIOUS?" CHLOE CAME FROM AROUND THE SIDE OF the dogleg coffee bar to greet Arlo at the door of Books and More. After three x-rays, two stitches, and a tetanus shot, Arlo had found herself in the casting room at the Sugar Springs Medical Clinic.

Fern had found the term incredibly funny, considering there was a movie premiere on the horizon, though that irony had taken one step back when the X-rays returned with the news that Arlo had broken her ankle instead of her leg. Not that she would have found either scenario particularly humorous. She knew the ladies meant well, and that humor was sometimes the best way to deal with an uncomfortable situation, but if she heard one more...

"You know when they say, 'Break a leg'—" Chloe started, but Arlo cut her off fast.

"Don't. Say it."

They had been best friends for years, and Chloe knew when to abandon something, but the grin on her face told Arlo the joke would rise to the surface once again.

"It's my ankle," she reminded them. And she was thankful that it was. At least her cast only reached from just under her knee to the second joint on her swollen, purple toes.

"Which is soooo different than your leg," Fern drawled.

"At least your cast is nice," Chloe said. "*Nice* being a relative term."

Arlo used a cane she'd gotten at the clinic and hobbled over to the reading nook.

"What's happening, hot stuff?" Faulkner trilled.

"They had a yellow," Helen said with a shake of her head. "I thought that would be so much cheerier. Or even purple."

To match my toes, Arlo thought drily.

Fern made a face as she followed Helen and Camille into the reading area and gathered around Arlo. "At least the black will look good for the funeral."

"Hoo-rah," Arlo said sarcastically. And she had thought Sunday had been bad. Though she was pretty certain she would rather plan another funeral than piss off a New York shark agent, break her ankle, and lose her second-best pair of jeans. She had loved those jeans. Now the right leg was cut off at the thigh. She supposed she could make them summer cutoffs. Under normal circumstances, that probably was exactly what she would have done. But it was too soon to make those lemonade decisions.

Arlo sighed and propped her leg up on the coffee table in front of her. With what she was sure was visible effort, she tried to relax. But how could she? There was simply too much to do. She had books to shelve, accounting to catch up on in the office, orders to put through, a house to clean, the Coliseum to get ready for the movie premiere. And an Alayna Adams Lookalike Contest to host. There was simply too much to do, so relaxing was out of the question. Even if the day's events had worn her down to a nub. Because all too soon, she knew that the dull throbbing in her leg—which had been a white-hot searing pain and only reduced to a dull throb by the pain medicine that was currently making her sleepy—would turn back into the white-hot pain from just after the accident. It was a vicious circle. So for now, she just wanted to sit. Pretend to relax. And wait for whatever shoe she knew was going to drop.

Across from her Fern jumped to her feet. "Mads!" the woman greeted.

Arlo couldn't say it was *the* shoe, but it was definitely *a* shoe.

She turned in her seat to watch her longtime friend advance toward her.

Normally Mads stopped at the coffee bar for a mocha java, but this time he came straight for her. "I tried to catch up with you at the clinic, but…" He trailed off.

"Why are you trying to catch up with me?" Arlo said. She felt so conspicuous sitting there with this large black cast on her leg. It was cumbersome and heavy and seemed to be pulling all of her strength down with it.

"I wanted to talk to you about the accident at the theater."

Fern shook her head. "That was no accident."

Arlo tried to summon the energy to tell her to hush, but she just couldn't quite muster it at the time.

"Did you see the look on Veronica's face?" Helen asked.

"That was way beyond RBF." Fern nodded emphatically.

"What do you know about RBF?" Chloe asked, coming into the reading nook and handing Mads his coffee.

He murmured his thanks and blew over the top of the cup as Fern retorted, "A lot. And that was more than resting bitch face."

"She was mad," Helen agreed.

"So Veronica was there at the time?" Mads asked. He set his coffee mug down on the coffee table and plopped himself on the couch across from Arlo. He took out his notebook and jotted down a couple of notes before turning his attention back to her. "And you're okay?"

If it hadn't been for the elbow nudges shared between Helen, Fern, and Camille, Arlo might have suspected that she imagined the concern in his tone. Mads was nothing if not matter-of-fact. He was a strange hybrid of the things he had done in his life. He was laid back, to a point, organized, flexible, and for the most part tough as nails. It wasn't often that people got to see his softer side. And by *not often* she meant *never*.

"I'm fine." At least she would be until the pain medicine wore off. She hadn't figured out how she was going to sleep tonight, but all things in due time.

"Who else was there?" he asked.

"Alvin and Calvin." Fern ticked off on her fingers. "And Johnny Bob. They were the ones moving that beam."

"And the four of you?" Mads confirmed.

"Yes," Arlo said.

"I'm told that the beam is something that would have held backgrounds and backdrops in times past."

Helen nodded. "Yes, and they can't remove it because of the historical society stipulations. They were just trying to make sure it didn't interfere with the new movie screen that we're having installed for the premiere."

Mads shook his head. "So you can install a new movie screen, but you can't take down the old things?"

"Pretty much," Helen said. "There's a lot of guidelines and things like that. The movie screen isn't permanent. They can install it because it's supposed to be temporary."

"But the beam was supposed to remain in place."

"That's right," Helen said.

"That's some accident," Mads said.

Fern threw her arms in the air and scoffed. "It was no accident," she said. "It was the ghosts, I'm telling you."

"Or Veronica," Camille added almost a little hesitantly.

Mads wrote a few more notes in his little notebook, then looked back up at the four of them. "But none of you believe that Calvin and Alvin or Johnny Bob are responsible."

"Of course not," the three ladies said in unison.

Arlo might have answered, but she was still a little dreamy at the time. The whole conversation was surreal. Were they really talking about beams falling and movie screens?

She might lay off the pain medicine tonight. That is, if she wanted a clear thought in her head. Right in that moment, she wasn't sure whether she cared one way or another.

"And Veronica," Camille said again. "I mean, I like the woman, but if you could have seen the look on her face."

"So describe it to me," Mads said. He buried his nose back in the little notebook and was again writing furiously. Or so it seemed to Arlo.

"Mad, angry, furious," Camille said, sounding somewhat like a thesaurus. "She was not happy."

"And why was she angry?" Mads asked.

"We were discussing who could have been responsible for Petro's murder." Fern crossed her arms and spread her feet shoulder-width apart as if taking a stand, daring Mads to tell them to butt out.

Arlo supposed he might have to, but he seemed to change his mind after his gaze fell softly on her then and darted away again.

"I'm guessing she didn't cotton to being a suspect?"

Arlo blinked as if to make sure she had read his expression correctly, but it seemed as if regret had taken up camp. She supposed it was accurate, seeing as how all three women burst into explanation of the hows and the whys all at once.

She caught the words *shark, killer, motive, money,* and *Yankee.*

"I'm sorry I asked."

Arlo supposed he had only said that so she could hear, because there were no protests from her geriatric book club.

"Or the ghost," Fern said. "We can't rule out the ghost."

"I'm pretty sure we can," Arlo managed.

"Here." Chloe appeared at her elbow. "Drink this. I think you need it."

Good friendship is never having to ask, Arlo thought, and she took a big sip of whatever was in the cup Chloe had passed her.

"And this." Her friend handed her the largest sugar cookie Arlo had ever seen.

"What is this?" Arlo asked. "Did you make this?"

"Daisy did."

"That's what she should name the bakery." Arlo laughed. "Daisy Did It. 'Cuz that's what we keep saying. 'Did you make this muffin?' No, Daisy did it. 'Did you make this cake?' No, Daisy did it. See? It's funny."

Chloe nodded slowly, and Arlo was certain she could see the track of her motion as she moved. She blinked once to try to clear her eyes. Apparently her pain meds had kicked in. Hard.

"Just eat."

Arlo nodded as her friend moved away. Sometime during the exchange, the chatter from her book club had died to nothing. And once again Mads's attention was centered on her. "How do you feel about the accident?" he asked.

Three bites into the cookie and the fog covering Arlo's brain was starting to lift. At least enough for her to realize as she had eaten a big breakfast, then she had spent her lunch in the emergency clinic, which was followed by tons of drugs to ease the pain in her broken leg. OMG! She had broken her leg in a theater.

No, wait. It was her ankle. Only her ankle.

Only her ankle.

Maybe the fog was better. She wasn't quite sure. She took another bite of the cookie as Mads patiently waited.

"It was an accident," Arlo said.

The Coliseum was over a hundred years old. It needed repairs monthly, weekly, sometimes even daily, and with everything that everyone in the town was doing to get ready for the movie premiere, it was a wonder they hadn't had more accidents before now.

"Just between friends," Mads said as he stood. "Don't talk to any reporters. We can't handle any more bad press surrounding this premiere. Not if we want to come out even on the deal."

Arlo nodded.

"Let me know if you need anything," Mads said. For a moment she thought he was reaching for her hand, to squeeze her fingers in maybe a reassuring, friendly sort of way, but she must've been mistaken. He gave her a quick nod and headed for the exit.

"You know what we should do," Fern said no sooner than the door had shut behind their chief of police. "We should not let her out of our sight."

Arlo was afraid of something like this. "That's all really sweet, but you don't have to do that—"

She stopped as Fern shook her head. "Not you. Veronica. She's dangerous."

Arlo closed her eyes and said a brief prayer for serenity.

It didn't work.

"I can watch her when she's at the inn," Helen offered. "But not all the time. If I can't leave, we'll need somebody to follow behind her."

"You're not really going to do this, are you?" Arlo asked.

"So now what we need is Camille or myself going to the inn to 'quote-unquote' visit, and if Veronica leaves, we'll just follow behind her. Simple, right?"

"Not simple. Not going to happen." Arlo said. On a normal day, under normal circumstances, she would've stood, glared at the three ladies in turn, showing them how serious she was, but coming out of her cloud of whatever pain medicine they had given her at the clinic had made her realize that she had to adjust. Jumping to her feet in indignation was completely out of the question, seeing as how she had to use her hands and arms to remove her leg from the coffee table and again to hoist herself out of the armchair.

"Where you going?" Helen asked.

"To the bathroom." Arlo looked at her one-time guardian as if daring her to deny her that.

She didn't, of course. Instead she gave a small nod.

Arlo grabbed the aluminum cane they had provided at the clinic and hobbled awkwardly toward the space under the stairs where the bathroom was located.

Thank goodness it wasn't on the second floor. She wasn't up to trying to maneuver stairs. Not yet, anyway.

Still it took her approximately three and half times longer to pee than it ever had before. Some of it might've been lingering vestiges from her painkiller high, and some of it was simply the awkwardness of balancing herself with a bulky cast in her way. She finally managed to complete her task. She flushed the toilet, washed her hands, and stared at herself in the mirror above the small sink. She had broken her ankle. At the movie theater. If somebody had told the story she wasn't sure she would believe it herself. It was too close to leg—literally and figuratively—and was simply too much of a pun. Or a joke. Or a play on words. She wasn't quite sure which. But it was funny. Or at least it would have been if it hadn't happened to her. With a sigh, she tossed the paper towel into the trash and hobbled back out into the bookstore.

Fern, Camille, and Helen were conspicuously absent from the reading nook where they had just been—she checked the clock—ten minutes before. It had taken her ten minutes to pee? It was going to be a long six to eight weeks.

"Where's the book club?"

Chloe shot her an apologetic look, and Arlo knew immediately she wasn't going to like what her friend was about to say. "They went over to the inn to see if Veronica was there. They were looking to start tailing her this afternoon."

Arlo sighed and tried to slip onto one of the barstools around the coffee bar, but her cast was just too cumbersome. Instead she leaned a hip against one stool. "I must've done something really, really wrong in a past life."

Chloe chuckled. "Do you feel better?" she asked.

Arlo smiled at her friend. "Lots. Thanks."

Chloe returned the smile. "That's what friends are for." She didn't have to say that she missed the time that they got to spend together, the time that she was now spending with her son. Arlo knew. Chloe knew. There was no reason to say the words.

"Oh," Chloe added. "Fern wanted me to tell you that you shouldn't expect her to be your slave since you—and I quote—saved her hide today."

"I wouldn't dream of it," Arlo said. Pushing Fern out of the way from the beam was second nature. Though she had to admit she still might get some mileage out of this. Telling Fern that she owed her for saving her from broken bones, or worse, could possibly be the perfect way to keep the book club in line. But Arlo knew that was just wishful thinking. The ladies were wild cards, and she loved them all the more for it. "I suppose I should go out there."

Chloe frowned. "You do not need to be driving."

Arlo looked down at the cast encasing her right foot. It might have been possible if her car had been an automatic, but it seemed like she wasn't going to be driving for quite some time. Not to mention the drugs they pumped into her at the medical clinic.

Chloe couldn't close. Somebody had to take care of the bookstore. Sam was definitely not in his office today, nor would she feel comfortable asking him to run her around, all things considered. They were burying his mom in two days. She supposed Mads could just stomp around and yell and scream and tell her how she needed to get them in check, but some things just weren't possible.

She had just about settled herself to staying put when the bell over the front door rang out its warning that someone had entered Books and More. Arlo and Chloe both turned to the door at the same time.

Daisy rushed inside, her cheeks a little pink, most likely from the ovens at her bakery and the exertion it had taken her to run across the street in five-inch heels. "Oh my gosh! Phil just told me! Are you okay?" She buzzed around the dogleg side of the coffee bar and began squeezing Arlo's limbs as if that held the answer to her health and well-being. Then she noticed bulky black cast on Arlo's right leg. "You broke your leg!"

Arlo smiled at her newfound friend. "It's my ankle, actually."

"At the theater," Daisy said. "You broke your leg at the theater. It's kind of funny. But only if you're okay."

"I'm okay." She gave Daisy a reassuring smile. It was just a broken leg, er, ankle, and people broke their ankles all the time. Every day. Right? But seeing as how she was stuck at Books and More and unable to chase after the book club, she wondered if somehow Fern had conspired with a voodoo doctor to make the injury happen so they would be free to solve who killed Petro.

Or maybe there were still quite a few drugs in her system. It was anybody's guess.

"Daisy," Chloe said, shooting Wally's widow an enticing smile. "Arlo can't drive."

Daisy gave her a wide-eyed look. "It's a little scary riding with her, but I wouldn't say she can't—oh. You mean with her leg."

Chloe nodded indulgently. "That's right. But she needs to go out to the inn. Do you think you could give her ride out there? Is someone at the bakery who can take care of it while you're gone?"

"Yes, of course. I could give you a ride," Daisy said. "I would be happy to do that."

"That would be great." Arlo said. "Can we go now?"

13

Arlo picked her way over the stepping-stones that led from the driveway to the porch of the Sugar Springs Inn. She had never noticed before, but she could see what Veronica meant by the pathway being lethal on heels. The large stones had grown unlevel with time and probably needed to be reset. She would talk to Helen about that later. Right now she needed to get inside and possibly save Veronica from a fate worse than jail—her Friday-night-turned-every-day book club.

She knew they were inside. Undoubtedly Helen was there, even though her Smart Car was firmly stored in the garage and Fern's Towncar was parked off to one side. She didn't know if Camille hadn't brought her own car or if she was off on her own adventure. But two out of three ain't bad.

"Hold up," Daisy called. She had caught her heel on one of the stones and was trying to work it free without losing the tap of her shoe.

That was something Arlo wouldn't have to worry about for a while considering she wouldn't be able to wear anything that lifted her left side above the walking cast on her right. Joy of joys.

She stopped and waited for Daisy.

"That's the third pair of shoes I've ruined out here."

"That's a shame" Arlo said. "But for now I think we need to go save Veronica."

Daisy's eyes grew wide. "What's the matter with Veronica?"

"The book club," Arlo answered.

Daisy stopped just before they entered the inn. "Are they trying to solve mysteries again? Exciting!"

Arlo shook her head. "It's not exciting. It's annoying. And Mads has had enough."

"Pee-shaw." Daisy flipped one hand in the air as if whatever Mads said had no significance whatsoever. "They're sweet little old ladies. They don't mean any harm."

"They may not mean harm," Arlo started, "but they sure can bring some." And with that she opened the front door of the inn and prayed that the scene she found wasn't something from the Three Stooges.

"Elly?" she called, stepping into the foyer.

Daisy was right behind.

"In here," Helen replied.

"I think it's cute that you have a special name for her," Daisy said.

Arlo didn't answer. Instead she made her way into the common room where she supposed the scene was about what she had expected. Veronica and the book club ladies were gathered around, lounging on the extra cushiony, overstuffed furniture that Helen provided. There were two decanters sitting on the coffee table. Well, if you considered Mason jars decanters. In one, the liquid was pure purple. In the other, it was a milky wine color.

"Come in. Come in." Helen waved her into the room. "Hey, Daisy good to see you, too."

"We're just having a drink," Fern said. "Introducing Veronica to some of the local labor, as it would be." She nodded toward the Mason jars on the table.

"We went out to Anderson's and picked up some moonshine so we could share it with Veronica." Helen said.

Arlo had seen Anderson's moonshine, and she had seen grape

Kool-Aid, and that was exactly what was sitting on the coffee table in the Mason jars. When it came to intoxication, they just didn't compare. Arlo wondered if Veronica had noticed that the ladies were drinking out of one jar while she was most likely getting her drinks from the other.

"Drink time's over," she said, swooping in and picking the jars up from the coffee table. Okay, so swooping in had been her plan, but it was hard to sweep with a cast just under her knee to almost the end of her toes. She managed to pick up the moonshine at least. She ignored their protests as she took it into the kitchen. She seriously thought about pouring it down the drain but decided against it. Anderson really did make some kicking corn liquor.

But she had seen this before, this bait and switch that the ladies engaged in when trying to break down the defenses of a suspect. Aside from being underhanded, it was a little bit tacky.

"Now," she said coming back into the room. She dusted her hands as if she had just completed a job well done.

"You are a party pooper," Helen said.

"It's okay," Arlo said. "I've been told that before. And I'm sure it won't be the last time, either."

Veronica pushed elegantly to her feet. "It's okay. I probably should go anyway. I need to go to town and get my shoes from the cobbler. He said they would be ready today."

Fern moved from her place in the armchair and linked elbows with Veronica, as if they were old sorority chums. "Come on. Stay a while more."

It was obvious to Arlo that Veronica was using every bit of her composure to keep from questioning the ladies about why they thought she was guilty of the murder.

She no more thought the thought before Veronica untangled herself from Fern's embrace and looked at the three ladies before her. Thankfully she didn't set that dark brown gaze on Arlo or Daisy. "This is some kind of Southern hospitality," she said with a shake of her head. "Tell me something. They say New Yorkers are abrupt and rude, but I walk in on a conversation about how I should be the number one suspect, and then you invite me to have a drink. Pardon me if I just don't quite understand."

"Oh, that," Camille said in that lilting accent of hers. "Love, we are always mulling over every possibility. We weren't serious about it, just trying to figure out all the ins and outs."

"Yeah, and we don't want our friends arrested. I'm pretty sure Mads is going to try to make an arrest by the end of the week," Helen added.

"You've been watching too many of those true crime shows on Netflix," Arlo said. "Mads will make an arrest when he has evidence to arrest someone. And until then, the three of you need to stay out of his way so that he can do his job."

"We're not in his way." Helen swept one arm around the room. "I'm at my home, my business. Talking with my friends. How can that be in Mads's way?"

Arlo sighed and stumped over to the armchair that Fern had just vacated. It was insane how much the stupid cast on her foot weighed.

"You know what I would like to talk about?" Fern said, sitting down and doing her best to tug Veronica down next to her. "I'm anxious to talk about Wally's new book."

"What's it like?" Camille clapped her hands together and smiled widely. "Please say you'll tell us what it's about."

Veronica allowed herself to be pulled down onto the sofa next to Fern. She braced her hands on her knees, the little gold bracelets she wore on her right wrist jingling with the motion. "It's really something else."

For a moment Arlo wondered if perhaps there was a second jar of moonshine involved in today's deception, for once Wally's new book was brought up, Veronica's entire demeanor changed.

"Tell us what it's about," Helen urged.

"It's a small-town mystery wrapped up in a legend. There's a lost

treasure—sort of *To Kill a Mockingbird* meets *Pirates of the Caribbean*."
She supposed Veronica hadn't told them one detail about the book,
but she had said enough. All three ladies leaned closer to her as she
spoke. "It's strangely melancholy," she said. "And unsettling at the
same time, but the thing is, it's so much better than *Missing Girl*."

"Different enough that two different people could have written
the books?" Arlo couldn't help herself from asking.

Veronica shrugged. "If I had to guess, maybe, yes. But I've seen
ghostwriters, and I've seen all sorts of people who copy other people's
style, so it could be the same author."

And of course they had no true way of knowing. The only person
who might possibly be able to tell them would be Inna, who had
served for years as Wally's assistant, or Daisy.

All eyes in the room turned to Wally's widow.

"What?" she said.

"Did he write it?" Helen asked.

"I have no idea." Daisy shook her head, her blond hair brushing across her shoulders. "Wally was such a private person. I always
thought he would eventually let me in, but he wasn't like that. This
part of his life was like a separate compartment from the others. I've
never seen anybody like that. He had no crossovers." She frowned and
gently dragged one finger across the corner of her eye.

Arlo wondered if she had an itch or if she was crying. If she was
crying, she cried prettier than anyone Arlo had ever seen in her life.

"I have no idea if he wrote it or not," Daisy continued.

"If it's true," Veronica started again. "If it's true and Inna wrote
Missing Girl, then it could very well be that Wally wrote *Under the
Buttonwood Tree*." She shook her head sadly. "If that's the case, the
world is now missing a literary genius. The next William Faulkner
here and then gone in the same instant."

The room fell silent. Listening to Veronica talk, Arlo couldn't
imagine that she had anything to do with the trouble at the theater.
Not that she had thought Veronica guilty at all. But she needed

that book as much as any of them did. Sure, it made sense that she wouldn't want the truth about Wally's other book to come out, but what if it could be proven that he had written this new book as well? Not one book in question, but two.

"Well, if you need readers," Camille said. "I taught English for years."

"I would love to beta read," Helen said. "It's kind of been a dream of mine."

"Mine, too," Fern said, not willing to be left out. "I never read a book before it's been published. How cool would that be?"

The words had no sooner left their mouth that Veronica shook her head. "The world's not ready for this to be read yet. But soon."

Arlo wasn't sure what that meant. Was the book truly not ready? If that were the case, why were there reader copies? Or perhaps she was simply not ready to share it. Was it just too much to have a murder and a new book back-to-back? Arlo had no idea. She supposed the whole situation was a PR nightmare.

"Whoo." Veronica stood, wobbled a bit, and nodded to the ladies gathered there. "I think I should lie down now. Thanks for the drink. What was it called again?"

"Muscadine moonshine." Helen replied.

Veronica paused. "And a muscadine is what?"

"Sort of like a grape," Fern said. "Lots of people grow them around here. They make great jelly, too."

Veronica nodded. "I'll keep that in mind." And with a small wave, she left the room. Arlo could hear her footsteps on the stairs as she made her way. She sounded as tired as Arlo felt. And she supposed that it had been quite the week so far, for all of them.

"How about some cake?" Helen asked as she stood and looked around at the ladies in the common room.

"Moonshine and cake?" Arlo asked.

Fern scoffed. "Why not?"

"Count me out," Camille said. "Last time we did that…" She whistled low and under her breath.

Arlo was sort of glad she didn't know what had happened then. At least they hadn't had a murder to solve. Or a murder they *thought* they needed to solve.

"And count Fern out since she's driving," Arlo said.

Fern stuck her tongue out at Arlo. "Spoilsport."

Arlo smiled. "You'll thank me later."

"Are you coming to get some cake?" Helen asked.

Helen's cake was always a treat, but she thought of the huge cookie she'd eaten. Add in the fact that she had skipped lunch, and she probably needed to eat a real meal so she could take the medicine the doctor had prescribed. And suddenly she felt tired—very, very tired. "Not now, thanks." She turned to Daisy. "Are you ready to go?"

"Whenever you are."

"If I leave y'all, you'll stay here, right?" She looked at each one of the members of the book club in turn.

The women all nodded innocently. It was the best she could do, given she had a broken ankle and all. And she was extremely ready to go home and rest.

"I'm going to hold you to it," she said pointing at each one of them.

Fern held up three fingers. "Scout's honor," she said.

Arlo just shook her head. She gave Elly a kiss on the cheek and made her way out of the inn once again.

"Watch those rocks," Arlo said as she hobbled down the stairs. She really hoped that this cast got easier to deal with. Right now felt like she was dragging around an anchor chained to her leg. And somehow that image brought up another, Johnny Depp with an anchor, which made her think of what Veronica said about *Under the Buttonwood Tree*. *To Kill a Mockingbird* meets *Pirates of the Caribbean*. How could that be? It sounded fantastic. Better than fantastic. It sounded like something the world needed. And yet if its authorship was in question, would anyone ever see it?

"I really appreciate you driving me over here," Arlo said.

Daisy palmed the keys and shot her a grin. "I'm 'driving Miss Daisy.'"

Arlo laughed. "That was terrible," she said between chuckles.

Daisy smiled back in return. "I know, but it made you laugh."

"Do you have something to eat at the house?" Daisy asked as they drove along. "We could stop and get something to eat, or I can take you by the diner and you can get something to take home." She chanced a look at Arlo as they sat at the red light to turn back onto Main. "It's whatever you want to do."

The thought of having dinner with Daisy somehow held great charm. But she was exhausted. As much as she wanted to spend a little time out, she knew that she needed to spend a lot of time in.

"It's okay if you don't want to," Daisy said. "I don't have a lot of friends in Sugar Springs yet, and I just thought it might be fun."

And then Arlo realized that Daisy had so recently moved to town, gotten busy opening a business, and had pretty much done nothing but bake since she got there.

"I would love to have dinner together," Arlo said. "But can we take a rain check? I really think I need to rest now more than anything."

"Sure." Daisy wasn't quite successful in hiding her disappointment. But Arlo could tell that she understood. "If you'll just take me by Harper's."

Arlo could get a barbecue sandwich minus slaw and head on to the house. Sounded like a perfect evening. Well, aside from the broken ankle.

Daisy chatted amicably as they meandered through Sugar Springs. Around the drive-through at Harper's Barbecue and back out to Arlo's tiny yellow house.

"What should I do with your car?" Daisy asked as she pulled into Arlo's drive. "I mean, I can leave it here and walk back to the store, I guess."

Arlo almost snorted. Only the smell of the barbecue in the sack she held in her lap kept her from laughing out loud. Her stomach growled in hunger and trumped everything else. "You cannot walk in those shoes all the way back to the bookstore."

Daisy lifted one foot. "I guess you're right."

"Just take it back and leave it at Books and More. Park it behind like Russell wants us to, and I'll figure something else out."

"How are you going to get to work tomorrow?"

"I have no idea," Arlo said.

She thanked Daisy once again and gave one small wave before she let herself into the house. She had no sooner set her house keys and the sack of food on the table when the front doorbell rang.

"What the heck?" she muttered under her breath. Using the cane for support, she stepped through the kitchen and into the living room. "I'm on my way!" she called just as the doorbell rang again.

"What do you—" She wrenched open the door but stopped when she saw Sam standing there. He held his own sack from Harper's, and he gave her a sad smile. "I'm a stalker," he said. "I followed you through the line at Harper's, and…" He didn't finish. Arlo stood back so he could come inside. "What have you done to yourself?" he asked.

Arlo shook her head. "Bring that sack on in here," she said. "And I'll tell you all about it."

"It's a good, sit-down story?" Sam asked.

Arlo nodded, somehow knowing he needed a little bit of normalcy in the turmoil that was his life lately. So let him feast on her drama.

She got them both paper plates and managed to scoot into the chair where she normally sat. They unloaded their food. In typical Southern fashion, Sam added his coleslaw on top of his pulled pork sandwich before putting the bun back down on top.

Arlo shook her head. "I consider myself a Southerner now, but that's one habit I've not picked up."

Sam shook his head and took a big bite of the sandwich. "You don't know what you're missing."

She grinned in return. "I don't suppose I do." It seemed there were a lot of things like that lately.

14

AN INSISTENT BLARE OF A FOGHORN BROKE THROUGH ARLO'S sleep. She knew that noise. That annoying wah-wah-wah noise. It was her alarm. It was morning. But she never remembered going to bed. She pushed herself up on her elbow, the bed beneath her so much softer than normal.

"Oof."

Hold on. A bed couldn't talk. She found a spot that wasn't quite so smooshy and warm and managed to push herself up into a sitting position. "Sam?"

They were on the couch. She remembered now. They had eaten supper and come in to watch a movie. She complained about not being able to get comfortable, and he had somehow managed to press her back against his front and snuggled down like they used to do in that short little time between prom and graduation. Between prom and *What makes you think I wanted to stay in Sugar Springs?*

"I guess we fell asleep." Sam rubbed his eyes and pushed himself up on the couch cushions. "What time is it?" he asked on a yawn.

"Seven," she said. "I think." She checked the clock to one side of the front door. 7:05. "Time to get up."

She grabbed her cane at the edge of the couch and somehow managed to hoist herself off him. She could always blame the cast for her difficulty and clumsiness, but it seemed there was a part of her that just didn't want to move. Sam was comfortable and warm and comforting. She supposed he needed her for the same reasons.

Although the night they spent together was completely innocent, she wondered how long it would be before news that his truck had been parked in her driveway all night reached the city limits of Sugar Springs.

"I gotta pee," Arlo said as she hobbled to the bathroom.

"Is there another one?" Sam asked.

"Just give me a minute."

Arlo locked the door behind her stared at herself in the mirror. She looked the same as she always had, perhaps a little more disheveled. She hadn't brushed out her hair last night, and she was still wearing yesterday's clothes, including the one-legged jeans. Then she decided it was too hard to look herself in the mirror. There were things in her expression she wasn't sure she was ready to see yet. Like the longing. The longing that she had felt so deeply for the last two days. Ever since she had helped Sam plan his mother's funeral. She supposed mortality could do that to a person.

"Arlo?" Sam's voice was questioning, almost concerned.

"Just a sec." She had to get a move on. She supposed with a little practice it wouldn't take her much more time at all in the bathroom. Especially if she avoided looking herself in the mirror. She washed her hands, dried them on a towel, and hobbled back out into the hallway. Of course Sam was standing there, handsome, rumpled from sleep, and sad. So very sad that she wanted to wrap her arms around him and pull him close. But something told her that wouldn't be a good idea. No matter how right the action seemed to be.

She stepped to the left to go around him, but he went right and they nearly bumped noses. She stepped back to the right, but he moved left and they bumped again.

He gave a small chuckle. "I'm going this way." He pointed to the right.

"Got it," she said. "I'll go this way." And she went opposite.

Somehow they made it through the morning-after awkwardness. Well, what there was of a morning after, and Arlo breathed a sigh of relief when Sam pulled out from her driveway. Now she just had to figure out how to take a shower, figure out what she was going to wear today, and somehow manage to look herself in the mirror and lug around a bulky cast at work. The joys just kept on coming.

It only took an extra half an hour to tape up her cast and take a shower. Thank heavens she didn't have to wash her hair. That would've really been a chore. As it was, she figured she might have to go into Dye Me a River and have someone there wash it for her, so she didn't risk falling in the shower with this cast.

As for something to wear…she managed to find a pair of khaki chino shorts that looked halfway decent. She paired it with one of her normal work shirts, a three-quarter sleeve button-down blue Oxford that was darted in the front to make it more feminine. But the shoes were another matter altogether.

The only thing she had in her closet that was the same height when she put it on with her walking cast were snow boots. And, as cute as they were with the black faux fur around the top and the snowflake pull on the zipper, she wasn't sure the ensemble really said "entrepreneur," small-business owner, or if she came across more as highborn homeless. Given no other choice, she pulled on one of her running shoes. The difference in height was slight, but she had a feeling that, by the end of the day, every bone from her hips down was going to ache.

Now she just needed to figure out how she was going to get to work. Her phone rang before she could make that final decision.

Elly.

And if Helen was calling her that meant only one thing.

Was she ready for this?

The phone rang again.

Did she have much choice?

No. No, she didn't.

She swiped the phone on and held it to her ear. "Good morning."

"Would you like to tell me why I'm hearing reports that Sam's truck was at your house all night?"

How to answer... How to answer...

"Because his truck was parked at my house all night." She hadn't meant for to sound like a question, but it sure came out that way.

"Arlo Jane."

Arlo couldn't tell if Helen's admonishment was truly admonishing or just surprised.

"Nothing happened. He just stayed the night." That didn't sound very innocent, now did it?

"Aha. Then can I say that next time you try something like this in a town the size of Sugar Springs that you be a little more discreet?"

"There was nothing to be discreet about," Arlo said. "We fell asleep on the couch."

Before Helen could respond, a beep sounded in Arlo's ear. She held the phone away from her face so she could see who was calling in.

Sam.

"Hold on, Elly." She switched over. "Sam, what's up?"

"I just got a call from Fern, and I'm thinking—"

"I'm already on the phone with Helen." Like she needed this right now.

"Sorry. I didn't mean to cause problems."

He didn't need to deal with this either. Tomorrow they would bury his mother; today he was having to fend off the rumor mill of Sugar Springs, Mississippi.

"Don't worry about it." Arlo shifted and sighed.

"I will, you know," he said. But that was just Sam. "I was wondering," he said, "if you might need a ride to work."

"I don't think so," Arlo said, her tone apologetic. But she knew he would understand. "Having your truck stay overnight at the house is enough for one day, don't you think?"

"I suppose," he said. Did he really sound disappointed or was that how she wanted him to be?

"I gotta go," she said. "I still got Elly on the other line."

"Yep, and there's Camille calling me now," he said. "Talk to you later."

Sam hung up, and Arlo switched back over to her one-time guardian. "You know...I just decided something," she said. "Talk all you want. I know what happened, and that's all there is to it. Now I've got to figure out how I'm getting to work. So, bye."

It was the closest she had ever come to hanging up on Elly. She had no sooner tapped the phone off than a car horn honked outside. Was that at her house? She peeked out the front and saw Daisy sitting in a cute little red Miata that she had no doubt bought with Wally's money.

Daisy waved. "I came to get you for work," she said with a big smile.

Arlo smiled in return. That was just Sugar Springs.

....

By seven o'clock that Tuesday, Arlo was ready to cut the cast off her leg herself, even though she knew she wouldn't. Daisy dropped her off with a sack from the diner and a promise to pick her up in the morning for Sam's mother's funeral. Just another joy of the week.

At least she had managed to deftly field any questions about why Sam's truck was seen at her house overnight. It helped that most people, like Fern and Camille, began their question with "I know this is none of my business, but..."

To which Arlo could say *You're exactly right* and not answer at all. The truth was, she didn't have an answer. She didn't have an answer for them, and she didn't have an answer for herself. Yet one thing was certain; she wouldn't be able to put off not dealing with her feelings indefinitely. But it surely couldn't be done the week of his mother's funeral.

Arlo ate her supper in front of the television, watching reruns of *Friends* and doing her best not to assign the characters to people in her life. Was Daisy Rachel? Or was that role reserved for Chloe? Or maybe Daisy was Phoebe and Rachel was Chloe. And don't even get her started on the guys…

She threw the remains of her dinner in the trash, and though she fussed about having to cook for one, she could do with a home-cooked a meal.

She supposed she could have gone out to the inn and had dinner with Helen and the many bachelors of Sugar Springs, but that opened up the whole Sam thing again and left too many opportunities for too many questions.

Sam. She couldn't read more into it than there was. They had fallen asleep. She supposed he hadn't wanted to be alone in his mother's house. Not when he had been there with her all these months. But tonight she was certain he had company of one kind or another, some relative come in from Meridian or Birmingham, who would keep him from being by himself. And hopefully keep him from thinking about her. Fretting over the rumors they had inadvertently started. He had other things—more important things—to think about other than her.

Not that he was. Because there was nothing between them. And there hadn't been for a long time.

Okay, so she was wrong. There was something between them, and it was called friendship. That's all there was to it.

She turned the air down and slipped into a pair of cotton gym shorts that would fit over her cast. Hopefully tonight she could get a little sleep. The only thing that had allowed her to rest last night was Sam. And just like that, he was back in her thoughts again.

She brushed her teeth, combed out her hair, and decided to make an early night of it. She was reading *Missing Girl* again. Trying to get a better feel for it this time than she had before. But she wasn't as disappointed as Chloe was over the writing style or even the topic; she just wanted one more pass through it. Maybe to tide her over until *Under the Buttonwood Tree* would be released. Of course, if Veronica was still walking around with it in her briefcase, then it would be a year or more before it even hit the shelves.

She turned off the lights in the front of her house and tromped her way back to the bedroom. Pillows. That's what she needed. Lots and lots of pillows. She grabbed the ones from the spare room, both the throw pillows and the regular ones, and piled them all up on her bed. She was just settling down when her phone rang from the other room. She had left it in the living room. With a sigh, she pushed up and stumped her way back down the hallway and to the front of the house.

She shouldn't have been surprised. Five of the seven days in any given week, she managed to go to bed without it, leaving it somewhere in her house instead. Which was bad, considering she didn't have a landline anymore and needed her cell phone were something to happen.

She snatched it up and looked at the screen a moment before the call disconnected.

Mads.

She thumbed the phone open and dialed him back. He answered seconds later, before it even had time to ring on her end.

"I was just coming over there." His voice was short, stern, typical Mads.

Great greeting. "Why?"

"You have a broken leg, and you didn't answer your phone."

"I have a broken ankle, and it was in another room." She thought about that sentence for a second. "My phone was in another room, not my ankle."

He chuckled, and some of the tension fell away from the conversation.

"So what's up?" she asked. She put him on speaker, then set the phone on the nightstand as she once again tried to make herself comfortable in the bed.

"Nothing, I suppose. I just wanted to check on you."

"I'm fine," she said. "Tired of this cast already, but fine."

"Yeah, I bet," he said.

"What about you?"

His tone was resigned, softly controlled. And she had heard it before. It was what she liked to call his "at the edge" voice. "Lot of stuff going on right now," he replied.

"Media getting to ya?"

She could almost hear him shake his head and shrug. "I was used to it when I was playing, but now..."

"Yeah."

He didn't have to finish. The same thing had happened when Wally was killed. The media had descended on Sugar Springs, making it hard for Mads to do his job. It made it hard for most of them to do their jobs. The town wasn't big enough for that many news trucks. And with all the attention on Mads and his lack of results in finding the killer, well, the pressure was mounting, and people were starting to wonder if holding the premiere was still a good idea and if Sugar Springs's finest could protect their important out-of-town visitors.

"Any plans for the night?" he asked casually, oh so casually.

"Yeah, I'm going roller skating later."

"How in the world—" He stopped. "You're joking, right?"

"I'm joking."

On the other side of town, Mads sighed. "Well, I won't keep you," he said. "I just wanted you to know that if you need anything, anything at all, you know you can call me."

"I know."

"And tomorrow?"

He didn't have to finish for her to know what he was talking about. Sam's mother's funeral. "Daisy's giving me a ride. I think she has taken it upon herself to be my personal chauffeur since I can't drive my car."

"I told you you should trade that thing in for something from this millennium as well as something with an automatic transmission," he teased.

"You should take that back. What if my car had heard you?"

"It might have driven itself off a cliff and saved the junkman the trouble."

"I'm going to pretend that you didn't say that," she said, her voice mockingly stern.

The other side of the phone grew quiet. "Anything at all," Mads finally said.

"I appreciate that."

"Good night, Arlo."

"Good night."

....

The weatherman had called for sunny days for the remainder of the week, but when Arlo got up Wednesday morning, it was raining.

Was there anything worse than a rainy-day funeral?

A rainy-day funeral while wearing a cast that had to be covered in plastic. But she wasn't going to let a little rain stop her from supporting her friend. She would just cover the cast with a black garbage sack, which would of course match her black pencil skirt and her black button-down that she had chosen for the day. It wasn't her best funeral attire, but it was the best she could do under the circumstances. Plus she had overslept because she hadn't slept much the night before. She was blaming the fact that she had been uncomfortable all night due to having a two-hundred-pound cast on her leg, but deep down, she knew it was more than that. It had taken a while for her to accept what her mind was telling her. Mads had called to see if Sam was there at her house last night. Why else would he have called?

Because he was checking on you, she argued back with herself. There was a part of her that wanted Mads to call and see if Sam was there, and she couldn't figure out if that part wanted it bad enough to make her think that it was actually true. Or maybe she just felt like shaking things up a little bit in quiet Sugar Springs.

As if her outfit wasn't bad enough, she couldn't figure out what to do with the shoes. Her hips were still killing her from the day before, but she was not going to wear snow boots. In Mississippi. In May. Aside from it being just flat-out too hot, she was fairly certain she would look like she needed to be checked into the mental hospital.

She eased down onto her hands and knees, shifting through the shoes that had collected in the bottom of her closet. She always had the best of intentions putting them in neat shoeboxes that were see-through so that she could stack them on the shelves above her hanging clothes. Then she could look at the shoes all lined up and know exactly what to wear any given day. Then again they all hid at the bottom of the closet. Shoes needed to be close to the ground, right? Well, that was her story, anyway. She eased to her hands and knees, still digging through the closet, and then she found them. The pair of pumps she was trying to break in when they found Wally's body on the sidewalk in front of Books and More. She pulled them from the closet. She hadn't worn them since then, which was a shame. They were great shoes. A little too tall for her walking cast, but great shoes. She went to set them aside when something fell to the carpet, a small piece of black plastic. A heel cap.

Not the great pumps from Wally's demise but another pair. A pair of black mules. And the little piece of black plastic made her think of the red one she had found at the inn. The one shaped like a diamond and studded with fake stones. At least she had thought they were fake stones. But what had she done with it? Maybe she had left it in the laundry.

She started toward the mudroom to compare the heel cap from her shoes to the one she found at the inn. But it wasn't there. What had she done with it? She remembered having it at Books and More. She had pulled it from her purse and shown everyone, then…nothing. It was almost as if it had vanished. But it had to be somewhere. Maybe she had left it at the bookstore.

Shoot! She had wanted to see the two side by side because the red one was such a distinctive shape. She didn't need to compare the two pieces—they were the same, heel caps. And yet not. So could it be that the tiny piece of plastic was important? Could it be a clue as to who killed Petro?

15

IN TRUE SOUTHERN FASHION, EVERYONE GATHERED BACK AT SAM'S
mother's house after the funeral. Marjorie Tucker had lived in Sugar
Springs for the majority of her life and was well loved, an adoration
that was distinctly noticeable in the number of casseroles, pies, and
mayonnaise-based salads that had been brought to the wake.

"It's not really a wake," Camille said as they stood shoulder-
to-shoulder in Marjorie's house with most of the town's residents
milling around. Everyone had a paper plate and plastic fork and a
snow-white paper napkin like the ones Sam's sister was handing
out a little too enthusiastically. Arlo supposed her mother's death
was completely out of her control, but making sure everyone had a
napkin was something she could accomplish. And she had set out to
do it with a fervor.

"Poor girl," Arlo said.

"Who?" Elly asked.

Arlo nodded toward Sam's sister.

"It's been called a wake my whole life," Fern said. She took a bite of
macaroni salad and pointed her fork at Camille. "Don't go changing
things now."

"This is a funeral repast," Camille explained gently. "The wake
is where they used to sit up with the dead body overnight to make

sure he didn't wake up. That way if there was a misdiagnosis and the person wasn't really dead, then they weren't accidentally buried alive."

"Thanks for that cheerful account," Helen said. "I don't know if I would've made it through the day without it."

Arlo decided to ignore the three women. Sometimes it just worked out better that way. She scanned the room, noting faces she hadn't seen in a while and some that she thought had come in from out of town. Perhaps Marjorie's family or even Sam's father Ken's family.

In her visual sweep, Arlo's gaze snagged on Sam's. He was sitting next to a large woman with short blue-gray curls and a strand of pearls that looked to be as old as Sugar Springs itself.

Arlo had been introduced to the woman at some point that day, and she remembered her to be an aunt of Marjorie's.

Sam gave her a small smile, which she promptly returned. She hoped hers was a little more cheerful than his had been. His sadness was understandable but heartbreaking.

He turned his attention back to his aunt, and the moment was broken.

"Elly," she said, turning to the woman next to her. "That little red plastic piece? Did I leave that at the inn?"

"I don't know, dear. We can go look. Why?" she asked. Helen tossed her plate in the trash and wiped her hands on a napkin. Helen tossed it into the can as well.

"I don't know. I just feel like I want to look at it again. But I don't know what I did with it." Which was beyond stupid, seeing as how it could possibly be a clue and she had carelessly tossed it aside somewhere. She supposed she wasn't thinking about finding clues in the hallway outside Petro's room, but more inside the room and perhaps in the theater where he had died. But the heel cap came off a pair of shoes, naturally. It might have been loosened by the flagstones that led up to the inn and then lost in the hallway by…anyone. A visitor to Petro's room or even Veronica, who was down the hall from Petro.

"Can we?" Arlo asked. "Can we go to the inn and see if it's there?"

And maybe dig through Veronica shoes while we're at it?

If only she had looked the first time she found herself in Veronica's room. Why hadn't she noticed then? She had been staring right at her shoes but couldn't remember one single pair.

"We're going to head out now," Arlo said, tossing the remains of her funeral meal into the trash. There was only so much Jell-O salad a person could eat without throwing their hands up in surrender.

Camille turned to Helen. "Are you going to the theater? There's still a lot of work that needs to be done."

Fern nodded. "We were just about to head over there ourselves."

Helen played it off perfectly. "I'm going to run by the inn first, and then we'll be there."

Camille and Fern nodded. "We'll follow you over," Fern said.

"Don't forget to tell Sam you're leaving, Arlo," Camille reminded her. "He's going to want to know that you're gone."

Arlo had no intention of leaving without telling Sam goodbye but nodded at her friend.

"See you later," she said to Fern and Camille and started winding her way through the crowd of people packed into Marjorie Tucker's house. It would've been a tight squeeze on a normal day, but dragging her cast around made it even worse. Add in a cane and... Well, maybe that was why she had it. So she could knock people out of the way to get to her destination.

Something snagged her arm. Arlo turned to find Daisy at her elbow.

"Hey," Daisy said. "Can I talk to you for a sec?"

"We were just leaving," Arlo said. For some reason, an impromptu conversation with Daisy seemed a little unappetizing.

Daisy's gaze shifted from Arlo and Helen. "It won't take long."

Unable to see a way out of it other than just flat-out refusing, Arlo waved Helen on and turned back to Daisy. "What's up?"

Daisy moved from one dainty foot to the other. If she looked glamorous on the days when she was going in to make scones and cupcakes, then she looked doubly glamorous, Hollywood elegant, the girl next door via ha-cha-cha today in her slinky black dress and tall black heels with her blond hair falling softly around thin shoulders. Arlo felt beyond frumpy in comparison.

She just had to go and break her ankle. Like that was the sole difference between the two of them.

"How serious is it between you and Sam?"

"Come again?" Arlo asked.

Daisy shifted once more. "How serious is it between you and Sam?"

She nodded. "That's what I thought you said."

"Then why did you make me ask again?"

Arlo shook her head. "We're friends," she said. Because that at least was the truth. From there, she had no idea what her relationship with Sam was or what it could be.

"Oh." Daisy looked down at her delicate pink fingernails then back up to Arlo. "So if you're friends, you wouldn't mind if I asked him to the movies."

Arlo stopped. "Of course not." But that wasn't the truth. Yet she *couldn't* mind. She didn't have a right to mind. And if she definitely didn't know her own mind and heart, then it would be grossly unfair to try to keep him on hold for something that happened over fifteen years ago.

Daisy visibly relaxed. "Okay. Good."

"I mean, I wouldn't do it today," Arlo said.

"Of course not," Daisy replied. "I would never do that. But I was just thinking, in a few days, maybe I would ask him."

"Sure," Arlo said. "That would be fun for the two of you."

"Would you like a glass of water?" Helen's question came just behind Arlo.

"I thought you went to tell Sam bye," Arlo said.

"I thought I might better get you a drink first to swallow down all those lies." Helen chuckled.

"I am not lying," Arlo said.

"Is there something going on between the two of you?" Daisy asked. "I mean, I don't want to step on any toes."

"You're not going to step on any toes," Arlo assured her.

"I don't know," Helen interjected. "There are a lot of toes to step on."

"Will you stay out of this?" Arlo hissed.

Helen shrugged. "Just saying."

"Well, stop saying," Arlo said. "Besides, when did you get on Team Sam? I thought you were all about Mads."

Helen glanced over to where Mads stood, talking to one of Sam's uncles or cousins or some secondary male relative.

"He's too brooding," Helen said.

"I've got an idea. Why don't you stay out of my love life?"

"Yeah, that's not going to happen," Helen said, and on that note, she turned. Despite her height, Arlo lost her in the crowd.

"Arlo?" Daisy wanted a definitive answer.

Arlo nodded. "Sure," she said, somehow the words not stabbing at her like they had previously. "Ask Sam to the movies. I'm sure he would appreciate it."

....

"Are you sure it was in here?" Helen asked.

Arlo looked around the large, spotlessly clean kitchen at the Sugar Springs Inn.

"The last time I remembered having it, I was here. At the inn. Could it be on the floor somewhere?" Arlo asked. Not that she could get down there and look. Not with all the tile underfoot and a cast on one ankle.

"I don't remember you having it at all," Helen said. "Are you sure you had it here last?"

"Positive. I mean, I think so." It wasn't that she really needed it. She just wanted to take a look at it one more time. She had gone through all of her shoes that morning, and every pair she owned had black heel caps, even her tan pumps. Which of course she couldn't wear because she had broken her ankle. And who knew if she'd be able to wear them after she got the cast off? But that was for another day. Another day when so much wasn't looming overhead. Still, with movie premieres, lookalike contests, murders, accidents, and stars and star-wannabes all over the place, she was looking for what might only be considered trash when it was all said and done.

Still the red heel cap was unusual. What color shoe would have a red heel on it? *Red*, she thought. Though with as fancy as it was, she supposed it could be on just about any color under the sun. White, black, silver, even clear. But who didn't like red shoes?

"Who do you think would have red shoes?" Arlo asked.

Helen stared at her as if she'd grown a second head. "How would I know?"

"I don't mean in the universe," Arlo said. "I mean here in Sugar Springs. Have you ever seen Veronica wear red shoes in Sugar Springs?"

"I'm not in the habit of taking inventory of people's feet," Helen said. "I stopped doing that a long time ago. You know, that time when shoes become less important to a woman because her feet age in dog years."

Arlo nodded. "Got it." And it would be highly unethical to go into Veronica's room and look at her shoes. So she wasn't even going to ask about that.

"Yoo hoo!" It was Camille and Fern.

"In the kitchen," Helen called.

"Do you think the inn is haunted?" Fern asked, coming into the room, Camille right behind her. "We keep telling everybody about the ghosts in the theater, but no one seems to want listen. So what about the inn? It's older than the theater. Do you have any ghosts in any of the rooms?"

"No," Helen said emphatically. "And I like it that way. Don't start any more rumors."

"Did you see Mads today?" Camille asked.

"Did Helen put you up to that?" Arlo returned.

Camille filled the teakettle with water and set it on the stove to heat. Then she turned back to Arlo. "Up to what, love?"

Arlo shook her head. "Never mind."

"I saw him," Fern said. "He's extra brooding these days, don't you think?"

"You'd be brooding too if you had three ladies sticking their nose into police business constantly."

"I resent that," Helen said. "It's not constant, and we only want to help."

Fern lifted her glass in salute. "Hear, hear," she said.

"I think you'd be brooding too, if you didn't have any clues for this case." Camille said.

"He's got clues," Fern said.

"Like what?" Helen asked.

Like the little red heel cap that Arlo lost.

"There's the lady in red," Fern said.

"The lady who we don't even know is real and who bears to close a resemblance to Inna, who is also in prison," Helen said.

"Jail," Fern corrected. "What about the note?"

"I'd forgotten about that." Helen nodded. "Except what good is it, really? We don't know what it says. There was only half of it. It was written in Russian. Or Ukrainian. Or one or the other. Is there much difference between the two?"

"If you can't speak either, it doesn't really matter, does it?" Camille said.

"It was signed with an S," Helen reminded them.

"S for Inna?" Camille shook her head.

"S for Sasha," Fern countered.

"I thought you said it was a love letter," Helen said.

Fern gave her an emphatic nod.

"Oh," Helen said. "If that's the case, and it is from Sasha, do we really even need to know what it says?"

Fern shrugged. "Maybe. Maybe not. And with Frances at the helm of translation"—Fern shook her head—"we might not ever know what it says. Maybe I should just figure it out myself."

"I doubt that very seriously," Arlo added.

"You know who he should get to translate it?" Camille said. "Sasha. I mean, they were friends, after all. And according to him, he's from that area, too."

"What if he was the one who wrote it?" Helen said. "Do you think he would honestly tell you what it said?"

"I'm sure Mads has already thought of all this," Arlo said. Mads was smart, and he knew the law. He had always been a problem-solver. It was just his nature, which was probably why he was so brooding these days, since the biggest problem in his life—a blown-out knee—was something he couldn't solve it all.

"I still think we should call him and tell him." Fern slid off her stool and started rummaging through her purse.

"Don't call him," Arlo protested, even though she knew they would ignore her entirely. She had to at least tell Mads that she had tried.

"No," Fern said. "This is a good idea. Plus," she continued, "I'll tell Frances. She'll love the idea because that means she won't have to do all the translating."

Turned out that Mads had already thought about Sasha as a potential translator, and he was scheduled to go into the police station the following day to look it over.

"Great," Fern said. "So you don't have to translate it anymore."

"I wish," Frances said. "That man still has me chipping away at this, though. This language is… Well, they say English is hard, but I don't know how anyone can learn Russian."

"So for certain it's Russian?"

"Fern Conley," Frances said. "You're trying to get me to give out proprietary information on a murder case. And I thought we were friends."

"We are friends," Fern said. "Don't I bring you tomatoes in the summer?"

"This is completely different."

"They're good tomatoes," Fern said.

"I'm getting off here now," Frances said. "And for future reference, it's only good manners, when you put someone on speakerphone, to tell them that you're doing that."

"Well, she's got you on that one," Helen said after Frances had hung up.

Fern thumbed her phone closed and shook her head at it as if the dark screen had somehow turned against her.

"Anyone up for a trip to the Coliseum to see how things are progressing with the remodel?" Camille's words slowed as she neared the end of the question just enough that Arlo knew she wasn't talking about the paint and gold leaf and new carpet and other items that had been restored in the old theater.

"Mads still has the balcony taped off," Arlo said.

"How do you know that?" Helen asked.

"It stands to reason that the balcony would still be closed," Arlo said. "Because the room here is still taped off, and Petro didn't die here."

"Someone may have," Fern said. "Are you sure you don't have any ghosts, Helen?"

"Maybe," Helen said. "Considering we lost the little plastic piece Arlo found the other day."

Fern frowned. "You lost it?"

Arlo sighed. "Not on purpose. I had it here when the publicist's assistant came in."

Fern nodded impatiently. "Then what did you do with it?"

Arlo shot her a look. "If I knew that, it wouldn't be lost."

"Veronica was fussing about that the other day," Camille said. "Didn't she say she lost one on the flagstones out front?"

"Well, now we lost one in the house." Helen said. "Or at the theater." They had gone from here straight over to the Coliseum.

Fern shook her head. "Or anywhere between here and there."

"And you think this might be a clue?" Camille asked.

"No," Arlo said as Helen answered, "Yes."

They glared at each other for only a moment before turning their attention back to the other two ladies in the room "It might be," Arlo conceded, "but it's definitely not if we can't find it."

"It's a little bitty thing, right?" Camille asked. She held up her both hands, touching her thumbs and forefingers together to create a large patch. "Shaped like so."

"Yes," Arlo said. "But much smaller."

"And would definitely belong to a pair of ladies' shoes," Camille deducted.

"That's what we figure," Arlo said.

"So perhaps if we find the shoes," Helen started, "we find our lady in red?"

Arlo shook her head. "That's a big leap, Neil Armstrong."

"Think about it for a minute. If the woman in red visited here and lost the heel cap off her shoes…" Helen started.

"Or if the heel cap actually belongs to Veronica and her shoes or that nice Andrews lady that was here just a few days ago or even someone who was here last week…" Arlo glanced around to see if they were paying attention.

But before she had even finished speaking, all three ladies were shaking their heads in eerie unison. That pretty much told Arlo she was sunk.

"What we've got to do," Helen said, "is find the missing heel cap. Or rather the shoes the missing heel cap came from. We find those, and no doubt, we find our killer."

16

"I THOUGHT YOU WANTED TO GO TO THE THEATER," ARLO SAID AS she followed behind Fern, Helen, and Camille. It was certain, she thought as she trailed them down Main, that the cast on her leg had slowed her down much more than their age had them. "And you promised you'd let Mads handle this."

"We did no such-a thing," Camille merrily chattered.

Okay. So they hadn't, but a girl could try, right? And she had to be a little bit grateful that they had waited until the following day before hunting down the shoe repairman.

In truth, she didn't know why she bothered. She supposed it gave her the ability to tell Mads that she had tried, even though she knew her book club had a mind of its own.

Well, three minds that somehow functioned mostly the same, in supreme annoyance and meddling. And that meddling was exactly why Arlo found herself stumping down Main toward Second in order to catch up with them at Barney's.

"You sure you don't want to go to the theater?" she prodded. "Check out the new carpet. Check on the paint. Sneak up onto the balcony."

"In a bit," Fern tossed over one shoulder.

Barney Adelman was the only cobbler in town, and seeing as how he would be the one to repair the shoes that potentially belonged to the killer who had lost a heel cap, then according to the book club, it seemed only natural they should question him first.

Arlo had to admit that the plan was logical. Though they shouldn't be the ones questioning Barney. When she told them as much, they replied back that if she hadn't lost the piece, they could have turned it over to the police, and Mads would be doing the questioning. And just like that, they made it her fault.

If only she could remember what she had done with the little plastic piece she found in the hallway outside of Petro's room. Because she needed to tell Mads about it and probably accept the verbal lashing she would receive for removing evidence from the crime scene or whatever else he wanted to call it. How was she supposed to know that every little thing she sucked up in a vacuum cleaner was potentially evidence?

When she did remember what she'd done with it, she was definitely taking it down to Mads. But for now...

She drew in a deep breath and marched into Adelman's Shoe Repair behind her book club ladies.

Barney Adelman looked more like a blacksmith than a shoe repairman. Not that she had seen many blacksmiths, so she supposed it was only fair to say that he looked like what she *thought* a blacksmith would look like. Leather apron, protective eyewear, and hands stained black from years of dye work. His arms were large and tattooed and currently crossed in front of him as he listened to what the book club was saying.

"We just want to know if someone brought in a pair of shoes, possibly red, to have them repaired," Camille said the words in a sweet, beseeching sort of way that only she could pull off with that Aussie accent.

"And I'm supposed to remember every pair of shoes I've repaired in the last two months?" He gestured toward the shelf of worn footwear behind him. Work boots, cowboy boots, ladies' pumps, even a pair of children's tap dance shoes.

"This pair would've been different," Fern said. "See, the little heel cap thingy on the bottom was kind of shaped like a diamond."

"Not a diamond-diamond, but diamond, four sided—" Helen broke off and drew the shape in the air in front of her. "But it does have little stones in it. Though I don't think they're real diamonds."

"Arlo!" Camille just caught sight of her. "Come tell Barney what we're talking about."

Barney shook his head. "Something like that has to be special ordered. Maybe you could get it in Memphis or down in Jackson, but I don't stock such things."

"You should," Helen reprimanded him. "We've been hearing that they are all the rage now."

"Bah," Barney said.

Arlo wished she had both hands free so she could guide the ladies out of Barney's shop and back down to Books and More, where they belonged. "Sorry, Barney."

"Bah," he said, waving one hand in front of him as if that would erase the last few minutes of interrogation by her wayward book club.

"But—" Helen started.

"No buts," Arlo said. "Leave this poor man alone so he can get his work done."

"We need to know whose shoes those are," Fern said.

"Of course you do," Arlo said. "But if the person who owns them hasn't figured out that they need repaired yet, then Barney here wouldn't know a thing about it, now would he?"

Even Fern couldn't argue with that logic, and she was the queen of the illogical argument. The irascible old lady turned back to Barney. "You get a pair shoes like that in, you call us, right?"

"Why do you need to know so bad?" Barney asked, a frown marring his broad forehead.

"No reason," Arlo said, deciding then and there that maybe her cane worked best as a herding device. She raised it to shin level and started poking the ladies. "They're just playing a game. A scavenger hunt."

"Yeah," Camille said. "Find the killer."

They just couldn't leave well enough alone. Arlo closed her eyes and waited for Barney's explosive response.

"A killer? Why should I call you? I should call the police, huh?"

"No need to call the police," Arlo said, doing her best to guide the ladies out the door. "Just a scavenger hunt."

"What has gotten into you?" Helen said when they finally made it back out to the sidewalk.

"I do believe that's my line," Arlo returned.

"Scavenger hunt?" Fern said. "We just about had him there."

"You didn't have anything," Arlo said. "He hasn't seen the shoes. And even if he had, that still doesn't mean that the owner is a killer."

"It's the best lead we've got," Camille said.

"You don't need a lead," Arlo said. "You are a book club. The only lead you need is on what to read next."

"I suppose you still haven't found that piece of evidence," Helen asked. Arlo didn't miss the slight emphasis on the word evidence. Helen was trying to make a point. One: that Arlo had dabbled in the investigation just as much as they had, and two: that she had lost something vital.

"I have not," she said, hoping that the words held enough finality that the subject would drop. No such luck.

"Where did you have it last?"

"I thought I had it at the inn. When I was vacuuming, I put it in my pocket."

"You had it at Books and More," Camille said grimly. "Remember? You showed it to all of us."

"Maybe it was at the coffee bar," Fern said. "Weren't we all standing around the coffee bar talking about it?"

"Yeah," Helen said. "What happened after that?"

Arlo had no idea. She supposed she had gone about her regular day, which could mean she had carried that little plastic piece anywhere in Books and More and set it down. Dropped it.

She didn't have to say the words for the ladies to understand.

"It could be anywhere in the store, huh?" Fern said.

Helen rubbed her hands together to show she meant business. "Then we got some work to do."

....

She supposed she should have been happy. Searching for something so small in the store the size of Books and More was bound to keep the ladies busy for hours and hours and hours. There was only one problem: they seemed to always be underfoot. If they had been talking about a book like a book club should be doing, then they would have been nestled in the reading nook, out of the way. But as it was, Arlo couldn't turn around without running into one of them asking if whatever chore she was trying to perform was something she had done the day she lost the heel cap as well.

Finally she could take no more and sequestered herself in her office to take care of the books, the business books, of course. Accounting was very, very low on her chore list. Just the fact that she went back willingly and with almost a smile on her face was testament that she needed a break. Badly.

"What are you doing back here?" Andy Baker, Sam's nephew, strode into the back room, pulling her away from numbers that were starting to swim before her eyes. Seriously, as soon as Books and More hit deep black she was hiring someone to do this. Even if it meant hiring Cassidy Langmore, the ditzy accountant from across the street.

"I'm working," Arlo said. "The question is, what are you doing here?" Andy had just buried his grandmother the day before. She had given him the week off to be with his family.

"Honestly," he said. "I'd rather be here. Mom's..." He shook his head. Arlo knew how hard Marjorie's death had been on Sarah, Andy's mom, but it seemed as if perhaps her grief was taking a toll on her family as well.

"I won't tell you to leave if you really want to be here," Arlo said. "But we've got everything covered if you need to go back home."

Andy jerked a thumb over one shoulder. "That out there is under control?"

Arlo briefly closed her eyes, then pushed up from her desk. She grabbed her cane and stomped around the side of her desk, Andy taking note of her cast once again.

"How's the leg?"

"It's my ankle," she said. "And if I hear one more joke about breaking a leg in the theater…"

Andy chuckled. "Just don't kill the messenger," he said.

She liked Andy. She really did. But at times like this, killing the messenger might just serve a greater purpose.

Books and More was in chaos. Or chaos, by her standards. Actually, chaos by most standards.

Fern was in the reading nook. She had all the pillows off both couches and all three chairs, and was systematically digging through every crease the furniture had to offer.

Faulkner was on top of his cage, bobbing up and down, squawking "Arlo's not gonna like that. Arlo's not gonna like that."

The bird had never been more correct.

Camille was methodically taking books off each shelf, searching behind them, and putting them back. Then she would take another section down and search behind it.

At least she is putting them back, Arlo thought.

Helen was crawling around on all fours, patting the carpet as if looking for a lost contact lens.

"Why didn't you come get me?" Arlo pinned Chloe with a stern look.

Chloe looked up from wiping down her cappuccino machine, allowing her gaze to wander around the shop. "Oh, they're fine. At least they're not down at the police station." She lowered her voice. "Trying to find out if Sasha is finished translating that love letter."

168   AMY LILLARD

"It's half a letter," Arlo said in a knee-jerk reaction.

Truthfully she had forgotten all about that. And it seemed possible that maybe the book club had, too.

"I don't think they remember it," Chloe said.

"Let's do everything in our power to see that they don't."

Chloe winked at her, then gave her a saucy salute.

Arlo supposed that explained why Chloe had let the book club continue their craziness. Because even if it was just at Books and More, their craziness was contained.

Camille turned, having seen her come back into the main shop. "Arlo, love," she started. "You didn't ship anything out during that time, did you? It would be terrible if it somehow it got mailed to another state."

"Or another country," Fern said.

"I didn't send anything out of the country." She tried. She really did. But she could not.

"Nothing like that," Faulkner squawked, bobbing up and down, clearly agitated.

"Fern, please put the couch cushions and the chair cushions back where they belong."

Fern propped her hands on her hips and frowned at Arlo as if what she just asked of her was beyond anything one human should ask another to do.

"And, Helen, you are eighty years old, please get off the floor."

"Spoilsport," Helen said. Then she sat back on her heels, hands braced on her thighs. "Though I'm not sure I can get up by myself."

"Here." Andy went over to where Helen knelt and reached down, offering her a hand up.

"Oh," Helen said. "Is that a tattoo?"

Andy looked down to his forearm, which he had extended to help Helen up. "Yeah." He turned a little pink around the ears.

"What does it say?" Helen asked. "I mean, I'm assuming it's some sort of Chinese word."

"I believe the proper term is *Asian*," Arlo said automatically.

Somehow her book club had turned her into the PC police. That more than her coming birthdays, made her feel old.

"Japanese actually." Andy replied. "It means *family*."

Fern had half the cushions back on one couch, but she wandered over to see Andy's ink. "How do you know it says 'family'?"

Andy shrugged. "I suppose you just have to trust the man who does your tattoo."

"Or woman," Arlo said. She resisted the urge to smack her hand over her mouth to stop any more political correctness from seeping out.

By now Camille had wandered over and was staring intently at the bold marks on Andy's forearm.

"Which way does it go?" Fern asked.

The pink in Andy's ears had seeped all the way down into his neck. "Like this." He held his arm up vertically in front of his face.

"You didn't research it or anything?" Camille asked. "You just took this tattoo artist at their word?"

Andy looked a little taken aback by all their questions. "They do a lot of characters in all different languages. They even do some of the Middle Eastern languages, too."

"What about Latin or Greek or even Russian?" Helen asked. She looked around at the other ladies in the book club, who nodded.

"I suppose they could tattoo anything in any language that you wanted it to be tattooed in, if you just ask." Andy frowned. "If you have the money. But I wouldn't recommend—"

"And did you use Google Translate or anything to figure out if you got the right word permanently inked onto your body?" Fern asked.

Andy shrugged, and Arlo could tell he was growing increasingly uncomfortable. But before she could step in and shoo the ladies away, he gave a casual shrug.

"I guess my generation is a little more trusting." He let out an uncomfortable chuckle, and Arlo did step in.

"Leave the boy alone." She didn't need to remind them that they had just buried his grandmother the day before.

The women nodded and gathered back in the half-destroyed reading nook.

"That doesn't look good," Chloe said nodding toward the little huddle that had formed in front of one of the dismantled armchairs.

"And while you're over there, put the cushions back," she called. But she knew that what Chloe said was correct. That looked like a plan being formed.

"You better get over there," Chloe said.

"Me?" Arlo coughed. "Why do I have to be in charge of them?"

"Just lucky, I guess." Chloe shot her a brilliant smile.

Arlo started toward the reading nook, but it only took two steps before Andy spoke. "What am I supposed to do?"

"I suppose you can try and figure out how much damage they've done looking for this heel cap."

He frowned. "What?"

Arlo shook her head. "Just straighten the shelves for now."

Andy nodded, and Arlo stomped over to where the book club ladies had returned the cushions to their proper places. Mostly anyway. The furniture was secondhand and had worn spots that Arlo had artfully concealed with careful placement of the cushions, but since they had all been removed and pushed back in a different manner, the shabby-chic look now just seemed shabby.

"It's settled then," Camille said just as Arlo grew even with them.

"What's settled?"

"Why should we tell you?" Helen said. "I mean, I love you, but you'll just try to stop us."

There wasn't much arguing with that. "I love you, too," Arlo said. "All of you. And I would surely hate to see you all in jail for mucking up a police investigation."

"Mucking?" Fern asked.

Arlo briefly closed her eyes and shook her head. "You can't go around trying to solve crimes in this town. We have a perfectly good police force willing to do just that."

"Should I remind you that you withheld evidence from the police chief?" Helen asked, one brow arched high on her forehead.

"I did not realize that it was evidence. And we don't even know if it's evidence at all. I don't suppose any of you have found it yet, have you?"

"No," Helen said.

"I didn't think so," Arlo said. "Now what's settled?"

"We're going to the police station to see if Sasha managed to translate Petro's love letter," Fern said absently.

"Half a letter," Arlo said automatically.

Fern stopped. Let out a small growl and stamped her foot. "Tricky, Arlo, very tricky."

"Yes," she said with a small smile. "I suppose it was. But now you're not going to the police station. I'll never hear the end of it from Mads if let you go down there and start meddling in this again. There's a movie premiere in a week."

"We know, love," Camille said. "That's why this murder needs to be solved."

"That's why y'all need to stay out of Mads's hair." He had way too much on his hands right now, what with all the media pressure he was facing in solving the case before the movie premiere. Just like the news to stir up everyone and get them worried about a potential murderer on the loose when chances were that one thing—the murder—and the other—the movie premiere—most likely had nothing to do with each other.

Fern shook her head with a tiny smile. "He does have good hair."

Helen elbowed her in the ribs. "Focus, Fern."

"It doesn't matter how good his hair is," Arlo said. And it was good. "You go do things that little old ladies do and stop acting like Charlie's Angels."

"We can't be Charlie's Angels," Fern said. "We don't have a Charlie. Or a Bosley. All we have is you trying to keep us from doing anything fun."

"Book. Club." Arlo crossed her arms and hoped her words would possibly sink into whatever part of their psyche they needed it to sink into so that these sweet little old ladies would stop trying to solve crimes and start reading books in the manner that sweet little old ladies in a book club should.

But all she succeeded in doing was dropping her cane. It clattered to the floor with a hollow aluminum thunk.

She sighed.

"I'll get that." Andy was at her side in a moment, fetching her cane and handing it back to her.

Six to eight weeks. Might as well be an eternity at the rate she was going.

The bell over the door to Books and More rang. Arlo braced on her cane and turned with the rest of the group just as Aleksandr Gorky ducked inside.

17

"Come in. Come in," Fern crooned.

Said the spider to the fly.

"Aleksandr," Helen said with more gusto than a normal greeting should have warranted.

"Sasha," he corrected.

"Sasha, right," Helen said. "Come sit down. What brings you into Books and More today?"

"Didn't you invite me here?" Sasha asked.

"What?" Arlo screeched.

"Hush, love," Camille said. "Let the Angels get to work."

Arlo started to protest, but Chloe waved her over to the coffee bar. Arlo limped over, expecting to find some sort of small coffee disaster, but instead Chloe nodded toward the reading nook where the book club ladies and Aleksandr, a.k.a. Sasha, Gorky were settling in. "There's no harm in that is there?"

Arlo watched the group for a moment or two. "I suppose not." They could question Sasha as long as they wanted. As long as he would sit there for it. And as long as they weren't interfering with Mads's investigation, then she supposed there was no harm in that at all.

Chloe gave a small, understanding nod. "Go. Hang out in the

cooking section. That way you'll be close enough if something crazy comes up."

Arlo shook her head. "The cookbook section is the cleanest section in the whole store for this very reason."

"Then let Andy take care of the rest."

Arlo laughed and started toward the cooking books.

Seriously, she was certain her cast got heavier as the day wore on. Maybe it was enchanted or cursed, just as the case might be. For the longer she had it on and was up and around in a day, the heavier the stupid thing seemed to get.

And the cane. Don't get her started on the cane.

"Why don't you just come over here and sit down with us," Helen said to Arlo. "You're not really fooling anybody when you stand there and rearrange the books that you just rearranged so that you can listen in on whatever we're talking about."

"Hear, hear," Fern cried. "Cop a squat and rest yourself."

Cop a squat?

Arlo hesitated a moment longer before reshelving a chocolate lover's cookbook and stumping over to the reading nook.

"Hel-lo," Faulkner chirped. "Hey, hey, good looking."

Sasha stared at the bird as if it might be as enchanted or cursed as her cast. "I never see a bird like that."

Arlo settled into the armchair, propping her casted foot on the coffee table. She rested it gently on a pile of magazines and sighed to have the weight not pulling at her hip. "Oh, he's one of a kind."

"I see one on TV," Sasha said. "But not alive."

Thankfully the book club understood his not-so-great-but-definitely-better-than-her-Russian English and didn't ask him how many had he seen dead.

Instead Camille leaned forward and patted the man on the knee. He settled down on the couch next to Fern. Camille was in the armchair where Helen normally sat across from Arlo, and Helen had draped herself on the couch across from Fern and Sasha.

Arlo had to wonder if the change in seating arrangements was some sort of tactical maneuver or simply a change of pace.

"So tell us how it went at the police station, love." Camille smiled sweetly at the man, and Arlo realized the tactics they were employing on this one. Helen was one hundred percent her own person. And her stature and confidence could be off-putting to someone who wasn't familiar with American culture. Or maybe who hadn't been born into the American culture.

Camille, on the other hand, was softer, gentler; her snow-white curls and creamy-white pearls could be indicative of grandmothers all over the world. Even if Sasha couldn't relate to them on a familial level, her size alone was enough to put him at ease.

It wasn't that Sasha was a small man. Probably a little shorter than average and slim enough that, had he been a woman, he might have been considered willowy. Helen was none of those things. She was more of everything. Taller, broader, more in-your-face. But that was just her Elly.

"It goes fine." Sasha glanced at each lady in turn, then shifted his attention to Arlo. The look he gave her was almost like he was in pain, as if somehow he had wronged her, then he switched his attention back to Camille. "I do the translation." He paused, shook his head. "But some words, they not translate. So…" He trailed off with a shrug. "There is half only."

"Of course, love," Camille said. She leaned back in her chair but didn't quite keep the disappointment from her face. Arlo could almost read her thoughts. They might have been better off with Frances and her Google Translate. No one doubted that Sasha knew the words written in the letter, but he couldn't very well translate it if he didn't he know the English word for it. "What can you tell us about it?" Camille leaned forward again as if inviting him to share.

He looked around at the ladies and once again glanced back at Arlo before answering. "It was just a note, a message."

"Of course." Camille had the patience of a saint, but it seemed as if it was running a bit thin. "Perhaps this will help." She opened that magical white handbag of hers and pulled out a Russian to English dictionary. She smiled and offered the book to Sasha.

He stared at it as if she had pulled an alligator from hat. Then in a split second, he composed himself and shook his head. "That won't help."

"Of course it will," Fern said, obviously growing impatient. "You find the word in Russian, and then we look and see what the English word is for it. Then we know what the letter says."

"But not Russian," Sasha said.

"Of course it is," Fern said.

Helen cleared her throat, and Arlo knew it was taking everything she had not to jump into the conversation.

"No." Sasha said.

"Of course it is," Camille said.

Once again Sasha turned his gaze to Arlo, and this time she understood. "It's not in Russian," she said. "There are many Eastern European languages. Russian is only one of them."

Fern's eyes grew wide, and she nodded, mouth slightly open in understanding. "Oh. I get it, like the Chinese thing."

PC police to the rescue.

"Yes," Arlo said. "Kind of like the Chinese thing. Except we should say Asian, and this is with Eastern European languages."

"So it's not Russian." Helen picked this time to break her silence. "Then what language is it?"

"Ukrainian."

"Ukrainian." Fern mulled over the word as if she'd never heard it before.

"That's where Petro was from, right?" Camille said.

Sasha nodded. "*Da*, and Inna."

Which stood to reason since they were siblings, Arlo thought.

"So what do you make of it?" Fern asked.

Sasha shrugged. "It is just note."

"From?" Camille prompted.

The man nodded and shifted uncomfortably in his seat. Arlo didn't know if it was the line of questioning that had him squirming like a worm on hot cement or if it was Fern's rearranging of the cushions that had a wayward spring poking him in the rear. At any rate, he looked about ready to bolt.

"It was his lover, right?" Fern asked. "All those hearts and things."

It had been their standard suspicion all along, that Petro's lover had gotten jealous over something, tore the love letter in half, and pushed him over the railing at the Coliseum. And that lover was the woman in red.

Sasha shook his head.

"Would you like a glass of water?" Arlo said. She waved to Chloe who nodded. "You're looking sort of pale."

"I am okay," Sasha said. But he accepted the glass of water when Chloe offered it to him. He drank half of it in one gulp and looked markedly better.

"The letter," Camille said gently bringing them all back on topic. "You didn't happen to write it, did you? You know, since it's signed with an S."

He swallowed hard and shook his head.

"Then who did?" Camille asked.

"Inna, of course."

Of course? It didn't appear to Arlo to be the letter of a sister to a brother. Even if it had been written in another language that she knew absolutely nothing about.

"But those hearts," Camille said.

Sasha shrugged. "They were loving," he said. Then he shook his head. "Close, maybe, friends as well as brother and sister."

"I get that," Helen said. "They were close. And loved each other very much."

Sasha smiled in relief as if happy that someone finally understood.

"But Inna would have signed it with her name," Fern said. "Wouldn't she have?"

"It was signed with an S," Helen added. "Not an I."

"S for *sonechko*," Sasha explained. "It means sunshine. Petro called Inna 'Sunshine.'" He nodded again as if satisfied with the exchange. Then he turned to Helen. "Tomorrow policeman say."

"Tomorrow what?" Helen asked.

Sasha stood. "Policeman say tomorrow I am able to move into Petro's room." He paused as if in question. "In your big house," he continued.

"He's going to release the room tomorrow, and you're moving in?" Helen repeated for clarification.

Sasha nodded.

"I suppose I could double-check with Mads and see." But Helen didn't look convinced.

"I see you then." Sasha nodded to them all, then made his way to the door. "I come in for coffee, and I get conversation in place. Good trade." And with that he left.

"Conversation over coffee," Fern said. "You must be slipping, Chloe."

Chloe waved away her words and went back to restocking all the doodads she had in her sweet little coffee bar.

"You really think Mads is going to release Petro's room tomorrow?" Camille asked.

"Are you really going to let him move in there?" Arlo countered. That was the real question. All of Petro's things were still there, and apparently Sasha was the closest thing to next of kin who could take over.

"Petro had the room for two weeks," Helen said. "It's not like I can tell him that it's already rented out to someone else."

"Why do I get a bad feeling about this?" Fern asked.

"You get a bad feeling about everything," Camille said. She slipped the Russian-English dictionary back into her purse and snapped it shut.

"And where was that when we found the note?" Fern grumbled.

"It wouldn't've made any difference," Camille said. "Sasha said that the note was written in Ukrainian."

"And we only have his word for it," Fern said. "It could be written in Swahili, and he could tell us that, and it would make no difference if we don't know the intricacies of each language."

"Kind of like Andy's tattoo," Helen mused.

"What about my tattoo?" Andy ducked out from where he was straightening the display of Wally's books and looked at each of the ladies in turn.

"You have to trust the tattoo artist to give you the right word in the right language, right?" Helen pressed.

He frowned. "I did, and I'm a little uncomfortable with all this talk about my tattoo," he said.

"But you got it," Fern pointed out.

"Yeah." He shrugged. "Just…don't tell my mother."

"I don't think we'll ever have the opportunity," Fern said. "But you had to trust someone to translate it for you, or else you wouldn't know that it means *family* in Japanese."

"Right."

"That's all I'm saying," Fern said. "Without our own translation of that letter, we are trusting that Sasha is telling us the truth: that Inna wrote it, that it's written in Ukrainian, and that S stands for sunshine." She paused, no doubt for effect. "That's a lot of trust in someone none of us knows from Adam's house cat."

18

"Do you have a Ukrainian to English dictionary?" Fern asked that evening.

Arlo had been beyond exhausted when she finally made it home. And still she had managed to start a load of clothes and cook herself a light supper, and had been about to settle down in her most comfortable pair of gym shorts and a T-shirt that was two sizes too big to watch some television before finally stumping off to bed.

And then the phone had rung.

"Ask her about the translation app," Camille said in the background. "The one for your phone."

"Why exactly do you need one?" Arlo said. Somehow she knew deep in her bones she was going to regret asking that question even as she knew it was inevitable to be asked.

"We found the other half the letter." Fern's voice was filled with the giddy excitement, which for Fern was saying something.

"What letter?" Arlo asked. "*The* letter?"

"Of course *the* letter," Fern shot back. "What other letter could it be?"

Good point.

"Where?"

"We thought we might look through Petro's things before

tomorrow," Fern said. "You know, when Sasha moves in. I still can't believe he allows himself to be called Sasha."

Arlo chose to ignore that last part. "So you crossed a police tape barrier and started digging through the dead man's things."

"Exactly." She was entirely too pleased with herself. "Now we need to translate it."

Arlo shook her head and pushed herself a little deeper into her couch cushions. She could tell that her downtime was about to end, and she was reluctant. For just one night, she would like to be able to rest and not be chasing around after these ladies. Or maybe that was just the cast talking. And tomorrow she had the Alayna Adams Lookalike Contest at the store. Yippee.

"Now you need to take it to Mads," Arlo said. Like they would do that on their own.

"Of course we will," Fern said. "Just as soon as we translate it."

"The app," Camille said again. "You haven't asked her about the app."

"I'm getting to it," Fern grumbled.

"No," Arlo said. "You don't need to take it to him *later*. You need to take it to him *now*." Which meant she needed to get up off the couch *now* and head over to the inn *now* and snag the letter for herself. *Now*.

"Camille seems to think that there's an app for the phone that will do the same thing," Fern said. "But we looked through the app store and can't find one."

Thank heaven for small miracles. "No," Arlo lied. "I don't believe I've ever seen one. But I think I have a dictionary at the store. Let me get on some shoes—shoe," she corrected. "And I'll be right there."

"She's on her way," Arlo heard Fern say before the line went dead.

With a sigh, Arlo tossed her phone down next to her and hoisted herself off the couch. She no sooner managed to stand and check her balance before her phone rang again.

Great. Now what did they want?

When she looked at her phone. Daisy's name was in place of the caller.

When it rains it pours.

Arlo retrieved her phone and thumbed it open. "Hello?" she asked as she made her way without her cane to her own laundry room. She couldn't head out in the gym shorts. Well, she supposed she could, but she didn't want to. That was a little too casual, even for casual Wednesday.

"Hey, Arlo, it's Daisy."

Of course it was. "Hey, Daisy. What's up?"

"Are you sure about Sam?"

At the moment she wasn't sure about anything. "What about Sam?"

"That you don't mind if I ask him to the movies or something," Daisy replied. "I just want to make sure there's not really anything going on between the two of you and that you're okay with it, since we're friends and all."

"Of course it's fine," Arlo said. When truly she wasn't sure how she felt about the whole situation. She supposed there would always be a little part of Sam that belonged to her and that she might always be a bit jealous of anyone he had a relationship with. Wasn't that just human nature? And then when that someone happened to look like Daisy James-Harrison and could bake like Betty Crocker…well, that put a whole new spin on things, didn't it?

The dryer still had close to ten minutes to dry, but she took a chance and opened the door anyway. Something clinked against the metal drum, and for a moment she figured it was the button on her jeans or maybe even the zipper pull off a pair of her slacks. But the missing red heel cap came tumbling out of the dryer. She bent down and picked it up. "Listen, Daisy, it's fine. But I gotta go for now."

She definitely couldn't talk dating with Daisy and mull over the importance of this find. She would need to take it to Mads as soon as possible. Or she supposed she could run over tomorrow with a half a love letter that her wayward book club had claimed to "find."

"Oh. Okay," Daisy said. "I'm sorry. I didn't mean to bother you."

"You didn't bother me," Arlo explained. "I just have a lot going on at the moment and can't talk right now?" She hated that her voice to rose on the end and made it an inquiry, but Daisy didn't seem to notice.

"Yeah. Sure. We can talk later. Okay then. Bye."

"Wait!" Arlo cried.

"Yes?"

"I uh…need a ride. Could you possibly—"

"Of course," Daisy said. She was silent for a heartbeat. "Oh, you mean now."

"Yes," Arlo replied. "I need to run out to the inn for a bit."

"Sure thing," Daisy said. And then she was gone.

Arlo set her phone on top of the dryer and examined the little plastic heel cap. She had no idea how it got there. But there it was. And she was glad she had found it. But it was one piece of evidence that would have to wait.

It turned out that her jeans were still too wet to wear. And she didn't have time to wait for them to dry. Who knew what the book club would do if she waited an extra half an hour before going out to the inn? Plus with any luck, Daisy was already on her way.

Arlo grabbed her phone and took the heel cap with her into her bedroom. She set her phone on her nightstand and placed that tiny little plastic piece of a clue on top of it so she didn't lose it again. She found a T-shirt that fit, sighed at the sight of herself in her gym shorts, and picked up her phone and the heel cap once more. She didn't like running around town looking like a bum now that she was a business owner, and especially not with Daisy in tow. But some things just had to be. And right now it was a skirt or the shorts. And she wasn't wearing a skirt.

She slipped her phone into her purse, palmed her keys, and started for the front door. She might not be able to leave yet, but she could wait for Daisy at the end of her drive. She wrenched it open to find Mads standing there, one hand raised to knock. The other was wrapped around a thick red leash.

Dewey, his extra-hyper Airedale terrier, barked in response.

"Dewey, hush."

The dog let out one more bark and whined as Mads tugged on his leash. "Sit," Mads commanded.

The pooch's tail dropped to the porch.

"Hey," Arlo greeted him. "What are you doing here?"

"Yeah," Mads said. "It's good to see you too, Arlo."

She shook her head. "I'm sorry. I'm just on my way out."

He looked at her outfit. He knew full well how she felt about presenting a professional exterior to the good people of Sugar Springs.

"My jeans are wet, and I don't have time to wait for them to dry. Just going over to see Elly."

"You're driving?" He frowned.

"Daisy's coming to get me."

Mads nodded. "Dew and I just thought we might stop by for a minute."

She glanced from her driveway to the street, but didn't see Mads's big black Ford parked anywhere.

"Did you walk?"

"From the park." That wasn't nearly as far as if he walked from his own house, but it was still a good ten blocks from the park to her house. And that was still quite a jog. But Arlo knew that Dewey Keller had more energy than three dogs his size and could have managed that distance in a matter of minutes.

"Is everything okay?" Mads asked.

She supposed it might look like something was wrong since she was rushing out in gym shorts to see Elly.

"No," she lied. "Nothing's wrong." Thank goodness she wasn't Pinocchio, or her nose would already be at the inn while her feet were still planted at her house.

"Okay. Just making sure. I guess I'll be going now. See you later?"

Arlo nodded. "See you later." More like *See you tomorrow with evidence that you're surely going to be upset about, but until then, at least you are not mad at me,* Arlo thought. Though it seemed like that man spent a lot of time these days angry about one thing or another. Or maybe *angry* was too harsh of a word. He definitely was the brooding type. And he seemed to be brooding a bit more lately than he had ever before.

"Mads?"

He stopped at the edge of her yard, Dewey still tugging on the lead. "Yeah?"

"Did you need something?" He seemed a little off, not entirely like himself.

Mads shrugged as if nothing was amiss. "Just walking the dog."

"Okay," she replied, then watched him walk away with a mixture of confusion and dread. But she didn't have long to ponder how he would react to the news of extra evidence or even the exact reason why he had walked ten blocks from the park just to see her. For just then, Daisy arrived.

First things first.

It was no surprise when she and Daisy got to the inn that Arlo spotted both Fern's Towncar and Camille's Mercedes. She was certain neither woman was going anywhere until that letter was translated.

Then they were staying at the inn for a while, if Arlo had anything to say about it. She was grabbing the letter and heading back home. After she chased the book club out of a not-yet-released crime scene and shooed everyone on home. Then tomorrow she would take both the heel cap and the other half of the letter in to Mads. She wanted to give them to him directly. She supposed so she could listen to him shout about evidence and meddling and how her book club had gotten out of control, and then that would be that.

Arlo told Daisy to wait in the car as she hoisted herself out of the vehicle and up to the front door. She didn't bother to call out a greeting as she went into the inn; instead she just made her way upstairs, each footstep echoed by her cast clunking hollowly against the wooden stairs. Four steps up and Camille poked her head out of what had once been Petro's room.

"There you are, love." Camille retreated back inside. "Arlo's here," she heard Camille say.

The ladies hadn't even bothered trying to preserve the integrity of the caution tape strewn across the doorway. They had simply peeled away one side and left it dangling from the other. Arlo shook her head as she stepped inside the room. "Don't you think it would have been better to wait until Mads officially releases the room?" she asked.

Helen looked up from her place on the floor. She was on her hands and knees searching under the bed. For what, Arlo had no idea.

"It's good to see you too, dear." Helen pressed her cheek back to the floor and shone the flashlight from her cell phone under the bed.

"What are you looking for now?"

"I don't know," Helen answered.

Fern turned from her place next to the side table where a suitcase had been placed. The suitcase, Arlo assumed, had belonged to Petro. "But we'll know when we find it."

"Clues," Camille said simply.

"Jason and Mads both searched this room. What makes you think there are more clues to be found?" Arlo asked.

Fern held up the half a letter triumphantly. "We found this, didn't we?"

Helen pushed herself to her feet and dusted off her hands and knees. "That's right. Mads and Jason searched his room, and yet we came up and found this letter."

"Just where was it?" Arlo asked.

"Under the pillow." Fern gestured toward the bed.

"Let me see." Arlo started into the room, her cane clicking with each step she took. And then there was an extra click. She stopped, her hand still outstretched for the half sheet of paper Fern still held.

"What was that?" Helen asked.

"Your cane hit something," Camille said.

"Don't move!" Fern put out one hand as if to stop her from across the room.

Camille bent down next to where her cane rested in the carpet and dug around for a moment.

This room, like the hallway, had the outdated shag carpet that somehow still worked in the old house. The only problem was fuzzy carpet had a tendency to hide things.

"Look at this." Camille pushed back to her feet. Between her thumb and forefinger she held a tiny black piece of something plastic, maybe some kind of acrylic.

"What is it?" Helen said. "I don't have my glasses."

Fern squinted and took three strides across the room. She pulled her glasses up from the chain around her neck. "Is it a cap for an air valve?"

"It's a heel cap," Arlo said. "Like the one I found except a different shape."

"See all the evidence we're finding?" Fern said with a satisfied nod.

"I see all the mess you're making." Arlo held out hand for the heel cap.

Camille dropped it into her palm and frowned. "Sasha has no idea whether Petro was messy or not."

"You don't know that," Arlo said.

"The police are notoriously messy when they a search the room." Fern nodded emphatically. "I've seen enough episodes of *NCIS* to know that for a fact."

That might be true, that the police were messy and that Fern had seen a lot of *NCIS*, but the point of the matter was these ladies weren't supposed to be in this room at this time. Especially not if they were finding evidence that the police missed. Which just didn't seem right.

Jason was about as half-assed as they came, but Mads was thorough. Almost methodically so. She couldn't imagine him missing a letter and a heel cap all in the same scene.

"That's another thing," Arlo said. "Maybe they need to come back in and re-search this room. Where was the letter, exactly?"

"I found it stuck underneath the pillow," Helen said.

Arlo shook her head. "That doesn't sound right. Didn't Mads and Jason have the bed completely unmade when they were here?"

"They did," Helen confirmed. "I offered to wash the sheets, but they said they didn't want me to mess with them until they released the room. They piled everything in the floor." Helen gestured to a spot toward the end of the bed where the pile had been.

"But the bed was made." It wasn't a question.

"When we got back in here?" Helen asked. "Yes. It had been remade. But I hadn't thought about it until right now."

"And the letter was under the pillow."

"Like it was waiting for someone," Fern said.

Or like someone had made the bed and pushed that half letter under the pillow.

From out in the front, Daisy tooted her car horn.

"Who was that?" Camille asked.

"Daisy," Arlo replied. "She brought me over here."

"You just left her in the car?" Fern demanded.

"Yes, and now I think we should all get out of here. It seems like perhaps some clues have been missed." Or planted, Arlo thought grimly. Or maybe someone else had been in the room since Jason and Mads had searched it. Someone or someones besides her wayward book club. Either way, they needed to get out of the room.

"That sounds like all the more reason to stay," Fern interjected.

Camille and Helen nodded.

"Someone was in here," Helen said, her voice filled with awe as if the concept had just occurred to her. "Someone came in and made the bed and placed that letter there and probably dropped that heel cap. Mads vacuumed in here and took the vacuum cleaner bag with him," she told them. "If it had been here at the time, he would have sucked it up in the vacuum then. And it wouldn't be here for you to step on today."

"Oh, this is good," Fern said.

"What does it mean?" Camille asked.

"It means we need to call Mads and have him come out and check this room again," Arlo said.

"If we do that, will we have to tell them that we came in here?" Fern said. "I don't like when he yells."

"If you don't like when he yells, then you should stay out of his crime scene." She knew she should've made that last word plural, but she didn't want to give them any more ideas than they already had. She needed them stay out of this crime scene and any crime scene that happened upon in the future, which would hopefully be none. But at the rate her luck was holding out...

"Okay. I'll make a deal with you," Arlo said, thinking fast. "Give me the letter and the heel cap."

An immediate hum of protest rose from the three ladies.

"Hear me out. You give me the letter and the heel cap, and I'll take them into Mads and explain what happened."

Fern pressed her lips together and shook her head. "Works for me. I hate to say it, but..."

"But what about the app?" Camille asked. "I thought we were going to translate the letter."

"It's only half a letter," Arlo said. "And we don't have the other half. The police do."

"I still have the copy," Fern said.

Arlo shook her head. "This is the best way to handle this." She looked to Helen for help. Of the three of them, Helen was usually the voice of reason. Well, of more reason than Fern and Camille at least.

"I think Arlo's right," Helen said. "Let's give her the clues, tape the room back up, and pretend this never happened."

Arlo wasn't certain the last part was possible when these ladies were involved, but at least it would get them out of the room, and she would have the evening to figure out what exactly she was going to say to Mads when she took the evidence into him the next day. Three pieces of evidence, possibly hidden, a murder in a small town, with a movie premiere looming on the horizon. One thing was for certain: Mads was not going to be happy.

19

THE IDEA OF MAKING HER WAY DOWN TO THE POLICE STATION ON the bright sunny day, by herself, was something of a wistful dream.

First of all she had one foot in a walking cast and needed a cane to make sure she kept her balance at all times. So the walk itself was a struggle—at the very least laborious. And she had no sooner set her bag down in Books and More that morning when Fern, Helen, and Camille all showed up to walk with her to see Mads. For three ladies who didn't like when he yelled, they were certainly ready to get front-row seats to the show.

Then when she got back to Books and More, she had an Alayna Adams Lookalike Contest to oversee.

At least the weather cooperated. It was a beautiful, sunny day in Mississippi. The sky was blue with a small spring breeze blowing through, though Arlo knew by midafternoon temperatures would be close to ninety. There was really no such thing as spring in Sugar Springs.

"Arlo," Frances said as she walked into the police station. "Fern, Helen, Camille." Frances paused, waiting expectantly for them to state their business.

"I need to talk to Mads about something," Arlo said.

Frances nodded as if she had known all along. "Go right in."

Arlo stepped into Mads's office. Camille, Fern, and Helen all crowded in behind her. Talk about front-row seats.

"Arlo," Mads greeted as she appeared in front of his desk. He seemed almost happy to see her. Well, happy for Mads anyway, then his smile froze as he saw the book club behind her. "Ladies." That almost-pleased to look grew slightly darker.

"I have something for you." Arlo took another step toward Mads. She fished into her bag and pulled out the paper sack where she had stored those three precious items, one definitely and the other two possibly evidence to a murder.

"A party and breakfast," Mads quipped.

Arlo gave him a smile, but it felt more like a grimace on her lips. She unrolled the top of the bag and poured its contents onto the blotter on Mads's desk.

"What—" he started, then stopped immediately. He might not know what the red or the black plastic items were, but he recognized the letter for its value immediately.

He started to reach for it then opened his desk drawer and pulled out a pair of gloves. He quickly snapped them into place. "Where did you get this?"

"We found it," Arlo said. It was simple and straight to the point and really told him all that he needed to know, but she knew that Mads wouldn't let it stop at that.

"Where did you find it?"

Arlo shifted in place. She would like to tell herself that it was due to being a little off balance in her running shoes and walking cast, but the truth of the matter was, when Mads pinned her with his dark stare, she felt a little like she been called into the principal's office.

"See, it's like this—"

Helen took that moment to step forward. "I found it," she said.

"Really, I found it," Fern said. She gave a tiny wave. Mads turned to Camille. "You don't want to make this unanimous, Spartacus, and say you found it, too?"

Camille shook her head. "No, it was them." She pointed to Helen and Fern in turn. "Well, actually, it was Fern."

"That's right," Helen said. "Fern found it."

"So you didn't find it?" Mads asked Helen.

Helen shook her head.

Mads turned his attention to Camille. "And you didn't find it?"

Camille shook her head as well.

Mads turned his attention to Fern. "But you did find it?" he asked. Well, it was close to a question. More like a statement that wanted confirmation.

"That's right," Fern said.

"So what's Arlo doing with it?"

Fern shrugged. "It's a long story."

"Okay," Mads said. "We'll put a pin in that. So you found it where?"

Fern grimaced. "In Petro's room at the inn."

Mads sighed. He briefly closed his eyes, then opened them once more. That's when he turned his gaze to Arlo. He kept it on her as he asked, "And what were you doing in Petro's room at the inn?"

Helen eased forward a bit more. "That's on me," she said. "I wanted to go in and get it ready for Sasha."

Mads's gaze was still trained on Arlo. "Who is Sasha?"

"Aleksandr," Helen explained. "Aleksandr Gorky."

"And he goes by Sasha?" Mads asked.

"I know. I know," Fern said. "I have trouble believing it, too."

"Sasha said that you said that he could have the room starting today. I just wanted to get ready for him. You know, change the sheets and all that."

It was mostly the truth, Arlo supposed.

"But Jason and I took the sheets off the bed when we were there."

"See, that's the weird thing," Helen said. "I thought so, too, but then when I went in the room the bed was made."

"That's when we thought we should search it," Fern chimed in.

Mads shot her a look but didn't speak. Fern crossed her arms as if daring him to say something more. For someone who didn't like when he yelled, she sure like to push his buttons.

"And did you know about this?" Mads turned his attention to Arlo.

"Only after it happened."

Arlo could see the wheels ticking behind Mads's eyes. He was trying to figure out the best way to get the entire story without getting every detail that he didn't need as well as those he did. Turning the ladies loose on their own version could take days to unravel.

"And where was this letter in the room?" he asked.

"It was under the pillow. On the side where it looked like Petro had slept. I only say this because that's where his things were. He had a book, an ink pen, and a piece of paper," she replied.

Mads frowned at her but just lightly. "We moved all that when we were there," he said. "Jason and I. We moved all of that out, so how did you know..."

Fern tapped her temple and gave Mads a shrewd look. "Like a steel trap."

Thankfully he didn't address that response. It was probably just as well.

"I think his lover came in and remade the bed, laid down in his spot, was crying for him, then pushed the letter under the pillow and eventually left," Fern said.

"It doesn't make sense," Camille said. "Why would they leave the letter there? Why wouldn't they want to keep it?"

Fern shrugged. "It's only half a letter."

"That is true." Helen shrugged.

Mads turned to Arlo. "Are they still trying to solve this?" he asked. "In my office? Right this minute?"

Arlo shot him a look. "I'm not a miracle worker."

"Think about it," Fern said. "Where else would the heel cap have come from? We decided that it wasn't there when Jason and Mads vacuumed, or it would've been sucked up in the vacuum cleaner on the day they searched the room, right?"

Mads sighed, though this one was bordering on a growl. "What are we talking about? What heel cap?"

Arlo took a step forward and pointed toward the little black piece of plastic lying on his desk. "That is a heel cap."

Hands still encased in the latex gloves, Mads picked up the little piece of black plastic and turned it this way and that.

"And it's for?" he asked.

"It goes on the bottom of women's dress shoes," Helen said helpfully. "It protects them, but apparently I have a flagstone in the front of the inn that needs some work. So it seems that women are losing their heel caps left and right out there."

Mads continued to study the tiny item. "So you're saying that whoever went into Petro's room lost this while they were in there."

"That makes sense then, doesn't it?" Fern asked. "His lover comes in wearing nice heeled shoes, she climbs into the bed cries, stuffs the letter under the pillow, and then leaves. All without realizing her shoes are practically ruined."

"That's about as far-fetched as it comes," Arlo grimaced apologetically at Mads.

"Especially since the room was taped off with police caution tape," Helen said.

"Which completely stopped you in your tracks," Arlo pointed out dryly.

"Not helping, love." Camille leaned in close to Arlo but uttered the words so everyone could hear.

Mads set the black heel cap on the blotter and picked up the red one with the stones. "So what's this?" he asked.

Arlo's turn on the hot seat. She shifted in place. "See, it's like this," she said. "I was helping Elly vacuum at the inn. And that got sucked up in the vacuum cleaner in front of Petro's room."

"No, I mean, *what is it*?"

"It's a heel cap for a different pair of shoes." Arlo tucked a strand of waist-length brown hair behind one ear and waited for Mads to respond. It wouldn't take him long to figure it out. The two heel caps came from two different kinds of shoes. The red one was found after their investigation and search through Petro's things, but before the other items were found last night.

"I'm not sure I understand," Mads said. "Why didn't you bring it to me?"

"I didn't think it was important at the time." She shot him another apologetic grimace-slash-smile.

"If you didn't think it was important, why did you keep it?"

"I misplaced it," Arlo said. "Then I found it again last night."

Mads paused for a moment, and Arlo could almost hear the whirring of his brain gears as he started to piece together the things that she wasn't telling him.

"You guys have been out looking for the shoes that this belongs to." He held up the little red heel cap studded with sparkling clear stones.

"Us?" Fern shot him an astonished look.

"Nice try, sister," Helen said out of the corner of her mouth.

"Yeah, see, I was in the grocery store couple of days ago, and Barney Adelman was fussing about people coming in and bothering him. Those people being the four of you."

Arlo wanted to protest at being lumped in with her book club and their sometimes-annoying search for clues, but she thought it best to keep that to herself.

"He was complaining?" Fern crossed her arms and harrumphed. "Like he's got something to complain about."

Arlo figured it best to stay on the topic at hand. "But the bright side is you now have both sides to the letter, and now you can know exactly what it says."

"I already know exactly what it says."

"That's impossible if you only have half of it." Fern thumped one foot as if to back up for her frown.

"I know enough."

"Doubtful," Camille said in something of a singsong tone.

As expected, it didn't set well with Mads. He rose to his feet, his considerable height and width dwarfing them all, including Helen.

"What makes you say that?"

Camille shrugged. "It's just that you have Sasha—Aleksandr—doing your translation. How do you know what he's telling you is the truth? It's like Andy's tattoo."

Mads turned back to Arlo. "Andy's tattoo?"

"Not worth it," she said with a shake of her head.

"All I'm saying is," Camille started once again, "if you put all your trust in Sasha, how do you know what he's telling you is the truth?"

Fern nodded to back up to Camille's points. "I think you should have Frances get right back on that translation," she said. No doubt trying to get one in on Frances for not sharing what little translation she did have.

"I thank you ladies for bringing this in and, if you have any more clues in the future, don't."

"Don't bring them in?" Helen asked as he escorted them toward the door.

"No," Mads said. "Don't have any clues."

....

"Can't you feel it?" The young, blond-haired woman raised her arms high above her head. She twirled around slowly, right there in the center of the Coliseum, downstairs and about ten feet from where Petro had met his demise. Her spin gave everyone on the main floor a free shot at the fact that she did not shave under her arms.

Not that Arlo was surprised. She had met a lot of people like Fern's niece, Ariel, from Meridian. Hippies, not just people from Meridian. Arlo's own mother fit that category nicely. Arlo was fairly certain the woman didn't even own a razor. And she was fairly certain that Ariel didn't either. Not that she was holding it against her. To each his own, she had always believed.

"Feel what?" Helen asked. She looked up at the ornate ceiling as if Ariel's hands were pointing toward whatever it was she should feel.

"The lost souls." Ariel dropped her hands to her sides and spun back to face the four of them. Arlo wasn't certain how, once again, she got shanghaied into time at the Coliseum, but she kept telling herself she was giving back to the community. In more ways than one, actually. She was helping the economy by employing a part-time person and working that person more hours than she could afford when she needed to be working at the store to get ready for the Alayna Adams Lookalike Contest. The contest that would surely be "no bother at all" was bound to be more bother than it was worth. And she was also putting in hours doing her part to help restore the old building so that the movie premiere would be the largest success it possibly could be.

"You can feel them?" Helen shook her head.

"Hear her out," Fern demanded. "These ghosts are going to ruin everything if we don't get a handle on them."

"The ghosts didn't kill Petro." Helen pointed out.

"But they could have tipped over the paint," Camille said. "Or dropped that sandbag."

"The ropes attached to the sandbag and the screws securing the scaffold where the paint was sitting were tampered with," Arlo reminded them. Though she wasn't sure why she bothered. No one was listening to her. Yet again.

"Or even broken Arlo's leg," Fern said.

"It's my ankle." Arlo shook her head. "It was an accident. All of these things have been accidents."

Fern shook her head. "You don't know that a hundred percent."

Helen frowned. "I'm not sure an exorcism is in the budget for the restoration."

"And new carpet was?" Fern countered.

Arlo could almost see Helen weakening.

"And it's not an exorcism; it's more of a friendly request for them to leave." Ariel turned back to Helen with a bright smile. "So many people have died here. So many have lost their lives." She closed her eyes and twirled in a circle again, somehow managing not to bump into either side of the rows of chairs as she spun her way down the aisle toward the stage. She stopped near the steps that led up onto the wooden platform. "They're good spirits. They don't want to hurt anyone."

"Except for Petro," Camille said.

"Are you talking about him alive or his ghost?" Arlo quipped.

Fern glared at her. "I thought you were on my side."

"I didn't think there were sides," Arlo returned.

"You know what I mean." Fern frowned. "Now let her do her job."

"She does this for a living?" Arlo asked. "Like she has no other job but this?"

Fern shot her a pointed look. "You'd be surprised at all the ghosts we have lurking in our midst. All those poor souls from the Civil War." She shook her head sadly. Arlo had a feeling that, if she'd been Catholic, she would have crossed herself.

Ariel picked that time to twirl her way back up the other aisle. "Turbulent times lead to turbulent spirits."

"That's a great sentiment," Fern said, smiling at her niece. Great-niece, Arlo thought it was, but she hadn't been paying too close to the particulars when Fern had introduced them.

"Maybe we should get it printed on a T-shirt," Helen quipped.

"Will you be serious?" Fern scowled.

Helen had the wherewithal to at least look chastised and pressed her lips together as if to prove perhaps that, if she couldn't be serious, she could at least be quiet.

"He's here, you know," Ariel said.

"Who's here?" Arlo asked. Then immediately she wondered how she fell into the trap.

"Petro. Isn't he why I'm here?"

"Yes and no, love," Camille said. "We're just looking for a little peace."

Amen to that. At least Arlo managed to keep that to herself.

Fern elbowed Arlo in the ribs. "See? What'd I tell you? She even knows his name."

She could have gotten it from the paper, but Arlo knew better than to point that out to Fern. It seemed as if her best bet at the current time was to let this play out in whatever direction it did, then go home and try to get some sleep once again.

"If he's here, then why don't you ask him how he got murdered?" Helen asked.

"I thought you were going to be serious about this," Fern admonished.

"I am being serious! If he's here, then she should ask him how he got murdered. And this is done."

Ariel folded her hands together as if praying. "If it were only that simple. We would have no unsolved murders. We would merely ask the dead who killed them, and that would be all there was to it."

Anyone else, and Arlo would have thought that speech to be laced with sarcasm. As it was, she knew Ariel Phillips meant every word with the most sincere sincerity that had ever been felt.

"So you can't just ask him?" Helen wanted to know.

"She just said she couldn't," Camille said.

"And you just said you would be serious," Fern said.

"Again," Helen said, "I am being serious."

"Shhh." Ariel put one finger over her lips and started sweeping around the room. Much like she had earlier, spinning in circles. Going down each aisle, she did her little float-walk throughout the downstairs.

Arlo and the book club ladies merely watched.

"I'm still not sure I can work an exorcism into the budget," Helen said.

Fern practically growled. She let out a grumbling sigh and tossed her hands into the air. "Okay, I'll pay for it. Does that make you feel better?"

Helen smiled. "I suppose so, yes."

"Oh, you entrepreneurial types," Fern grumbled. "Always worried about the bottom line."

"And you're not?" Camille asked.

Fern shook her head. "I'm more of an artist," Fern said. "We are more concerned with the finished product."

"Speaking of the finished product." Arlo nodded toward the carpet that had been recently laid in the lower half of the Coliseum.

"It looks great doesn't it?" Helen asked.

"Much better than what had been there," Camille agreed.

"What about the seats?" Arlo asked. "Who was supposed to be checking out the seats?"

"I almost forgot," Helen exclaimed. "Arlo, you and Fern go up to the balcony. Camille and I can stay down here and check these. Just make sure that they all work, there's no tears in the fabric, and that any previous repairs are holding."

"Upstairs?" Arlo asked. The last thing she wanted to do was stump up and down stairs in the stupid cast.

"Oops," Helen said. "How about you and Fern stay down here and Camille and I will go upstairs; sound good?"

Arlo gave a thankful smile to her one-time guardian. "I appreciate that. More than you'll ever know."

"I'll start down at the bottom," Fern said. "You start up here, and then we'll meet in the mid—"

"What is that smell?" Helen's exclamation broke across the remainder of Fern's sentence.

"Is that smoke?" Camille asked. "Is something on fire?"

"It's sage," Fern said.

They all turned to Ariel, who had taken a bundle of dried sage from somewhere, most likely the big canvas hippie bag she wore across her body like a free-spirited mailman. "The burning of sage purifies the air and chases away the wayward spirits," she explained.

"I thought they were friendly," Helen said.

Arlo shot her a look.

"Of course they are," Ariel said. "But friendly or not, you don't want them hanging around for this premiere. Not if they're tipping over paint cans and dropping sandbags on people."

"The poor publicist," Camille murmured.

"Not to mention poor bookstore owners who have to dive in front of falling beams in order to save someone else," Arlo said.

Fern gave her a pointed look. "I thought you didn't believe."

Arlo gave a light shrug. "My broken leg says otherwise."

"I thought it was your ankle, love," Camille said.

Arlo closed her eyes. There was no winning that one for sure.

"You'll be careful though," Helen said, eyeing the smoldering mass of sage that Ariel was carrying around the historic theater like the Olympic torch. "No sparks or anything, right?"

Arlo could tell that Helen was torn between shutting down the circus show and trying to do everything she could to make her friend happy.

Ariel closed her eyes and somehow maneuvered through seats and down the aisles and crossed up and over in a crazy non-pattern pattern that only she understood. "No." She kept her eyes closed as she smiled. "It's the smoke we're after. It's the smoke that sends them away."

"And how long will they be gone?" Helen asked. Arlo caught sight of Camille already upstairs examining the chairs in the balcony while Helen loitered downstairs trying to make sure that Fern's well-meaning great-niece from Meridian didn't burn the whole thing down.

"For a good two weeks. Maybe even three, if you're lucky," Ariel added. "Some of the older ghosts may not come back at all. Sometimes they just get the hint and decide to cross over. It's glorious."

Glorious, Arlo thought. That was a word she needed to use more often herself. It was just glorious.

"Arlo?"

She turned at the sound of her name to find Mads standing just inside the entrance of the theater itself. "Can I talk to you for a second?" He watched Ariel spin around. "What is she doing?"

Arlo shook her head. "Don't ask. Just…don't ask. What's up?"

"Listen, I don't mean to be hard on you. About the ladies. It's just…"

Arlo shook her head. "I understand. Everyone is under a lot of stress these days."

"Then Sam's mother," Mads said. In the last year, the two men had made up, so to speak. They weren't mortal enemies any longer, and the years between prom and the present day had diluted the animosity and competition between the two of them. And for that Arlo was grateful. Unaccustomed to it, but grateful all the same. "I know. Made me call my mom," Arlo said.

Mads nodded. "Makes me miss mine all the more."

Mads's mother had died his second or third year in the NFL. During the fall, of course. He had buzzed home, said his goodbyes, and buzzed right back to play the following Sunday. It wasn't required, but it just seemed to be something that was done. Plus she knew that, for Mads, football had its own healing properties.

"How's your dad?" she asked.

"He's Dad."

Mads didn't need to say more. Arlo knew how difficult Roger Keller could be. He was a stickler, a war vet, and old-school. A Southern gentleman, a dying breed, and a pain in the butt. But she knew Mads loved him.

Mads shook his head and gave her a small smile. Until that moment she hadn't realized that he didn't smile near as much these days as he should have. When he smiled, he was still as handsome as ever. "Anyway," he said, "just do me a favor and try to keep them out of the way. We're doing our best to hone in on a suspect, and I need to be able to concentrate on the evidence I have."

"And not evidence that is scattered all across the county."

"Something like that."

"No problem," she said.

He turned and started for the door of the theater. "You're coming to the premiere, right?"

"I wouldn't miss it for the world," she said.

He smiled again, one of those rare Mads smiles, and made his way out the double doors of the theater and into the bright Mississippi sunshine. Arlo turned back to the inside of the theater, hoping Ariel's exorcism had come to a complete and full stop.

"What did Mads want?" Helen asked.

"Nothing, really," Arlo said. And she was thankful she didn't have to lie. He didn't want anything from her that he hadn't already asked for in front of the ladies. And he really hadn't asked for anything all.

Camille and Fern joined them from whatever corners they had been hiding in, checking chairs and making sure the upholstery was in order. Then Ariel marched toward them, her eyes bright with excitement. "He's gay, you know."

"Mads?" Helen asked. "Where'd you get that information?"

"No, not Mads," Ariel said. "Petro. Petro is gay. Or I guess he *was* gay. Sometimes it's so hard when you're talking about the dead."

"I suppose it must be," Arlo said.

"How do you know that?" Camille asked.

"He told me of course," Ariel said with a flip of her curly blond hair.

"He can tell you that he's gay, but he can't tell you who murdered him." Helen crossed her arms.

"Well, he didn't tell me so much as I can just tell. I have a good nose for that kind of thing."

"Must be all the sage," Arlo said. Once again she managed to keep her face straight and her words as serious as a heart attack. Then she decided she needed to be nice.

Sarcasm was not a beauty mark; her mother taught her that, and then there were the lessons that Elly had taught her. Plus the *hush up* look that Helen was giving her at that very moment.

"I had a feeling he was gay," Fern said.

"I'm not sure it's a good thing to be talking about the dead," Ariel gave a hesitant, almost apologetic smile.

Helen nodded. "I'm sure you're right."

"Are they gone?" Arlo said. She couldn't help herself. She looked around as if the ghosts were lingering above their heads.

"I'm not sure they're completely gone," Ariel said in that "everything will be just glorious" voice of hers. "But they are subdued and will stay that way for at least another week. That will get you through the event, right?"

"Right," Helen said.

"Good." Ariel smiled. "I'll send you an invoice."

She breezed out as Arlo and the book club watched her go. "How much are you paying her, again?" Arlo asked.

Helen shook her head. "Whatever it is, it was too much."

....

"Four hundred dollars!" Helen exclaimed a couple of days later. She held up the invoice as if anyone could actually see it. "And she didn't even get rid of them. She said they were just 'subdued.'"

"That's all we need," Fern said.

"No, we didn't need anything. The Coliseum is not haunted, and if it is, then a haunting should be part of the whole experience of coming to see something at that particular theater." Helen flopped down with an exasperated sigh. "I was thinking fifty bucks."

Fern shook her head. "Oh, the nonbelievers."

"This has nothing to do with believing or not believing," Helen said. "This has to do with being completely over budget for the restoration. I certainly hope this premiere brings in enough money to warrant the work we've done."

"Give me that." Fern reached out and snatched the invoice from Helen's hands. "I said I would pay and I will."

Arlo pushed the cart of new books past the reading nook and tried not to smile.

"Surely it will be fantastic," Camille said. "The premiere."

"Glorious," Arlo said, feeling prideful that she managed to get that word in again. It was a good word, and she did need to start using it more often.

"We've only got a few days before the premiere, and people are already starting to arrive," Helen reminded them.

"Did you say that the inn was completely full?" Fern asked Helen.

Helen nodded. "I even rented out the attic room."

"I didn't think you had a bed up there," Arlo said, trying to imagine some of the professionally pressed and carefully blown-out Hollywood types poking around the inn's attic. At that very moment, another of the Alayna Adams lookalikes was carefully peeling books from the shelves and holding them with the tips of her fingers as if she might get some sort of backwoods fever from them.

Of course they weren't all that bad, but most walked around Sugar Springs speaking loudly of its charm, its eclectic citizens, red-dirt crusted pickup trucks, and whether or not the water was safe to drink.

"There's a bed," Helen replied. "The rest of the space is full of a lot of junk. But I put it on Airbnb as a 'vintage experience.' Someone snapped it up within two days." She smiled, self-satisfied. That explained where she had been for the last two days. She was probably scraping dust off every surface in the tiny, slanted-roof room just up the stairs from the main hallway.

"And I've heard that the motel is full," Fern said.

Arlo briefly closed her eyes. "Please tell me you didn't go out there to bother anybody again."

"Ah, love, we don't bother," Camille said sweetly. "But we do find out what we need to find out."

That they did.

So everything should be going just as planned.

The bell over the door to Books and More rang as Daisy swept in. "Hey, y'all," she greeted.

Chloe, Fern, Helen, Camille, and Arlo all greeted her in return. "Arlo, Chloe, I need your opinion on something." She held a bag, a long dress bag that could only contain an evening gown of some sort or another. Or a wedding dress, but Arlo didn't think that was a possibility.

"I can't decide. And I'm going to have to take one of them back. I mean when am I gonna wear it here?" she asked rhetorically. "So I need to know which one is the best."

Arlo abandoned the cart of books and went to stand next to Chloe, who waited for Daisy to unzip the long bag.

"Got to be the best! Got to be the best!" Faulkner squawked and bobbed on top of his cage.

The book club ladies were also watching to toss in their opinion, Arlo was sure, should it be asked for. And maybe even if it hadn't been.

"There's this one." Daisy pulled out a pink dress. Barbie pink with a silver crisscross pattern in the front that connected to tiny, rhinestone-crusted spaghetti straps. It looked elegant and breezy and somehow fun and flirty at the same time even as it reached the floor.

"That could be a good color on you," Chloe said.

That's what Arlo thought too, but she was withholding her opinion for as long as possible.

"But I wonder if pink might be…" One of Chloe's hands fluttered about as if the simple motion was a necessary adjective. "I don't know. A little trite."

Arlo knew that, if Daisy wore that dress, she would be a life-sized Barbie and might actually steal the show from the Hollywood sorts who were coming to strut their stuff.

"And then I found this one." She pulled out a second dress, this one a pale, shimmery blue. The fabric itself held a sparkle and seemed as if it was made from dragonfly wings. Gossamer, Arlo thought. "I think this will look better with my eyes."

"They're both beautiful," Camille said.

Daisy laughed. "I know. That's why this is so hard. Which one will look the best?"

"Blue," Chloe said nodding emphatically.

And though the blue one was pretty, when Arlo's turn came, she shook her head. "Pink." Something about a walking Barbie appealed to the little girl in her, whether she had been allowed to have a Barbie or not.

"Well, you both are no help." Daisy turned to the book club. "Okay, there's three of you. That's a good odd number. What do you say?"

Helen studied the dresses for a moment. "I have to go with Chloe on this one. Sorry, Arlo. But I think you should wear the blue."

"Pink," Fern said. "The blue one's too froufrou."

Daisy held it out looked at it. "I like froufrou. And I don't want to have the same dress as anyone else," she said. "The pink one I had made especially for me. There's nothing worse than showing up to the party in the same dress as someone else."

"I suppose not," Fern murmured.

"I guess I'm a tiebreaker," Camille said.

Daisy nodded. "It appears so."

Camille looked from one to the other.

Pink or blue. It was like a real-life Sleeping Beauty. Where the fairy godmothers couldn't make up their mind or wouldn't allow the other to choose the color. Pink-blue-pink-blue.

"Well," Camille said, "I love the pink. But I love pink. Yet I have to say that for a red-carpet event, I definitely think the blue is more suitable."

"Pink, blue, pink and blue, blue and pink," Faulkner chatted. "Go with the pink. In the pink."

"And Faulkner likes the pink," Daisy said.

"He's a bird," Arlo said unnecessarily. But sometimes it was good to remind the people around Faulkner that he had no true opinion of his own and his vocabulary was merely a mimic. Sometimes he was eerily spot-on with things.

"But I do like the pink," Daisy said.

"Then you should wear that one," Arlo said. She would never be able to pull off such a girly-girl dress. But it would suit Daisy just fine.

"So you think the pink?" It was obvious which one Daisy wanted them to pick even though it wasn't obvious to Daisy.

"Pink," everybody said at the same time.

Daisy laughed once more. "Okay, pink it is. Sorry. I just want it to be perfect. After all, it is my first date with Sam."

For a moment, Arlo thought she might be sick.

....

"So did you know?" Chloe asked a little later that afternoon. The book club had dispersed after an afternoon of not talking about books. Oh but they did mull over every clue they had concerning Petro's murder, including the obviously bogus information that Ariel received almost straight from the ghost.

"Know what?" Arlo said as the two of them got ready to shut down Books and More for the day. She played it off, but she knew exactly what Chloe was talking about, the same thing that had been knocking around in her mind since she heard the words.

"That Daisy and Sam are going to the premiere together."

"No, but why shouldn't they?"

"I thought…you and Sam…"

Arlo shook her head. "There is no me and Sam. Daisy came to me and asked if she could ask Sam to the movies. So there you have it." At the time she had thought they would drive over to Corinth and see the latest blockbuster or chick flick or animated children's cartoon. She didn't think Daisy was talking about the movie premiere right there in Sugar Springs. But there you have it. Sometimes things weren't always what she thought they were going to be. And she had no reason to be upset. And she wasn't. She absolutely wasn't. Because she and Sam… Well, she just didn't know. And last time she checked, this was a free country. And Sam was a red-blooded American male. And Daisy was a beautiful bombshell.

Okay, maybe that last part bothered her just a little. But you couldn't change the world to suit yourself. Arlo had a more classic look, her mother used to say. Which just meant that she had good bone structure and would look great as she aged, but what it didn't mean was that she was beautiful. She had come to terms with that a long time ago. She had heard herself referred to as striking, and one teacher had even said that she had a classic beauty, but that was almost as bad as saying she had good bone structure.

"And you're not the least bit upset," Chloe prodded.

"Okay," Arlo said. "I'm not upset, but it's a little disconcerting. Let's go with that. No, that word's too strong. Maybe unnerving. No, disconcerting."

"Enough," Chloe said. "It's disconcerting. I got it. And I think I might be disturbed too if someone were dating Wally right now."

"Well, considering he's dead," Arlo said.

They locked Books and More and started around the building where they parked their cars. Well, where Chloe had parked her car and Arlo normally parked hers She still had weeks and weeks to go with the cast.

"You know what I mean," Chloe said. "When you love somebody for a long time, it's really hard to let them go. Even if it means they're going to be happy."

Hadn't she thought the same thing just a couple of days ago? A part of Sam would always be hers. But in truth, she and Sam had only dated for one summer. She and Mads had been a thing long before that—two years in fact.

But Mads wasn't going out with beautiful Daisy James-Harrison. And Daisy's looks were another thing that shouldn't bother her but somehow did anyway. Arlo hadn't been raised to be overly concerned with outer beauty. Maybe she needed to go spend a week with her mom and have Henny Stanley's inner peace over outer beauty rub off on her some. It seems that what she been given during the first sixteen years of her life was starting to wear thin these days. Or maybe she had more feelings for Sam than she might have realized.

"What?" Chloe asked. "I know that look on your face, and it's not always the best. What are you thinking?"

"I don't know," Arlo said. "I mean, I've been so wrapped up in making sure we have books and trying to figure out who killed Petro and trying to keep the book club from interfering with Mads while he tries to figure out who killed Petro and doing all this volunteer work at the Coliseum—"

"And getting the store ready for the Alayna Adams Lookalike Contest," Chloe added.

Arlo rolled her eyes. "That too." She sighed. "With all that going on, I haven't given one thought to what I'm wearing to the premiere."

She had formal dresses from forever ago. She hadn't worn one in a long time. Her weight was pretty steady, so she ought to be able to slip into something she already owned. But now having seen that gossamer blue and the Barbie pink that Daisy had at her fingertips, she wanted something different. She might not be as elegantly beautiful as Daisy, but she did want to be the best Arlo at the event she could be.

"I'm taking Jayden tomorrow into Corinth to the formal wear store there and getting his tux for the event. Want to ride along and see if they have any dresses?"

"Who's taking care of the coffee bar?"

"Fern said she would watch the counter from ten to one. Maybe you could get Andy to come in to watch the books part. There shouldn't be too much extra traffic coming in since there are still a couple of days till the premiere. What do you say?"

What did she say? The part of her that wanted to believe that inner beauty was the most important, so much more important than the outside and was all that should matter, warred with her feminine core—the inherent spirit of her that wanted to be beautiful both outside and inside, especially at a huge event, the biggest event to probably ever take place in Northeast Mississippi, and taking place right in her backyard. Almost literally, considering how close she lived to the Coliseum and—

Okay. Deep breath. The fact of the matter was she wanted a gorgeous dress, too. She wanted to look beautiful. None of her mother's hippie teachings could get her out of that one.

"I say that sounds like a deal."

20

THE STRANGEST PART OF FRIDAY BEFORE THE PREMIERE WAS BEING surrounded by Alayna Adams lookalikes. There were at least two dozen girls walking around who favored the star. Some were dressed in costumes from her movies; the remake of *Cleopatra* seemed to be the favorite with at least eight girls in Egyptian gowns and golden snake headdresses. For Alayna, the movie hadn't been quite the rise to fame that she wanted. She wanted to be catapulted to the top, Arlo had read yesterday online, and Alayna was certain that *Missing Girl* would be the thing to take her to the stars.

Missy herself was easy to spot. Of them all, she favored Alayna the most. She wore a fuchsia-colored dress that hugged all her curves ended at the knee, giving a great view of her toned calves and designer shoes. Beautiful shoes made from some sort of floral material with platform soles and high, high heels. If Arlo's ankle wasn't broken, she would have broken it in those, but Missy pulled the style off with ease.

"How's it going?" Arlo asked just before midday. The girls were huddled together upstairs in Sam's office to shield them from the crowd and prevent them from seeing the others as they performed. Everyone else, locals and out-of-towners alike, were waiting downstairs for them to begin. Arlo had made the mistake of putting everyone in Sam's office for privacy, not realizing that, in order to check on them, she herself would have to climb the stairs, dragging a cast on her right leg.

Joy of joys.

"Good, I think." Missy was confident. Arlo could see it in her eyes, though she pretended to act nervous. "How do I look?" she asked, smoothing her hands down her slim waist.

"Awesome," Arlo said. "Really great."

"I got my breasts done, you know." She turned to the side so Arlo could better see them. "They are exactly the same size and shape as Alayna's."

But her hair was a wig. "And your—" Arlo didn't know what to call it, that fake beauty mark.

"It's a tattoo."

"Why would you go to all that trouble?" Arlo hadn't meant to ask, but the question had been rising up inside her ever since she had met Missy the Alayna Adams lookalike.

"Money," she said simply. "People pay me to come to parties and such. I get to play like I'm Alayna, and the more famous she gets, the more money I can make."

Incredible. But this time Arlo kept the comment to herself. "Good luck," she said, with a small nod to Missy.

But the girl was having nothing of it. She grabbed Arlo by the shoulders and gave her a big hug. "You don't know how much this means to me," she said, still holding Arlo tight. "After all that trouble at the theater and the awful man who was saying that he was going ruin the premiere. I'm so thankful that you let us have the competition here."

Arlo stepped back and managed to extricate herself from Missy's clinging embrace. "You're welcome."

She smiled then and bit back any more comments and made her way carefully back down the stairs to the first floor. Fans, she thought. What wouldn't they do for their celebrity crushes?

....

The competition itself was part Broadway show, part high-school talent follies, and all bad community theater.

Each contestant came down the stairs, then took their place on a raised platform that Andy had borrowed from the Boy Scouts. It lent itself to be the perfect stage for the performances. Most of the entrants couldn't act a lick but had joined on their looks alone. And a good number of the contestants did look so very much like the starlet. But it was Missy Severs who captured everyone's attention. Her acting was spot on, and she emulated every nuance of Alayna Adams's personality. Things that Arlo hadn't even realized the actress did, like tilt her head to one side as if listening for a faraway sound even when the person she was talking to was right in front of her. She performed perfectly and received more applause than any other of the competitors combined.

Perhaps she had her own little following.

Her self-satisfied smile as she exited the stage was enough for Arlo to realize that Missy felt she had won. She shook hands in the crowd, though Arlo noticed it was not the strong handshake of Missy Severs but the limp-wristed greeting of Alayna Adams.

"I wonder what she thinks of all this," Andy said from beside her.

Arlo had been so lost in her thoughts that she hadn't realized he had come up next to her. "Missy? She's eating this up."

He shook his head. "Alayna Adams. The real one."

What would the starlet think? And why hadn't she been involved in the production? It seemed like a fairly good publicity stunt and a good way to keep your face in the papers. But even with so many lookalikes floating around, the real Alayna Adams was nowhere to be seen.

"I think she would hate it." Arlo had never met the actress, but she had seen enough interviews with her to suspect. Alayna Adams wanted all the attention on herself.

She glanced over to where Missy stood at a practiced angle that Arlo recognized as being classic Alayna.

Needing to be the center of attention. It was one thing both women naturally had in common.

....

"I heard you went dress shopping with Chloe," Helen said after supper.

"Is that what this is about?" Arlo used her fork and pointed to the orange cream cake that Helen had just served her. "You invited me over for dessert, and even made my favorite, just so you could find out about my dress for the movie premiere."

"Honey, you forget I helped raise you," Helen said. "I saw the look on your face when Daisy told you she was taking Sam to the premiere."

Arlo shook her head. "It's nothing. I'm happy for them both." And as she said the words, she realized that she possibly could be happy for the two of them. She couldn't honestly say she was happy at that very moment. Something about it. Maybe because it was out of her hands.

The fact of the matter was she cared about Daisy, and she cared about Sam—a lot. She had for a long time. And she cared about herself. And more than anything, she wanted all three of them to be as happy as they could be. Wasn't that everybody's wish?

"I wouldn't say the look on your face is happy. And it wasn't then, either."

"It was just surprise," Arlo said. She would probably feel the same if Mads was dating somebody. Just a little bit possessive, kind of crazy ex-girlfriend-y, but not too much. "No big."

"And you went and bought a new dress for the occasion? That's not like you."

"Did you buy a new dress for the occasion?"

"Of course I did," Helen said. "It matches my hair."

"It's gray on top and red on the bottom?" Arlo asked.

Helen nodded vigorously. "Isn't that great? I took it in to Dye Me a River to make sure that my ends are the exact color of the dress. Wanda matched it perfectly."

God bless Wanda.

Charlene, Teresa, and Wanda, along with the rest of the staff at the local beauty shop, were something of folk heroes around Sugar Springs. They listened like bartenders, counseled like therapists, and filtered the gossip through a sieve. Oh, and they were really good at their jobs as well.

"If you bought a new dress for the occasion, why are you giving me a rash of trouble over buying one, too?"

"Is that what you think?" Helen shook her head. "I just want to make sure that you're happy and not lamenting telling Daisy that she could go after Sam."

"How did you know that I told Daisy she could 'go after Sam,' as you put it?" Arlo asked.

Helen gave a tiny shrug. "Maybe she asked me first before she asked you?"

"Leave it to Daisy." Arlo shook her head.

"I'm sorry I missed dinner," a male voice said from the kitchen doorway. "I had to go to Memphis today."

They both turned as Sasha came into the room.

"What'd you do there?" Helen asked, her tone open and conversational.

Sasha shrugged. "I had shoes for a cobbler."

Helen penned Arlo with a look. "You know we have a shoe repairman here in town."

"He could not fix mine," Sasha said. "They need a special part."

Despite the incriminating sound of his words, Arlo knew it was no good. Sasha could take all of his shoes to a repairman, and it wouldn't matter to them at all. Not with the shoes they had seen him wearing.

Helen opened her mouth to say something, but Arlo shook her head. Helen closed it again and sighed.

218 AMY LILLARD

"I hope a plate would still wait for me?" Sasha asked.

Helen nodded. "You pay for supper, and I make sure you have one." She took the plate from the side table where she had placed it just moments before cutting the cake for Arlo and herself. "It's still a little warm. If you want it hotter, I can put it in the microwave."

Sasha nodded. "I understand. Is good just this way."

Helen handed over the plate wrapped with foil. "Go ahead and take it into the dining room. I left a place setting for you. I figured you'd be along directly. Though everybody else is almost done eating now."

Sasha nodded again. "Thank you."

He turned to go, but Helen stopped him with one quick question. "Sasha," she started, "was Petro gay?"

....

Later Arlo would swear it took Sasha five minutes to answer, though she knew that it could've only been a matter of seconds. Five…ten… maybe as much as twenty. In that time, he bobbled his plate, almost dropping it as if the question had stopped the muscles in his hands from working properly. He opened his mouth and closed it, trying to get his squeaky jaw joint working once again.

When he finally did answer, his voice was at odds with his wild eyes. He looked as if he was ready to bolt to one side or the other, maybe jump through a door or a window and run out into the night. Instead he tilted his head back and waved one hand in front of him as if such a concept was utterly impossible.

"No," he said. "No, no, no, no." He shook his head. "Petro was not gay. Why do you ask such a thing?"

Arlo turned to Helen. "Some things are better left private," she reminded her one-time guardian.

Helen shrugged. "I thought your generation was all about full disclosure."

Arlo shook her head. The subtleties of disclosure and privacy were completely lost on anyone above the age of sixty-five. She was fairly certain anyway. Then again, sometimes she didn't think she understood it herself.

"The ghost person today"—she looked to Arlo for the word; getting nothing. She turned back to Sasha—"she brought it up. I guess I just wanted to know if maybe she really did see ghosts."

Arlo was amazed at the sheer number of people who simply wanted to believe in the supernatural and would look for any indication of its reality.

Sasha shook his head. "Where I come from," he started, "we do not discuss these things."

Helen flipped her braid over her shoulder and shot him her sassiest look. "Well, you're in America now. We talk about such things all the time."

A cloud seemed to descend over Sasha's expression. He gave an almost imperceptible shake of his head. "Not so much as you think." And with that, he stepped out of the kitchen and headed toward the dining room to eat his not warmed up supper.

"What you make of that?" Helen asked when Sasha was gone.

"I think you should probably stop asking strange men about their sexuality."

"I didn't ask about him. I asked about *his friend*."

How to delineate that difference? Arlo had no idea. Instead, she slid off her stool and reached for her purse. "I think I need to be getting home now."

"You haven't even eaten your cake," Helen protested.

"I know." But Arlo felt a sudden urge to be by herself. Maybe to mull over the events of the last few days, or maybe she just needed time alone. Then again… "Take it to go?" she asked.

Helen shot her a loving look. "You know you can."

"And maybe a second piece?" she asked with a smile.

"For tomorrow?" Helen asked.

Arlo nodded. And just that easily, the lie slipped from her lips. "Absolutely."

The two words that tumbled around in her head were two words that she wasn't even sure she wanted to say. But all the way to Mads's house, they taunted her, demanding release.

Mads lived a little further out of town than Arlo, just on the edge where the lots were a little bigger and the houses a little more farm-like. Arlo supposed that some of them might have even been on larger tracts of land until houses started to go up in between them when farms closed and people went to work in the factories and industry in surrounding towns. Somehow this had formed a haphazard neighbor-hood full of clapboards and bricks with huge trees in the front yards, tire swings hanging from their limbs. Almost none of the houses out this direction had garages. But most boasted carports or awnings to shelter vehicles when the weather got bad. Mads's house was no exception, and she was grateful to see his big black truck parked in the carport attached to his house. He was home.

She grabbed up the two pieces of cake and rang his doorbell. From the other side, she heard Dewey barking furiously, convinced an intruder had just summoned them to the door. As she waited, she heard Mads holler back a command, and she could only imagine him turning the big dog out into the backyard. He was a great dog, just a little…exuberant. But glorious in his own way.

Arlo smiled a little to herself and waited for Mads to open the door.

"Arlo?" His brows raised at the sight of her. "Come in, come in." He stood back so she could enter the house. "Dewey's in the backyard."

She stepped inside. "I figured."

Mads shook his head. "I guess I should try to take him out more. He gets way too excited when we have company."

"He's a terrier," Arlo said with a small shrug. "I have cake." She held up the two containers as if to prove her words.

Suddenly Mads grew a little defensive. She could almost see the wall go up as he crossed his arms and waited for her to continue. "Nothing about the case," she said. "Just something happened today."

"And?"

She lifted the containers once more. "Cake?" she said hopefully.

Mads motioned the way to his kitchen where the old-fashioned aluminum and Formica kitchenette set waited.

She settled into one of the chairs and doled out cake as he went to the refrigerator. "Milk? Coffee? Tea?"

Arlo shook her head. "Water is fine."

"Water, it is." He took an old-fashioned glass pitcher from the refrigerator and poured them both some of the cold liquid. Then he gave them each a fork and sat down across from her. "Now what is it?"

Arlo took a deep breath and tried to decide where to start. "Fern's niece, or maybe it was great niece, came up from Meridian this morning. Fern hired her to appease the ghosts in the Coliseum so they wouldn't create any more mischief as we get ready for the premiere."

"This is a joke, right?"

Arlo shook her head. "Afraid not. But Fern insisted that it was necessary, and you know Fern."

Mads nodded and began to eat. "This is good," he said.

Arlo smiled and took a small bite of her own. "It's my favorite."

"It might be a hard second for me," Mads said and took another big bite. His favorite had always been banana rum with extra pecans.

"Back to Fern's niece," she said.

Mads nodded.

"She claimed to talk to the ghost today."

"And we're still not in a joke, right?" Mads asked.

"If I start to tell a joke, I'll let you know, okay? Now focus on what I'm saying."

"I'm trying. Believe me, and I've heard a lot in my time. But seriously, Arlo. She came to appease the ghosts?"

Arlo nodded. "I know. I know. But in all of her talking to the ghosts—"

"Wait. If she could talk to the ghosts, why didn't she just ask who killed Petro? I mean, he was among them, right?" She could hear the teasing note in his voice.

"I asked the same thing. Apparently, it's more complicated than that."

"Of course it is."

"Will you be serious for one minute, please?"

"I'm trying; it's just really hard when someone starts up a conversation with 'Let's appease these ghosts.'"

"Do you think Petro's murder could have been a hate crime?"

There were those two words, those two vile words she'd been choking back the entire drive from the inn to Mads's house.

"So this ghost buster said that Petro was gay, or is this because he was an immigrant?"

"Gay. Maybe."

"So she could ask him about his sexual orientation but not who killed him?"

"I don't know all the ins and outs, but it just made me think. If he was gay, then could this be a hate crime?"

They both sat in silence for a moment, and Arlo knew that, like her, he was thinking about Cable and Joey. Cable worked at the menswear store owned by his family, and Joey worked at the dry cleaner. They were obviously a couple, but not obviously a couple. The South was doing its best to be progressive, but change was hard. Still the two men were well-liked and well-received. As far as Arlo knew, they never had any trouble, not that had been recorded anyway, but the South was slow to change. Small towns, even slower.

"What do you think?" Mads asked. He had stopped eating cake, stopped joking, and turned into thoughtful, brooding Cop Mads again.

"I don't know what to think," Arlo said. "I mean, it's not like he was trying to start a movement or anything. He was here to ruin Wally."

Mads nodded and finally resumed eating. Arlo sat and watched him as Dewey scratched at the back door and howled the way only an Airedale could.

"No," Mads finally said. "I don't think it was a hate crime. Hate crimes are usually more…violent," he finally finished.

"Being tossed off the balcony was not violent enough?"

Mads shook his head. "Now you're talking about hate. Hate does crazy things to a man's brain. This could possibly have been a crime of passion, maybe jealousy, or even anger, but it was not fueled by hate."

He sounded so sure that Arlo wanted to believe him. But somehow it just seemed as if they were missing something in the whole deal.

"And why are you wondering this again?" Mads asked.

"I wasn't trying to solve anything," she said. "I had what could possibly have been new evidence, and I brought it straight to you."

He smiled at her. "Good girl."

She shook her head. "Just for that, I'm leaving before you pat me on the head."

His eyes grew dark, and he stood as she did. "You can stay for a while," he invited.

She shook her head. As tempting as it was, she needed to get home. Her nights had been terribly restless of late. And she had taken to going to bed a lot earlier, so when she woke up in the middle of the night in pain from her ankle, she still had time to rest and get back to sleep. "I've got a big day tomorrow."

Mads nodded. "I understand. I'll wash these up and bring them by tomorrow," he said pointing to the plastic containers on the table.

She nodded. From outside she could hear Dewey scratching and whining, trying his best to get in to see her.

"Sorry I got him all riled up."

Mads smiled. "It was worth it."

....

It was worth it.

Those words came back to her at the oddest times over the rest of that evening and the following day. They seemed to float around her head as she took the sponge bath and got ready for bed. She had decided that sponging off was a heck of a lot easier than trying to shower with a bag on her leg.

Then those words again as she drifted to sleep. And all through the morning as she greeted customers and did her best to keep the book club in check. Oh and tried not to think about Sam and Daisy and basically their last day of normalcy before *Missing Girl* the movie.

"You'll be happy to know that there were no accidents at the Coliseum today." Fern gave a satisfied nod. "Ariel to the rescue."

"Did everything get done?" Arlo asked as the book club trudged back in late Thursday afternoon.

Helen sighed and collapsed into the couch in the reading nook. "Yes, thank heavens. Everything done, and the gold leaf finally came in…. That took everyone. But we got all pulled together, and the place looks beautiful."

"And tomorrow we'll open it up to the public. And start doing everything for the red-carpet walk," Camille said. "Did you know that sometimes the red carpet isn't even red?"

"What?" Fern shot her an incredulous look. "How can the red carpet not be red?"

Helen sat up straight and waved a hand as if trying to dispel all the rumors floating around. "I read about this online," she said.

"Way to go, you," Fern said.

Arlo silently nodded. It had taken a long time, but they were finally managing to get Helen into the twenty-first century. Though Arlo couldn't imagine that she wouldn't keep a couple of toes in the '70s. It was just her style.

"Sometimes they have a theme, you know, so like if there's a movie with a lot of snow, then the red carpet will be white, or if it's a movie about the ocean, they might have a *blue* red carpet."

"That makes absolutely no sense," Fern scoffed. "You cannot have a blue red carpet. A red carpet is a red carpet, and a blue carpet is a blue carpet. End of story."

"Hopefully, the carpet will be red for our premiere," Camille said.

"I'm pretty sure it is," Helen replied.

Chloe came around the counter and brought them all a cup of coffee. She set them on the coffee table in the reading nook. "I do hope we all get to walk it. After all, how many times do you get to say that you walked the red carpet at a Hollywood premiere?"

"Well this isn't really a Hollywood premiere because we're not in Hollywood," Arlo said. "But it is exciting."

Except she wasn't too excited about trying to walk down the red carpet with her cane and her pitiful black cast. The more she thought about Daisy and her pretty pink dress, her "Barbie doll come to life" demeanor, and her going out with Sam, the more Arlo wanted to look her absolute best for the event. She had even made herself an appointment at Dye Me a River. Not that she was getting her hair cut. But she would like a wash and a style, maybe something a little interesting to add to her arrow-straight hair.

They all turned as the bell over the door chimed its cheerful warning that someone was coming into Books and More. Arlo half expected to see Phil for an afternoon coffee. That was his normal routine. But instead Alayna Adams, the *real* Alayna Adams, rising star and lead of *Missing Girl*, swept into the store. She had her arm looped through that of Tyson Dell, her costar. Cameramen trailed them as they walked in, and a barrage of paparazzi followed behind that. Arlo was certain she had seen a few call letters from local stations trailing in the mix. But one thing was certain. Hollywood had come to Sugar Springs.

21

ARLO TOOK A STEP BACK AND ONCE AGAIN SCRUTINIZED HER reflection in the full-length mirror behind her bedroom door. From the top of her head to her knees, she was completely satisfied. But somehow the cast seem to ruin the aesthetic of her outfit. Not that there was anything she could do about it. She had done the best she could, given the hand she'd been dealt this go around.

She decided it safest to go with an above-the-knee dress. Not as formal as normal red-carpet attire, but it would keep her dress away from her cast and maybe protect her balance. The last thing she needed to add to the bulk of her cast was delicate fabrics swishing all around and snagging on the fiberglass.

Her dress was probably as simple as they came. Black, cap sleeves, scoop neck. The ultimate little black dress. But it had been dressed up with sequins. The whole thing shimmered when she walked, and it held kind of an old-school feel, like a majorette in a marching band, but all grown up.

Teresa at Dye Me a River had enjoyed getting her fingers on Arlo's hair once again, though she couldn't hide her disappointment at not being able to cut even a little off her mane. But Arlo was adamant about the length. The beauty shop girls did like getting everyone ready for this big event.

Her hair had been pulled up in an *I Dream of Jeannie* ponytail that had been threaded with sparkles as if strung with stardust. She couldn't say the look was elegant, not like the dress she seen Chloe pick out or the one Daisy was wearing. But such was life. Still, she felt dressed up, sassy, and just like herself.

But the cast. Oh, heavens, the stupid cast.

She managed not to let anyone write on it, mainly because she would be showing it to the world this evening. Not that anybody out there cared, but truthfully, she did. So she promised everyone they could take a set of paint pens and go to town, but only after the premiere. And if she had thought that getting a black cast would somehow make the whole look a little more elegant, she'd been terribly wrong. It simply looked like a black cast, an ugly black cast, a little dingy around the edges from the dust that seemed to spontaneously grow in a bookstore. She turned from the right to the left, her dress sending prisms of light across the room. There wasn't anything she could do with the cast.

She sighed and made her way into the front room to wait on Chloe.

Daisy might've been running Arlo to work most days since she had broken her ankle, but since Sugar Springs's newest resident was going out with Sam tonight… Well, that was something Arlo was not allowing herself to dwell on. And Chloe had stepped in and offered Arlo a ride. Now she and Jayden were swinging by to pick Arlo up for the event.

Arlo didn't have to wait long before she heard short honk from her driveway. She flipped on the kitchen light for when she got home, grabbed the tiny sequined purse that just matched her sexy little dress, then made her way outside. It'd taken four stores in Memphis to find shoes that were the exact same height as her walking cast and yet still dressy enough to go with the dress. Her black fabric heel with a three-quarter strap had a band of rhinestones across the toes. They were delicate and dainty and understated, and thank heavens she could walk in them. Well, it. And she topped the look with a French mani-pedi that gave a simple yet clean finish.

Chloe hopped down from her Land Rover with the car still running.

"Look at you," Arlo said.

Chloe turned in a circle, showing a 360° view of her peach-colored Grecian gown. Her tight blond curls had been pinned into something that almost looked like an updo, but Arlo knew how unruly her best friend's hair could be. Still, she always thought it to be cute and fun and a sassy look, though she had stopped telling Chloe that every time she complained about her curls.

"What do you think?" Arlo asked.

"You look like super Batwoman or something," Jayden called from the truck.

Arlo laughed. She gave a small nod in his direction. "Thank you, kind sir." From a ten-year-old, she would take super Batwoman any day of the week.

"You do look nice," Chloe said. "Are you ready for this?"

Was she ready for this? Did she have a choice? Then again, with any luck, tonight would be great fun.

"Do you have to wear that?" a small, girly voice asked.

Arlo turned as a young girl stood staring at her intently. Tasha Anderson. The little girl who had been after Jayden as a boyfriend for quite some time now. It seemed they started early these days. And it seemed that Jayden didn't mind because Tasha "liked his curls."

"What are you talking about?" Arlo asked.

From the back seat of the Land Rover, Tasha nodded importantly at Arlo's cast. "That. It doesn't go with your dress at all."

Arlo wanted to sigh, but she managed to keep it to herself. "Yes, I have to wear it, and yes, I know it doesn't match my dress at all."

"We could make it look a little better," Tasha mused.

Arlo shook her head. "I don't see how."

"Ms. Chloe." Tasha turned and respectfully addressed Jayden's mother. "Do you still have my craft supplies in the back of the Land Rover?"

Craft supplies?

"Of course. Aren't you taking them to the children's event tonight?"

Tasha gave another important nod. "That was the plan, but we may have to use some now because that just doesn't go."

Out of the mouths of babes.

"Will you get them for me, please?"

Chloe nodded and started toward her hatchback.

"Craft supplies?" Arlo asked.

Tasha nodded once more. It seemed to be her schtick. "You just leave this to me."

....

Thirty minutes later, Arlo could have declared Tasha Anderson a pint-sized Picasso. Somehow she transformed Arlo's cast, using what seemed to be the largest privately owned craft supply in the free world. Tasha had a tackle box setup, but instead of lures, the pink box contained beads and string and spray and glue and paint and glitter and glitter and glitter. In the end Tasha had sprayed the whole thing with glue, dusted it with fine stardust glitter, then sealed it all off with glitter spray so that her cast sparkled as brightly as her dress. Then she took some sort of silver tape and covered the burgundy part of her ugly cane so at least it didn't look as matronly. At first Arlo thought the tape was merely silver, but it had a prism to it, and when the light struck it just right, it shone like a disco ball high above the dance floor. Arlo had never been so glittery in her entire life, and she wasn't a hundred percent sure she was comfortable with the whole effect. Though she had to admit, it did look better than it had before, and as much as a cast could go with a formal dress, her cast definitely went. Seeing as how the cast had to go with her, that was a good thing.

Coliseum parking was a nightmare, so the plan had been previously made to park at the high school and take shuttle buses to and from the actual theater. The *red* red carpet had been set up outside, roped off with velvet partitions. It looked so Hollywood in front of the old-timey theater, and so out of place with the magnolia trees blooming in the background. It was somehow South meets West, a clash of the Titans, old world and new. Arlo knew that, once this event was over, Sugar Springs was most likely go back to being the sleepy little town that it had always been. And tonight would be one blip on the radar of the time when Hollywood came.

Chloe gave the valet her keys, and the four of them climbed aboard one of the shuttles.

"This was a good plan," Chloe said looking at the crowd of people gathered in front of the Coliseum. It was unlike anything Arlo had ever seen. Flashbulbs seemed to be going off in every direction. A large wall had been erected in front of the jewelry store that sat next to the Coliseum, and celebrities and townfolk alike stopped there to have their picture taken first before their actual walk down that luxurious red carpet. The wall boasted the *Missing Girl* title and was surrounded by the sponsors for the actual event in town. Some local, most national, all proud to be displayed here tonight.

The shuttle dropped them off at the end of the block, which honestly was the only place to stop without clogging up the entire system. Arlo was not looking forward to walking so far, but a girl had to do what a girl had to do. She and Chloe walked side by side, taking it slow, which was good for Arlo's gait, but it also allowed them time to take in everything around them. Jayden and Tasha walked side by side in front of them, brushing hands every so often but not quite getting brave enough to hold. Tasha had strapped her pink tackle box full of glitter back onto the rolling rack she pulled behind her like a glitter stewardess.

"She is something else," Arlo said as they followed the pair.

"I'm just not sure if I like her not," Chloe said. Definitely the words of a mother who had just realized her son was growing up.

"But she likes your son," Arlo reminded her, lightly bumping her shoulder companionably.

"I know," Chloe said.

"And he likes her," Arlo said.

Chloe frowned. "I'm not sure if he likes her as much as he likes that she likes him." Her frown deepened. "I think."

Arlo laughed. "I know what you mean."

The line in front of them was long and snaked out from in front of the wall. The red carpet itself dumped into a circle that was surrounded by velvet rope, kind of like a mini cul-de-sac with paparazzi, photographers, and anyone else who was lucky enough to be invited to the premiere snapping pictures. It seemed everyone around had their phone out, either taking their own shots or trying to get the spectacle on video. Arlo had never seen anything like it.

Jayden and his "date" were going to walk the red carpet, then head over to the children's event, since the movie was rated R. But as the son of the author—or suspected author—he was at least going to be able to honor his father tonight by making that walk. Chloe had insisted. She wanted Jayden to realize that, whatever Wally had been or done, he had accomplished something in his time on earth, and that something was what was supporting them and would support him for most of his life. It was a matter of respect and acknowledgment.

They stopped in front of the *Missing Girl* title and took their pictures. People were posing while others snapped off their own shots. They took one of the four of them: Chloe, Arlo, Jayden, and Tasha. Then the kids moved out of the frame. Chloe and Arlo stood side by side, best friends for so long.

"There you are!"

Arlo turned and did a double take. She might not have recognized them except for Elly. She would have known her anywhere. With her gray and red hair pulled back into a side ponytail that laid across one shoulder. Her dress was a stunning long-sleeved mermaid silhouette that began in a wispy silvery-gray and ended in a pool of deep red at her feet. Across the bodice was an intricate design of tiny stones that made her waist look small and added to the princess vibe she had going on. And of course Camille. Such a traditional soul, Camille had on a short-sleeved gown of the sweetest rose color with a higher hemline in the front than in the back. The elegant crisscross bodice and empire waist hid all the wrong things, while emphasizing all the right ones. Her handbag was hooked over one arm, and Arlo would only admit to herself that she had wanted to see if tonight Camille would show up with a different, perhaps even smaller bag.

So really it was just Fern who took her by complete surprise. After having seen her in practically nothing but overalls for the past year or so, Arlo was shocked to find her in a silk dress made in the qipao style, with a high neck, lightly fitted all the way to her ankles. The dress had satin frog closures down its length, and the teal-colored fabric was strewn with black and gold Asian characters and springs of plum blossoms.

"Look at you," Arlo couldn't stop herself from saying.

Fern waved a hand as if her appearance was of no consequence. "Oh, stop," she said. "Y'all act like you've never seen me in a dress before. And I've worn dresses plenty of times."

That was true, but the navy-blue shirtwaist that she normally wore to funerals was nothing compared to the ensemble she had on this evening.

Chloe stepped forward. "You look beautiful," she said, glancing at all of them in turn. "All of you look so very beautiful."

Helen lightly touched the red ends of her hair as if assuring herself all was still in place. "We clean up pretty nice."

"Yeah," Arlo said. "For a hillbilly book club."

"Hillbilly?" Fern frowned. "Speak for yourself." But Arlo knew she was teasing.

"Let's have our picture taken together," Camille said. She grabbed Arlo by one arm and Fern by the other, and led them back to the place where the *Missing Girl* logo was painted on the wall in front of the jewelry store.

Arlo smiled as the photographer and the people around him

started snapping off pictures left and right. It did feel very glamorous to have so much attention on her at one time. Something she would probably never have again. And truthfully, that was okay with her. But she was glad to be here in this moment with these special ladies. And she was glad to have a memento from this evening.

Arlo looked up and caught Mads's gaze.

She felt her smile instinctively widen.

He gave a little wave. And she felt for him having to work tonight of all nights, such a big event in little Sugar Springs. But he was head of the police and backup for the security that the movie company had provided. It was a big job with so many people in such a little space. But everyone seemed to be having a good time.

"Who is that?" Chloe asked through her smile. They were still posing for the cameras.

"That's Cheryl." Arlo managed to say the words without moving her lips much. Cheryl was Wally's editor, a redheaded bombshell wearing a backless green dress and greeting folks as if she had had a greater hand in the creation of the book—more than editing anyhow.

"No," Chloe managed to get through her smile. "In the red dress."

Their turn in front of the *Missing Girl* logo was over, and they stepped a little closer to the red carpet. Arlo allowed her cheeks to finally rest, though she still felt obliged to smile some. She gazed around at the small crowd where they stood.

"Who are you talking about?" Fern asked. "I see three red dresses."

The first was on Alayna Adams, star of *Missing Girl* who was still locked-arms with Tyson Dell, her costar. Arlo knew that it was expected of them, this movie romance turned real-life romance, and it was suspected they would become the next Hollywood power couple.

Red dress number two was being worn by a woman that Arlo faintly recognized as someone from the production crew. She was certain she had been introduced to her some time during the renovation of the Coliseum, but she couldn't remember the woman's name for her life of her.

"Alayna is the star," Camille patiently explained.

"Not her," Fern and Chloe said at the same time.

"The other woman works in production," Arlo said. "I think."

"Not her either," Fern said as Chloe shook her head.

"Her." Chloe pointed in the direction she wanted them to look.

A slender woman in a full-length red dress stood, her back to them as she talked to someone from the movie company. Her long, dark hair had been sideswept with a rhinestone clip and cascaded gently down her bare back. Elegant and beautiful. "Have you ever seen her before?"

"This place is full of people I've never seen before," Arlo replied. "Why do you ask?"

Chloe shook her head as they inched closer to the roped off section of the carpet. "There's something about her that's familiar. It's like déjà vu."

"You can't even see her face," Helen pointed out.

"I don't need to see her face. I can see it, too," Fern said.

"Stop agreeing with her just to take sides," Camille admonished.

"I'm not. There really is something about that woman that seems familiar, though I don't think she was at the theater helping," Fern said.

Arlo tried to study the woman without appearing to study her. With a figure that could only be described as willowy, the red dress clung to boyish curves so gentle they were almost nonexistent. She had thick, luxurious eyebrows and icy-blue eyes that, as Chloe had said, were eerily familiar. But still Arlo couldn't place her. It wasn't like they had met a thousand people in the last week or anything.

"You don't suppose..." Chloe broke off.

"What?" Arlo asked.

"That she could be the lady in red everybody's been talking about?"

The description fit, to be sure, but Arlo hadn't seen the woman before tonight. "Just because she's wearing red tonight..."

They inched a little closer, still talking through their smiles.

"I know," Chloe said.

"What are the odds?" Fern asked.

"I don't normally wear red," Helen said. "Because it clashes with my hair. But with coloring like that…"

"She should wear red every chance she gets," Camille finished for her.

Dress them up one time and they were all fashion experts.

But Helen was right; with the woman's coloring, she should wear red regularly. But that didn't mean much of anything. Except if she was the lady in red from the other day and not just this evening, she might know who killed Petro or might even be responsible herself. Or once again Arlo's book club might be sticking their noses—and pulling hers along with them—into something that was none of their concern.

"Can you sign in, please?" A young man with a clipboard shoved it toward Arlo. She took it and the pen without question.

"We have to sign in?" Fern protested. Arlo was certain she was about to kick up a fuss purely because she could.

"Yes," she said, tapping the sheet with one newly manicured fingernail. "You sign your name right under mine."

Arlo turned her attention to the clipboard and the letter S seemed to leap off the page at her. A familiar S. The same S that was on the love letter that was found next to Petro's body. The love letter that Sasha claimed wasn't a love letter at all but a missive between brother and sister. So if the S belonged to Inna written as an abbreviation of her nickname, then why was it penned there, as the beginning of Sasha's name?

"Look." Arlo showed them the signature.

"We know he's here," Camille said gently. "He told us he was coming."

"Look at the S," Arlo said, but Chloe had already spotted it.

"It's the same," she breathed.

Arlo wanted to study the name a little more, maybe allow it to sink in. What did it mean? But she had to pass the clipboard and the pen around for them all to sign. Still she wanted one more look at it. But the crowd behind her was swelling, gently pushing them out of the way for the next people in line. She reluctantly handed the clipboard back to the attendant.

"What does it mean?" Helen asked through her smile.

They took a step closer to that sweet spot where the press had been stationed to snap pictures of all the attendees. It was time to do their thing as they had been taught from a YouTube video that Helen had miraculously found on how to preen for the cameras at a movie premiere. It was true: you could find whatever you needed on the internet. Everything but who killed Petro Chenko.

"It means Sasha wrote the letter," Fern said. Like the rest of them, she had her smile fixed firmly in place and yet somehow managed to push words through it.

Arlo turned one way and then the other as did the other members of her party. She had been certain she would trip and fall because of her casted leg, but she promised herself that she would do her best. Now add in all the shock of realizing that Sasha had written the letter to Petro... Well, her concentration was taking a hit.

She needed to find Sasha. She needed to talk to him, ask him outright if he hurt Petro. She didn't want to. She was afraid of the answer he would give. Between the letter and the trip to Memphis to fix a special pair of shoes, his guilt looked solidified.

Arlo smiled but directed her gaze around the crowd. The dark-haired woman was stepping onto the curb of the sidewalk. Her shoes were eerily familiar. Or at least the sparkle at the heel was. Silver shoes, red heel caps, clear, sparkling stones. This woman, she was their lady in red. She turned so that she was facing them and lifted her gaze, her eyes a beautiful and familiar ice blue.

"Sasha," Arlo breathed.

This lady in red was no lady at all but none other than Sasha Gorky.

22

SHE MUST HAVE SAID HIS NAME LOUDER THAN SHE THOUGHT.

Sasha's eyes grew wide.

"I need to talk to you," she called, then broke away from the crowd.

Not Sasha, she thought as she pushed her way through the throng of photographers. Why did it have to be Sasha? Arlo used her cane to sweep the people from side to side. Still thanks to her cast, she was not as fast as Sasha even if he was wearing four-inch heels.

"Sasha!" she called again, keenly aware of all the flashes going off around her and the crowd's attention shifting from the theater to the woman in red taking mincing steps down the street with Arlo hobbling behind. She just wanted to talk. She just wanted to ask Sasha about the letter. Why he had lied? She just wanted him to prove that he was innocent.

But he was fleeing.

And she was afraid that he was guilty.

Arlo hadn't gotten a good look at his shoes, only noting very quickly that they were tall. But what were the odds that he would be wearing the same pair today?

She hurried her steps, but she was falling behind. Somehow she remained on her feet as Helen, Camille, and Fern all passed her, each holding the hem of her dress up so they could speed past. Truth was, none of them were running very quickly, age, broken limbs, and full-length formal gowns a hindrance to all.

"Arlo!" She turned as Mads came up next to her. She was still running as much as she could run with a cane and a cast. He walked next to her, his breathing effortless.

"That's Sasha," she said, leaving out any explanation. "I think he might have lost the heel cap in the inn. We need to talk to him."

"*I* need to talk to him," Mads corrected.

Arlo stopped, holding her side. Man, she really needed to start running again. Okay, maybe she needed to start first.

As she watched, Mads passed the book club and captured Sasha by one arm. Sasha stumbled and nearly fell, saved from splaying across the sidewalk by the police chief's firm grasp.

Camille reached into her handbag and pulled out a set of handcuffs. "Do you need these?"

Mads just shook his head and walked Sasha back to the red carpet.

Cameras continued to flash all around, and Arlo was fairly certain the whole thing was being filmed. She hoped so. Not that she wanted to see herself hobbling after Sasha, but she definitely wanted to watch Mads chase after him again. It was a pretty sight, watching Mads do his thing.

"I need to talk to you," Mads said.

"I didn't mean to," Sasha said. Tears were running down his cheeks, ruining once-perfect mascara and smearing his eyeliner under his eyes. "I loved him."

"You don't have to say anything right now," Mads said. He pulled a card out of his pocket as one of the deputies came and slapped their handcuffs on Sasha's wrists.

With an expression that could only be described as disappointed, Camille placed her own cuffs back into her bag.

Arlo couldn't help but notice how the cold steel of the handcuffs looked against the delicate rhinestone bracelets Sasha wore.

"You have the right to remain silent," Mads read.

"It was an accident. He told me that he would not stop. He was going to ruin *Missing Girl*. And if he did—" Sasha broke off tears still flowing.

"You have a right to an attorney," Mads said.

"I do not need attorney," he said. "Alive in American prison is better than dead in Chechnya."

Arlo could tell that Mads wanted to get him out of there as soon as possible. Bystanders were still snapping pictures, video cameras were still running, and the whole ordeal would most likely take up half of the segment on *Entertainment Tonight*. It was a fiasco and not at all what they had planned for the movie premiere.

"May I have your attention please." Veronica Tisdale raised her arms, and everyone's attention turned toward her. She looked lovely tonight, close-cropped hair framing a beautifully made-up face. Shining diamond earrings. A magnificent dress of flowing lavender that made her skin look even darker and showed off her stunning figure. "I hope you enjoyed our excitement tonight. And I'd like to thank chief of police Mads Keller for joining in the fun. Let's all hear it for Mads." Veronica started clapping, and everyone else joined in.

Mads handed Sasha off to one of the deputies and gave a slight bow. Then he muttered something to the other law enforcement officer.

For a split second, Arlo was confused. And then she realized what Veronica was doing. Instead of allowing Sasha's arrest to ruin the movie premiere, Veronica was pretending it was some sort of publicity stunt. Now that was thinking on your feet. And that was something Veronica was very good at doing. "Now hurry along, the movie is about to start."

A round of applause and cheers and whistles rose from the crowd.

"No!" A cry rang out. "You're supposed to announce the winner of the lookalike competition." Missy Severs stepped forward. "The Alayna Adams Lookalike Contest."

Had Arlo not just seen Alayna make her way into the theater, she would have thought the starlet was standing right there in front of her.

"Right," Veronica sighed.

"It's me," Missy said. "It's got to be me." There was a wobbly tone in her voice, and it made her seem a little off-balance. Like she was slipping down an emotional slope toward unhinged. "I came all this way. I'd do anything for Alayna. Anything!"

Arlo stopped. Everyone stopped. There was a chilling note in her words.

And then it all clicked into place.

When she had seen Sasha tonight, she had thought that he had been the woman in red when the whole time it had been...

"Mads!" Arlo called. "Someone get Mads."

"I'm on it," she heard Fern say. She couldn't take her gaze from Missy. The fan club president was having her fifteen minutes of fame, and she was loving it. Flashbulbs exploded around her. Folks had their phones out videoing the scene as she spread her arms wide. "You should be thanking me," Missy was saying. "That nasty man came here and said he was going to ruin everything. The whole movie, but I couldn't let that happen to Alayna. To her career. To my career. I couldn't let him ruin the movie."

Arlo was grateful that she was one of the few who truly understood what Missy was talking about. She supposed that they believed that she was responsible for some other part of the program. Not a man's death. But as far as Arlo was concerned, it was close enough to a confession for her. And there were witnesses. And video recordings all around.

"Without me, none of this would be possible!"

Arlo just hoped she kept talking until Mads came back. She was certain he would need to talk to Sasha sometime tonight, find out his side of the story, but the killer...

"What is it?" He came up next to her in the crowd.

Arlo had never been so happy to see him in all her life. "Sasha didn't do it," Arlo explained. "Missy did. Petro was going to ruin her gig, and she killed him for it."

"How do you—"

"Just arrest her," Arlo told him. "Before she stops talking and decides to run."

As if on cue, Missy looked over, saw Mads standing there, and fled.

....

Arlo was torn between going back to the police station with Mads and going into the theater to watch the premiere. It seemed somehow anticlimactic to watch the movie after what had just happened, but she seemed to be alone in that thought process. She supposed the majority of the crowd had no idea what had transpired in front of the theater this evening, but by tomorrow, the whole country would be talking.

So she allowed herself to be swept along into the theater and down to the seats that had been reserved for her, Chloe, Fern, Camille, and Helen.

"This is so exciting," Fern said. "Aren't you excited?"

Someone in the row behind them shushed her, and Fern turned around and gave them a look. "Don't you shush me, Justin Carmichael. I know your grandmother."

Arlo thought she heard Justin mutter, "I'm thirty-four," before Fern turned back around and harrumphed.

Camille shifted her handbag in her lap and set her copy of *Missing Girl* on top of it. "I'm ready," she said. "I'm going to mark every place where the movie is different than the book."

Heaven help them all.

"How are you going to do that in the dark?" Arlo asked.

Just about that time, they lowered the lights to begin the movie.

Camille dug out her cell phone and turned on the flashlight as the master of ceremonies walked out onto the stage. He introduced himself and took the applause and then told everyone to turn off their cell phones.

"Dang it," Fern said.

"Ditto," said Camille.

"I got an idea," Arlo returned, whispering to the three of them. "How about you just watch the movie tonight, and tomorrow, you can discuss all the differences like a book club should."

Chloe grinned. "Now there is an idea."

....

Monday was almost as hectic as Saturday or even Sunday. With the exception of a murder arrest.

But anybody who hadn't read *Missing Girl* last year and who hadn't bought it before the movie premiere had definitely come in on Monday to make sure they had a copy. Arlo watched book after book walk out of the store with a satisfied smile on her face. They might not ever know if Wally truly wrote *Missing Girl* or if Inna had been lying about the whole thing. Arlo herself might not appreciate the style in which the book was written, but it was definitely popular.

And that made *Under the Buttonwood Tree* all the more desirable. Veronica never said if she thought Inna might have written it instead of Wally. Whatever her thoughts were, she wasn't sharing them with anyone Arlo knew. That evening Arlo fell into bed and went to sleep almost immediately, sleeping better than she had in the weeks leading up to the movie premiere. Even her ankle kept quiet, and she was allowed to rest fully. She supposed she was also a little more comfortable knowing that there wasn't a murderer running around Sugar Springs. Not that she would consider Missy a standard murderer.

"I'm not sure I understand," Camille said at Tuesday morning brunch at the inn. The guests had been served muffins and eggs and all the good things that Helen usually offered, and the book club, along with Arlo and Daisy, had gathered in the kitchen around the island. Arlo briefly wished that Chloe could be there, but it seemed the things, they were a-changin'.

The morning edition of the *Commercial Appeal* was on the counter in front of them. Headline: "Murderous Fan Threatens Movie Premiere." The article explained how Missy Severs, in her quest to keep Alayna at the top of the Hollywood heap, was willing to go to any lengths to stop Petro Chenko from ruining the premiere of *Missing Girl*. Though Petro claimed to have proof that someone else besides Wally Harrison wrote the bestseller, no proof had been produced before his untimely death.

Sasha was there at the inn as well, today decked out in his men's attire. It seemed he only dressed as a woman from time to time, which classified him as a cross-dresser. Thankfully none of the ladies asked the difference. Arlo wasn't sure how she would have explained that one. Or perhaps she simply wasn't the only one who was anxious to hear his side of the story, and all the questions of dress and gender were put on hold to learn the truth.

"I loved him," Sasha said. "And it was killing me that I thought I had killed him."

"There, there," Camille patted his hand.

Sasha had believed all along that he was the woman in red. He had dressed up that night and gone to the theater to talk to Petro. They had decided to walk up to the balcony for their visit because it seemed more romantic. Then Sasha gave him the letter telling Petro how much he loved him and how much he needed him not to blow the cover of *Missing Girl*. They had argued, and Sasha had grabbed him, leaving the bruises they had all saw. But he had left. He had torn the love letter he had written to Petro in half and walked away. The following day when he had heard about Pedro's death, Sasha convinced himself that Petro had taken his own life and it had been entirely his fault. The guilt and remorse was eating him up inside.

"I was afraid that if Petro got too much attention from saying that

Inna wrote *Missing Girl,* and not Wallace J. Harrison, then the police would come, and I would be deported," he explained.

"Just like that show I watched," Helen said.

"What show?" Sasha asked.

Helen shook her head. "I'm glad it wasn't you," she said.

"So am I," he agreed. "But still he is gone."

What he wasn't saying was, after he left, thinking that he had inadvertently killed his lover and his friend, Missy had come out of the shadows where she had been lying in wait. She had used her martial arts training to snap Petro's neck. No one told Sasha that if he had stayed around or gone for help instead of running off into the night, Petro might have lived. Then again, Missy might have killed them both. She was just that kind of obsessed.

But the thing that kept running around in Arlo's brain was Sasha's words at the premiere: "better off alive in American prison than dead in Chechnya." That was no life for anyone. And the idea of such hate and discrimination filled her with sadness. She had been raised to believe to each his own, and though she herself had not adapted to her parents' style of living, they didn't question her desires or her right to seek the life that she wanted by putting down roots in Sugar Springs. She had never realized just how lucky she was in that until today.

"So that's it," Helen said. "Mystery solved."

"What about the bed being made and the letter found in Petro's room?" Daisy asked.

"I did that," Sasha said. "I could not help it. I miss him so. Then I heard a noise from hallway. So I go out window."

"And on the way in, you snagged your shoes on the flagstone out front?" Daisy asked.

Sasha nodded.

"They always say the shoes are the most important thing," Camille said.

Everyone thoughtfully agreed.

He nodded at them all and grabbed the suitcase he had left by the door. "Thank you for allowing me to stay in your lovely home."

Helen grabbed him by the shoulders and hugged him close. "You come back anytime, you hear?" Her voice was thick with tears. "I'll always have a room for you."

Sasha nodded against her shoulder. "I will."

Not willing to be left out, the other two book club members slid from their stools and made their way over to hug him one by one.

Arlo smiled and gave the man a small wave goodbye.

"I wish he could have stayed," Fern said. "He needs good support right now."

That part was true, but they all knew that Sasha Gorky would struggle in a town the size of Sugar Springs. He would stand out far too much. He needed some place larger, with more diversity and understanding, but maybe soon…someday real soon…

Daisy picked up the copy of the paper and studied the picture on the front. Missy Severs with her arms open wide, obviously mono-loguing to the onlooking crowd. "So if Missy admitted to killing Petro, and Sasha wrote the letter and made the bed up in Petro's room, who messed with all the things at the theater?"

"The ghosts," Fern said unapologetically.

"There are no ghosts," Camille said gently.

"I wouldn't be so sure of that," Helen said. "I found out last night that the movie company had thought foul play was at hand so they installed cameras in the theater to expose the culprits."

"When was this?" Fern asked, obviously offended. She didn't like having her ghost theory tested with something as uninspiring as technology.

"Right after Petro was killed," Helen replied.

"That long ago?" Fern screeched. "And you're just now telling us?"

Helen shrugged. "I just found out."

"So you're telling us that the movie company had video of all the accidents?" Arlo said.

"That's exactly what I'm saying," Helen said. "And there's nothing on the footage that shows who cut the ropes or knocked over the paint. Nothing."

Fern sat back with a satisfied smile. She crossed her arms and nodded. "Ghosts."

Arlo wasn't sure the supernatural was involved, but without any proof one way or the other...

"Thank you for a lovely stay," Veronica said, coming into the kitchen, wheeling a suitcase behind her.

"You're leaving?" Helen said. She looked like a child who had just been told that Santa wasn't real. "First Sasha, and now you?"

"It's time to go back to New York," Veronica said with a smile.

Strange, but Arlo had kind of gotten used to having Veronica Tisdale around. Too bad that she was such a New Yorker; she would be a great addition to their little town.

"Be careful," Helen said. She reached out a hand to shake, and when Veronica took it, Helen pulled her into a quick hug.

How do you say, *Sorry for believing that you were a murderer when you really weren't?*

Veronica patted Helen's back uneasily, then pulled away. Such a New Yorker.

Arlo supposed, with Veronica, those words weren't necessary.

"Take care," Veronica said with a small wave.

"Hey, V," Fern started. "If you get some galleys of Wally's new book, you know that we can help you with it. You know, beta readers, check for mistakes. Camille taught English for years."

"I haven't decided what to do with Wally's book yet." She said the words, but no one believed her. Arlo supposed Veronica had her own reasons for lying. And they might never know why.

"But if it's fantastic," Arlo said. Perhaps she loved books a little too much, but sometimes it seemed as if it didn't matter who wrote what—only that it got written. What was a story if it was never told?

"It is fantastic," Veronica said.

"You should share it with the world," Arlo replied. Their eyes met, and an understanding passed between them.

"I'll give it some thought," Veronica said. Then with a small wave, she disappeared down the hall.

"I'll give it some thought?" Fern said. "What does that mean?"

Arlo shrugged. "It means she'll give it some thought."

Can't Judge a Book by Its Murder

1

THIS WAS THE LAST THING SHE NEEDED.

Arlo Stanley hurried around the building, barely missing the crumbling spot at the edge of the street. Her foot twisted, and a sharp pain shot from her toes up to her ankle. This was not the day to break in new shoes. And heels at that. Now she had a bum ankle to add to the equation. But she had already been dressed for work when the police called.

A dead body! Right there on the sidewalk! Directly in front of her bookstore!

Things like this didn't happen in their little town. Just. Didn't. Happen.

She could hardy grasp it. Yes, people died, but not on Main Street. At least not as long as she had lived in Sugar Springs. It was unthinkable.

And to make matters worse, this weekend was important to the residents of Sugar Springs and all the Main Street merchants. This weekend was the Tenth Annual All-School Class Reunion. Not many people usually came out for that sort of thing, just a few locals and whoever happened to be in the area. But this year they had a special guest, the most famous person ever to leave Sugar Springs, Mississippi: Wallace J. Harrison. Known as Wally to those who had graduated with him, he was an upcoming star in the mystery-suspense genre with ten consecutive weeks on the *New York Times* Best Seller list. Wally was a national sensation. And he was back in town.

Arlo had managed to convince Wally's assistant that he should do a signing at her newly opened bookstore. She was even going to host a special Sunday opening for the event. Now the store was currently sectioned off with bright-yellow police tape.

She picked up her pace, mincing along and trying not to grimace in pain. She needed to get to her shop as quickly as possible, but City Ordinance 52-B stated that all shop employees had to park in the alley behind their stores to allow for ample parking in the front for their paying customers. Joni, the town's petite meter maid—sorry, "traffic specialist"—was something of a stickler when it came to Main Street. So Arlo's slightly dented, vintage VW Rabbit was parked in the alley behind her shop.

Arlo groaned when she saw the crowd of people in front of her store. It might be 9:00 a.m. on Friday, but everyone was already out and about. No one was looking at the new display she had created of Wally's book along with choice murder weapons, making her window resemble an extra-large game of *Clue*. They were staring at the body. The one she could just see through their shuffling feet. Not quite a body, more a tangle of arms and legs, grotesquely twisted as if this poor soul had jumped from the third-story rooftop and fallen to the sidewalk below. Not just a death, but a possible suicide.

Arlo stumbled. A body. A real live dead body. On the sidewalk in front of her store. Goose bumps skittered across her skin. This was nothing like watching crime TV or reading about a death in the latest mystery. This was something altogether different.

There was one resident who wouldn't get to engage in the weekend festivities. Though she didn't know who it was. When the police had called, dispatch hadn't told her the identity of the person, only that it was a man and she needed to get down there fast. But Sugar Springs wasn't a big place. There wasn't any doubt Arlo would know the person who lay there on the sidewalk. Maybe she had even sold them a book. The thought was sad and sobering.

Yet she couldn't continue to stand there. She had to be professional, move forward, find out why this person felt the need to fling himself from the roof. See what needed to be done next. Keeping focus would help her handle the ordeal. At least she hoped it would.

Arlo tugged on the tails of her button-down shirt and smoothed her palms over the sides of her gray dress slacks. She pushed her waist-length, chocolate-brown hair over her shoulders and straightened her back. One deep breath in and she started forward.

"Excuse me." She nudged past Dan the grocer, Phil who owned the video store next door, Joyce the florist from across the street, and Delores the gum-smacking clerk from the jewelry store down the way. Arlo didn't bother with the niceties; she simply pushed through. She had to talk to Mads, the chief of police. She had to have him clear up this…mess? Disaster? *Crime scene.*

"Mads." She greeted him on a rush of air, then stopped when she got a good look at the body. "Is that…?"

He nodded, his normally stern face grim.

"But…" The one word was all she could manage. She looked back to the twisted form.

Wally Harrison lay dead at their feet.

....

Arlo's ears began to hum as Chief Matthew "Mads" Keller shooed everyone away from the body. "Go on now," he said.

Mads, so nicknamed from his high school football days, crossed his arms so everyone would know he wasn't budging. Most turned and trudged back to their stores, spinning around once or twice as if to make sure the scene was still the same, that their eyes weren't playing tricks on them.

"Do you think he jumped?" Jason Rogers, Mads's first officer, nudged the body with the toe of one boot.

"Would you stop violating my crime scene?" Mads growled.

Jason held up both hands and backed away. "Sorry, big-city cop."

Mads rolled his eyes.

Arlo rocked in place, staring in horror. Wally Harrison was dead. In front of her store. And dead.

"Well?" Jason asked.

Mads squatted down next to the body and used the end of his pen to lift the baseball cap from in front of Wally's face.

"The Yankees," Jason scoffed. "Of course he liked the Yankees. He left here and got all big-time on us. Too good to root for the Braves."

Mads let the cap fall back into place. Arlo knew he wanted to say something to Jason, but he was too controlled for that. One day though…one day he was going to blow. She hoped she was around to see it.

People continued to walk past, pretending to be shopping as usual, but slowing down to take in as much of the scene as they could.

The crime scene. In front of her store.

She had to get ahold of herself.

"Did he?" she finally asked. "Kill himself?"

It was a stupid question. Why would a man like Wally Harrison kill himself? He had a successful life. He was raking in the dough from his book; he was handsome. Once upon a time, he had been everything in their small town. He wasn't the geek who made it big. He was the golden boy, the one that got away. The one who would put Sugar Springs on the map if he ever admitted to being born there.

Well, Mads could have had that kind of life too, if he hadn't blown out his knee in the first game of the AFC playoffs his third season in the NFL. After that, he became a cop in Memphis and eventually made his way back home to Sugar Springs.

"Looks that way," Mads said on a breath of a sigh.

"Arlo."

She turned at the sound of her name. Chloe Carter stood in the doorway of the store they shared. Her face was a contorted mask of disbelief and horror with a little disgust thrown in for variety. After all, there was a strange past between Chloe and Wally, but that was a long time ago.

"Have you been in there all morning?" Arlo asked.

Chloe ran the "more" of Arlo and Chloe's Books & More, which included a coffee bar, cake counter, unique gifts, and fine chocolates. She had, on occasion, been known to offer flowers, but that had given Joyce at Blooming Blooms an apoplexy and so Chloe had dropped the idea before the roses even wilted.

Chloe nodded, but before she could say anything, a loud voice rang out, bouncing off the Civil War–era brick that lined Main Street. *"Bozhe miy!"* Inna Kolisnychenko, Wally's trophy assistant approached from the end of the block. Her thick Ukrainian accent added a hard edge to every word she said. "What is going on here?"

"Ms. Kolisnychenko." Mads stood and Arlo could tell by the look on his face that he would rather be anywhere but there, anywhere but telling this woman that her employer was dead—most likely by his own hand. Arlo had to give Mads points for correctly pronouncing Inna's name though.

"Is that—?" She stopped, almost as if posing, as she stared at the body on the sidewalk, one hand on her hip as she bit her lip in confusion. She was a study in beauty.

Inna was statuesque, with dark hair and a pouty mouth, like a Ukrainian Jane Russell, but she carried herself more like a half-asleep Marilyn Monroe. Though she was much taller than most men, including her boss, she had a tendency to make them want to take care of her. There was something a little helpless about her. At least that's what Arlo thought Inna wanted people to see. Arlo wasn't sold on Inna's presentation, though she wasn't certain why.

Inna wore her deep-plum-colored wrap dress like an Amazonian queen. She had paired it with platform stilettos that gave her another four and a half inches easy. In those shoes, she was nearly as tall as Mads. Her exotic blue eyes seemed almost impossible in her face, as if they could see straight through to a person's secrets, to their soul.

She was more than beautiful, a fact Inna already knew. And anyone who knew Wally knew Inna, the trophy assistant. Too beautiful to be much more than arm candy, Inna probably pulled in more in a week than Arlo had all last year.

The strange thing was Daisy, Wally's wife, was even more stunning than Inna, leaving the average person to wonder why Wally was fooling around. And the average person did know about his affair…or *affairs*, plural. He had all but admitted his dallying with Inna on *Good Morning America*. Everyone knew that she was nothing more than ornamentation. That much was obvious in her lack of skills, other than the savvy way she tucked her hair behind her left ear.

Wally's wife, on the other hand…

"Oh. My. Gawd." Daisy James-Harrison stood at the end of the block, fingers pressed to her mouth, but not so hard as to smudge her lipstick. Her kelly-green dress set off her blond hair and brown eyes to utter perfection.

Then Arlo remembered why the woman was there. Daisy was going to inspect the store and give Arlo the final instructions on how Wally liked his book signings set up. A job that Inna should be performing. But now…

"Mrs. James-Harrison…" Arlo breathed, completely unsure of what she was going to say. She felt like she needed to say something, but what? No one had taught her anything about this in business school.

"Is that…?" Daisy looked hard at the man lying on the ground at the officer's feet.

ABOUT THE AUTHOR

Amy loves nothing more than a good book. Except for her family…
and homemade tacos…and maybe nail polish. Even then, reading
and writing are definitely high on the list. After all, Amy is an award-
winning author with more than forty novels and novellas in print.

Born and bred in Mississippi, Amy is a transplanted Southern
belle who now lives in Oklahoma with her deputy husband, their
genius son, and three very spoiled cats.

When she's not creating happy endings or mapping out her latest
whodunit, she's usually following her teen prodigy to guitar con-
certs, wrestling matches, or the games for whatever sport he's into
that week. She has a variety of hobbies, including swimming (a.k.a.,
floating around the pool), any sort of craft, and crocheting, but her
favorite is whatever gets her out of housework.

She loves to hear from readers. You can find her on Facebook,
Amazon, BookBub, and Goodreads. And for more about what
inspires her books, check out her pages on Pinterest. For links to the
various sites, go to her website: AmyWritesRomance.com. Or feel
free to email her at amylillard918@gmail.com.

OH,
HAYATO
...

YOU'RE
...

...GOING
TO TAKE
OVER
THE SHOP,
AREN'T
YOU?

NO
WAY.

MENU 29   (Read the entire volume--all of it!--then please come back to read this.)
The cover illustration complements the illustration of the first chapter in Volume 4. It's the part where
Hayato explains why he wants to become a pastry chef. I had drawn that one with him looking straight
ahead, and another one in which his eyes are averted when he admits that he has given up on his dream.
Oddly, both of them were chosen as the first chapter cover illustrations in the collected manga version.
It's like this manga has a mind of its own.
    Well, I guess when you try to plan things a certain way, they tend to go wrong!
I borrowed a design that was in a manga by my friend, Sakura Konjou, for the shirt Hayato wears in this
volume. But my drawings look so off... Hmm. Konjou-san really has a great sense of design. I really like her. ♥♥
    This volume is an important one, so I've been careful to take time with the drawings.
  I really had a hard time from around this chapter on. I look back on Volume 5 and I get exhausted.
   It's not that I hate it, though. Hana's father seems to suspect Hayato's real intentions, doesn't he?
            At Oikawa High, there's cleanup during lunch break.

YEAH.

I PUT IT DOWN ON MY FUTURE PLANS SHEET FOR SCHOOL.

AND WE DISCUSSED IT DURING THE HOME VISIT.

7

MIX VEGETABLE 05

I have so few lines in this one.

We get to roast sweet potatoes too!

Mixed Vegetables Volume 5

Yay!

...LET'S GET BACK TO WORK. WE CAN TALK ON THE WAY HOME.

IT'S FOR...

...THE FOUNDING GRAND-FATHER...?

"I AM."

THAT'S WHAT HAYATO SAID.

... SNF ...

Here, give me your bag.

READY TO GO HOME?

HAYA- TO...

11

GOOD NIGHT.

HANA, WHAT'S ...?

COME INSIDE NOW.

HANA?

WELCOME HOME.

SQUINCH

17

NEVER MIND...

18

MORNING.

OF ALL DAYS...

MORNING, HANA.

GOOD MORNING.

NOTHING.

NO, NOTHING.

HANA, DID SOMETHING HAPPEN BETWEEN YOU AND HYUGA?

Cleaning up

THERE'S NOTHING I CAN DO.

POUND CAKE

SA BUTTER POUND AKE PAN

Thanks.

Okay.

OKAY, WE'LL CLEAN UP IN HERE, SO YOU CAN JUST GO STRAIGHT TO CLASS AFTER THAT.

I'M GOING TO TAKE THE INGREDIENTS BACK TO THE TEACHER'S OFFICE.

REALLY?

Blackboard and ingredients monitor

...

Umm...

...

Cleanup time has passed, and she already changed

WHUH?!

OH...

MATSU-YAMA, MATSU-YAMA.

FWP

HOW NICE...

I WONDER IF HAYATO...

I-I'M SORRY, MATSUYAMA.

I WISH...

...OPENS UP TO MATSU-YAMA?

OH, IT'S OKAY...

...I HAD BEEN LIKE YOU, MATSU-YAMA.

But he's crying.

NO, NOT THAT.

SNORF!

LIKE A NINJA?

I wouldn't mind it either.

I MADE HIM CRY!

I MEANT I WISH I COULD HAVE BEEN A FRIEND THAT HAYATO FELT COMFORTABLE CONFIDING IN.

JUST THE OPPOSITE, ACTUALLY.

ASHITABA-SAN...

...DID HAYATO SAY SOMETHING TO YOU?

HE DIDN'T TELL ME ANYTHING.

WELL...

SIDE DISH Mixed Vegetables 1

SO, HERE I GO!

ALL RIGHT, I'M GOING TO TALK ABOUT FOOD AGAIN.

AFTER ALL, THIS MANGA IS ABOUT FOOD.

THANKS TO ALL OF YOU, WE'VE REACHED VOLUME 5.

My hair is growing longer.

HELLO, IT'S ME, KOMURA! THANK YOU FOR READING *MIXED VEGETABLES 5*.

ARE YOU THE TYPE TO EAT THE THINGS YOU LIKE MOST FIRST?

OR DO YOU LEAVE THEM TILL LAST?

I'VE BEEN FRUSTRATED SO MANY TIMES.

GROANN

I THINK I'LL JUST EAT MY FAVORITE BITS FIRST!

Even steaks, I'll start right at the center.

...I HAVE A HABIT OF LOOKING AT THAT LAST MORSEL AND SUDDENLY FEELING FULL.

I can't eat another bite...

URR PP

HOW-EVER...

SQUINT

I LEAVE THEM UNTIL THE LAST. AFTER ALL, I LIKE TO END IT WITH THE TASTES I LOVE.

I pace myself and leave that perfect piece for last...

...to savor the moment. ♥

menu.30

EXCUSE ?

...

LIKE, THAT OUR DREAMS WERE DIFFERENT.

BUT THAT DOESN'T REALLY MATTER.

...I WANTED AN EXCUSE.

BUT...

menu 30

The cover illustration for this chapter is similar to the one I drew for Chapter 17 in Volume 3. In that illustration Hayato is supporting Hana. But this time Hana is leaning backwards, so she's now supporting Hayato. From the very beginning, these two have been opposites, but their feelings have been reflected in one another. They approached each other with the same motives, they nurtured the same emotions, they experienced the same doubts, so I think even when Hana first looked back on their relationship, Hayato was doing the same thing. That's also why when Hana's deception came to light, they were able to get together and really understand each other. It's like learning to walk all by yourself! Scary!

Usually for flashbacks I outline the cells with two fine lines, but for the scenes with Grandpa I subconsciously used dark outlines. This was done automatically. Hayato has strong feelings for his grandfather because I, too, loved my grandpa. When I told my grandfather that I wanted to become a manga artist, he declared, "To be a manga artist, you have to be talented like Osamu Tezuka." Get serious--that man's a god, Gramps!

Still, I was able to become a manga artist and I wish my grandpa could have read my manga.

36

... MY GRANDPA.

HE WAS SORT OF LIKE YOUR DAD.

LEAVING THE SHOP IN MY CARE...

...WAS SOMETHING HE LOOKED FORWARD TO MORE THAN ANYTHING ELSE.

HE CHERISHED THE SHOP.

AND HE LOVED HIS WORK.

"HAYA-TO!"

"HAYA-TO..."

SUCH A GOOD BOY! ♡♡♡

BUT...

...I LOVED CAKES TOO.

HEY, THAT'S NOT A FAIR QUESTION.

GRAMPS!

WOULDN'T IT BE GREAT...

...TO HAVE YOU STANDING NEXT TO ME AT THE COUNTER?

Grandpa Hyuga, you look so different now.

Whuh?

HEE♡

LOOK AT ME. AT THIS AGE, I HAVE A NEW DREAM.

AFTER ALL...

...I NEVER THOUGHT...

...SOME-THING LIKE THIS WOULD HAPPEN TO US.

THAT WAS MY LAST CHANCE...

...TO TELL HIM.

"SOMEDAY"...

...WILL...

...NEVER COME.

SIDE DISH Mixed Vegetables 2

DOES EVERYONE LIKE CHEESE?

CHEESE

...GET THE IMPULSE TO LEARN EVEN MORE ABOUT CHEESE.

Maybe I'm ready to try unusual cheeses.

AND THAT'S WHY SOMETIMES I...

Cheese that's a bit burnt.

IT'S SO IRRESISTIBLE!

I LOVE CHEESE! ON PIZZA AND GRATIN.

Cheese all melted and gooey.

...SO CHEESELIKE!!

I'VE HEARD THAT NAME OFTEN ENOUGH, AND THAT SHAPE IS...

AND AT SUCH TIMES, I ALWAYS REACH FOR CAMEMBERT.

BUT I'LL PROBABLY DO THE SAME THING AGAIN. **I'M SURE OF IT.**

Oh, no no no. This mold. I can't take it.

Camembert is a mold-ripened cheese.

I WONDER HOW MANY TIMES I'LL MAKE THE SAME MISTAKE WITHOUT LEARNING MY LESSON?

BUT HUMANS ARE SUCH SAD CREATURES. WE FORGET PAST MISTAKES SO QUICKLY. OR PERHAPS, WE REMEMBER THEM, BUT THINK "THIS TIME, IT'LL BE OKAY." AND WE OVERESTIMATE OURSELVES.

Huh? Really?

AND I'LL GO ON LIVING, BELIEVING THAT SOMEDAY I'LL ENCOUNTER A CHEESE I CAN HANDLE. HOW SAD.

menu.31

THERE'S NO ONE...

...I WANT TO HAVE TASTE ONE OF MY CAKES.

NOT ANY-MORE.

menu 31   With the sudden turn of events, I'm sure some of you thought, "Is it over?" But I just felt it was time I let Hayato release some of his tension. Hayato can't cry unless Hana cries. He's got a lot of pride, doesn't he? But after he released some of his pent-up emotion, I think Hayato had the most peaceful expression yet. Hana won't be happy if she gives up on Hayato, but it sure is difficult to deal with death. I'm a novice, myself. However, MV will continue, although the two will have to overcome a few more hardships. By the way, I once dried a screentone--which was first submerged in whiskey and water--and tried to paste it, but it didn't work! It got too wrinkled! I didn't fix it, though. Memories, memories. As for kibinago and hammerhead sharks, I did a bit of collaborating with Sango Tsukishima who did Ruu no Paradaisu for Margaret Comics. The popular Ruupara is now in tankobon (graphic novel) format and on sale! I bought one too!

I CAN'T COMPETE AGAINST SOMEONE SO DEAR TO HAYATO.

THERE'S NOTHING I CAN DO...

HIK KUP

I-I HAVEN'T CRIED IN SO LONG...

HIKKUP

SIGH...

?

HIK-KUP

EVERY-
ONE...

...IS
HAPPY
FOR
US.

ALL RIGHT,
HANA-CHAN,
LET'S DRESS
YOU UP IN
A PRETTY
KIMONO
TODAY. ♡

a pretty kimono!
Yes!

He revived.

I'M
SO
GLAD.

I KNEW
YOU
WOULD.

Y-YOU
LOOK
NICE
IN A
KIMONO...

THROB

GASP

ERR
...
...NOTHING.

WHAT'S
THE
MATTER?

Heh

MINE.

I DON'T KNOW ABOUT THAT COMPARISON.

It's not sour.

ERR...

...IT'S SORTA LIKE SHARI, SWEET AND SOUR.

BLUSSSh

O-OKAY....

...BACK TO WORK, BACK TO WORK.

ZWOOP

HMM? I'M CUTTING SHARI.

I've never seen you do that.

WHAT ARE YOU DOING, HAYATO?

LEAN

I ASKED IF I COULD DO IT.

BUT IT'S QUITE HARD TO BLEND THE SUSHI VINEGAR AND RICE PROPERLY.

I'M NOWHERE CLOSE TO...

...MAKING THE KIND OF SHARI THEY'LL USE IN THE SHOP.

YES!

HANA-CHAN! ♡

DELI-CIOUS!

Three times over!

...!!

OH, I'M GLAD.

OHHH! WHAT IS IT?!

MNCH

I WAS GOING TO PUT IT ON THE MENU TONIGHT.

I made tempura with it.

I GOT SOME REALLY FRESH KIBINAGO.

Maybe I'll make shioyaki too.

HA-YATO...

...SUDDENLY SEEMS EAGER TO LEARN.

YUMI♥

I also made it sashimi-style with bainiku sauce.

77

SIDE DISH Mixed Vegetables 3

CHEESE! PART TWO!

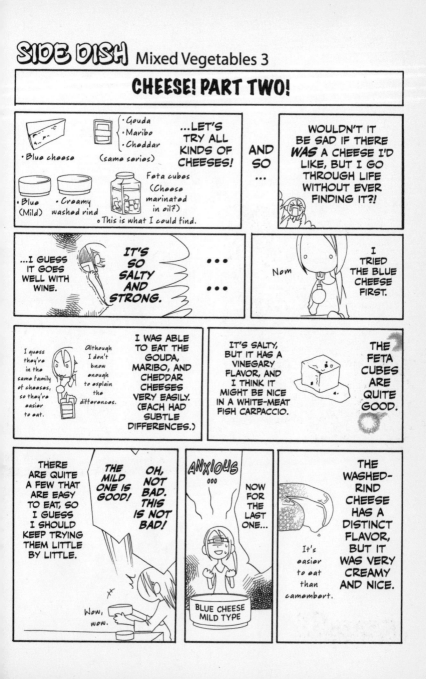

·Blue cheese

·Gouda
·Maribo
·Cheddar
(same series)

·Blue (Mild) ·Creamy washed rind

Feta cubes (Cheese marinated in oil?)

◦ This is what I could find.

...LET'S TRY ALL KINDS OF CHEESES!

AND SO...

WOULDN'T IT BE SAD IF THERE **WAS** A CHEESE I'D LIKE, BUT I GO THROUGH LIFE WITHOUT EVER FINDING IT?!

...I GUESS IT GOES WELL WITH WINE.

IT'S SO SALTY AND STRONG.

...
...

Nom

I TRIED THE BLUE CHEESE FIRST.

I guess they're in the same family of cheeses, so they're easier to eat.

Although I don't know enough to explain the differences.

I WAS ABLE TO EAT THE GOUDA, MARIBO, AND CHEDDAR CHEESES VERY EASILY. (EACH HAD SUBTLE DIFFERENCES.)

IT'S SALTY, BUT IT HAS A VINEGARY FLAVOR, AND I THINK IT MIGHT BE NICE IN A WHITE-MEAT FISH CARPACCIO.

THE FETA CUBES ARE QUITE GOOD.

THERE ARE QUITE A FEW THAT ARE EASY TO EAT, SO I GUESS I SHOULD KEEP TRYING THEM LITTLE BY LITTLE.

THE MILD ONE IS GOOD!

OH, NOT BAD. THIS IS NOT BAD!

Wow, wow.

ANXIOUS

NOW FOR THE LAST ONE...

BLUE CHEESE MILD TYPE

It's easier to eat than camembert.

THE WASHED-RIND CHEESE HAS A DISTINCT FLAVOR, BUT IT WAS VERY CREAMY AND NICE.

YOU TWO SHOULD BREAK UP.

HEHE

meh4 32

How about a cover illustration like this one?
It's a different interpretation of Hana's dilemma in Chapter 1.
But I agonized over this story. From about the previous volume on, I've been having a hard time. I mean, I need this space to explain situations that can't be fully described in the manga itself. In Volume 3, I boasted that "the way I draw manga has changed."
And it's very difficult to maintain that. In fact, it's impossible! Cripes! Also, I'm basically a pessimist and I tend to fret and obsess over things. My editor gave me an earful, and I was finally able to finish this chapter. Really, it was like Boss Osawa yelling at me.
(Smile) I hope one day that this page will be blank!
This was the first kissing scene I drew. Oh boy, I'm so bad. It's embarrassing. I'm really bad at it. Those two just went at it. How embarrassing! Ha ha ha! (Am I 12 or something?)
For this chapter, I got sushi ingredient ideas from Sushi Takahashi. Thank you very much!

AHAHA! NO, I GUESS NOT!

YOU WOULDN'T JUST SAY "OKAY" TO SOME- THING LIKE THAT.

JAB

WHAT ARE YOU SAYING, CHEF?! THERE'S NO WAY WE'D BREAK UP.

WHAT ARE YOU LAUGHING AT?

AHA- HA HA HA

HUH?! DIDN'T I COME ACROSS AS THE COMMANDING FATHER FIGURE?!

AHA- HA-HA

IT WAS SO UNLIKE YOU.

And you said it with so little force.

CHEF...

Welcome. ♡

Hana-chan, your face looks different.

Huh?! How can you tell ?!

OH, IT'S OKKA. ♡

SWSH

GOOD EVENING!

83

Extra MV

Confession.

It's very hard for me to distinguish between Grandpa and Mr. Okamoto when I'm drawing.

So I have these pointers.

Grandpa

- Hyuga eyebrows (Just like the Chef's)
- Hyuga eyes (whitish eyes) (Just like the Chef's)
- Slanted eyes (Just like the Chef's)

Okka

- Bangs →
- Curving
- Profile (aquiline nose)
- Potbelly

Also, they will never appear together in a scene. So, please try to tell them apart.

Umm, I'm really sorry.

IT'S OKAY. IT'S JUST HEAVY.

I can carry it.

HA-YATO!

LET ME HELP.

NO, I'M FINE.

BUT, LEAVE IT TO A GUY.

I'M PRETTY CONFIDENT ABOUT MY OWN STRENGTH.

...WOW.

IT DOESN'T MATTER WHAT THE CHEF THINKS.

BLSH

HE HAS RIPPED ARMS TOO.

92

IT'S
NOT...

YOU'RE
RIGHT.

...THAT
I WANT
TO BE
JUST THE
MISTRESS.

...
STRONGER
MALE
SUSHI
CHEFS, SO
I TRAINED
HARD.

I
SIMPLY
REFUSED
TO FALL
BEHIND...

I
MEAN
...
MY
STRONG
ARMS DIDN'T
COME FROM
SIMPLY
BAKING
CAKES.

...I
FULLY
INTENDED
TO TAKE
OVER AS
HEAD
CHEF.

THEN,
ONCE I
MARRIED
INTO A
SUSHI
FAMILY...

WORKING WITH HIM HAS NOTHING TO DO WITH CONTINUING TO DATE HIM.

THIS HAS NOTHING TO DO WITH THAT.

I WILL MANAGE BOTH.

THEY CAN CO-EXIST IN PERFECT HARMONY, JUST LIKE YOUR SHARI AND NETA.

GASP ...

WELL...

...IT'S A BIT TOO SOON FOR YOU TO CUT SHARI.

SIDE DISH Mixed Vegetables 4

A STORY ABOUT MAKING DESSERTS.

IN OTHER WORDS, IT'S ALL BEGINNERS' LUCK, **AND I QUIT WHILE I'M AHEAD!**

URK

That's nothing to be proud of. In fact, that's embarrassing.

THAT'S BECAUSE I RARELY MAKE THE SAME THINGS TWICE.

...I RARELY MESS UP WHEN MAKING SWEETS!

NOT TO BRAG, BUT...

Looking proud

Do it like we're on a cooking show.

PUT THE SUGAR AND WATER IN A SAUCEPAN, AND TURN ON THE BURNER!

Younger brother (loves purin) (Great at separating eggs).

Yeah!

FIRST, LET'S MAKE THE CARAMEL.

ONCE, I MADE PURIN FOR THE FIRST TIME IN TWO YEARS.

AND SO, NATURALLY, IF I MAKE SOMETHING OVER AND OVER AGAIN, I WILL FAIL SOMETIMES.

WITH CARAMEL, YOU DON'T START OUT MIXING IT CONSTANTLY, BUT WAIT A BIT UNTIL THE SUGAR STARTS TO BROWN.

It looks all powdery!

HUH ...?!

OF COURSE! I failed!

DO YOU REALLY HAVE A TEACHERS' LICENSE IN COOKING?

She has a license for nothing.

KRAK KRAK

BBL BBL BBL BBL

SCORCH SCORCH

I HAD TOTALLY FORGOTTEN HOW TO MAKE IT AND I STOOD AT THE STOVE AND STIRRED THE CARAMEL VIGOROUSLY. THEN...

GULUP GULUP

menu.33

BANNED FROM THE SHOP...?

WHAT'S GOING ON, MOM?

YOU WEREN'T AGAINST US GOING OUT.

I'M NOT TALKING ABOUT THAT.

menu 33

Okay, I had no ideas for this cover illustration.
And let me say this: I don't like to draw minute details. Can't do it!
This is about my limit! In the first place, I don't like to use rulers. (I hated desk boards too...)
In this volume, I liked how I did the boss's worried face. Speaking of this volume, each chapter
has one more page. So from Vol. 5 on, each book will have six chapters instead of seven.
However, the total number of pages won't change much, so please don't worry.
"If I fail, I'll quit the shop." I actually didn't want to use that line, but Hana said it and now I'm
in a bind. (worried) Although, I personally tend to like tests. You get to go home early and you
can scribble on the back of your notes. Please don't play soccer after eating dried kelp.
Seriously. That will really get you...I know because I've done it. The pattern on Hana's futon is
different. Probably because she's using summer futons.
It's not like I ran out of screentone or anything. Nope. Not at all. Okay, that's a lie. Sorry.

YOU FAILED YOUR MIDTERM, DIDN'T YOU?

BUT...

EVEN IF WE HAVE FINALS, WHY CAN'T WE WORK IN THE SHOP?

YOUR TEACHER TOLD ME DURING THE HOME VISIT...

...THAT WORKING IN THE SHOP MUST NOT GET IN THE WAY OF YOUR STUDIES.

YOU MIGHT BE RIGHT.

Yeah, that's true.

BUT YOU DON'T HAVE TO DO WELL IN SCHOOL TO BECOME AN ARTISAN.

111

HANA-CHAN... ...I WAS SUCH A FOOL...

NOW DON'T YOU GIVE THE TEACHER A HARD TIME OR YOU'LL HAVE TO ANSWER TO ME.

I'LL COVER FOR YOU WHILE YOU TWO STUDY UP.

You just want to kiss up to Matsuzaba Sensei.

SAKI...

UH-OH. HE LOOKS SO SORRY!

OH...

!

AFTER CLOSING WOULD WORK.

HUH.

YES!

SAKI-SAN, CAN YOU HELP US STUDY?

BUT WHAT ABOUT THE SUSHI SHOP? HAVEN'T YOU BEEN GOING?

PLEASE HELP ME!

SO YOU FINALLY REMEMBERED WE HAVE FINALS.

Sheesh.

"Sheesh" your-self!

HUH? I GO.

HUH?

TMP

OKAY! I'M OFF TO THE KITCHEN CLASS-ROOM.

TMP

IS IT...

KITCHEN 1

...REALLY HARD TODAY?

HEAVE!

＊ Today's Menu **＊**・**＊**・**＊**・**＊**
＊ ・ Ku lau jou (Sweet-sour pork)
＊ ・ Nai doufu (Milk gelatin)
＊ ・ Su mi tang
      (Chinese-style corn soup)
＊・**＊**・**＊**・**＊**・**＊**・**＊**

Hoho! ♡ Keep the compliments coming. ♡

FLIP

Wow, nice one!

Forget it.

OKAY...

...WHOEVER'S IN CHARGE OF ORDERING INGREDIENTS FOR THE NEXT CLASS NEEDS TO COME TO MY OFFICE LATER TO PICK UP THE ORDER FORM.

ITADAKI-MASU.

OKAY, LET'S HAVE A TASTE.

WE CAN GET EVERYTHING READY TOMORROW MORNING AFTER WE GET THE SUPPLIES.

YES, AND WE'RE IN CHARGE OF THE TASTING NOTES FOR THIS.

...ARE WE IN CHARGE OF CLEANUP NEXT?

MONITOR...

IF THIS HAS TO BE TURNED IN BY TOMORROW, I WON'T HAVE MUCH TIME TO STUDY TODAY.

I don't feel like drawing the plating either.

BUT THE TASTE IS A PLEASURE.

TODAY'S DISHES REQUIRED SO MANY INGREDIENTS. PUTTING ALL THE TASTING NOTES TOGETHER IS SUCH A PAIN.

COOKING NOTES

NOT ARTISTIC

SIGH

WE HAVE TWO MORE COOKING SESSIONS THIS WEEK.

Why do we have to cook before exams?

MATH AND GYM.

GYM...

Did you just eat something strange?

WHAT ARE OUR AFTERNOON CLASSES FOR TODAY?

124

...BACK HOME, ALONE.

THEN HE WALKS THE SAME DISTANCE...

HAYATO WALKS ME HOME EVERY NIGHT.

AND IT'S PRETTY FAR.

...I WANTED TO TRAIN AT HIS SHOP.

ALL BECAUSE...

...

SIDE DISH Mixed Vegetables 5

I'M RUNNING OUT OF WAYS TO SAY THIS, SO

THANK YOU!

I'M AGAIN INDEBTED TO SO MANY PEOPLE!

- MY EDITOR
- THE EDITORIAL STAFF AT *MARGARET* MAGAZINE
- SHUEISHA
- ALL THE PEOPLE AT THE SHOPS WHO LET ME DO RESEARCH
- MY FELLOW MANGA ARTISTS (THANKS TO YOU ALL, I'M ABLE TO TASTE THE FAMOUS LOCAL PRODUCTS OF SO MANY PLACES. I'M GETTING FATTER AND FATTER!)
- MY FRIENDS (IT'S HARD FOR ME TO GO OUT, BUT PLEASE KEEP INVITING ME)
- MY FAMILY (MY CAT AND DOG TOO!)

There are many prep school students who are readers. Thank you! Study hard!

AND LAST BUT NOT LEAST, **ALL OF MY READERS!**
ALL OF YOU OUT THERE WHO READ MY MANGA!
OH... I LOVE ALL OF YOU! (I CONFESSED!)
THANK YOU TO ALL OF YOU WHO TOOK TIME TO WRITE!
PLEASE BE PATIENT FOR A REPLY.

I'LL BE WAITING FOR YOUR COMMENTS, OPINIONS AND CRITICISMS!

AYUMI KOMURA

SHOJO BEAT MANGA/MIXED VEGETABLES
C/O VIZ MEDIA, LLC
P.O. BOX 77010
SAN FRANCISCO, CA 94107

ASHITABA

menu.34

MAEZAWA-SAN COLLAPSED?!

meny 34 The desserts in the cover illustration are the winning cakes from the "Autumn Cakes" entries in "Seconds!!" I thought about making it a pinup illustration of Dad Ashitaba, but I wasn't brave enough. Everyone--please give Komura some courage! I wish I had more guts... (What's that?)

Anyway, since I began MV I've been noticing uniforms at bars and restaurants. Like Hayato's uniform in this chapter. I love uniforms! (Is this leading to another confession?) I think when someone looks good in a uniform, it shows how much pride and care they take in their work. And that's why a manga artist's shabby attire is also... No? No good, huh? I'm also not good at drawing cars. I'm so bad, in fact, it's laughable. In the culinary arts department you have to take a lot of specialty classes, so you only take five regular subjects. During exams, you take a total of 12-13 tests.

LUCKILY WE DON'T HAVE ANY SPECIAL ORDERS RIGHT NOW.

UNTIL THEN, I'LL MAKE THINGS IN ADVANCE AND DO PASTRIES THAT LAST LONGER.

AND IF WE RUN OUT, WE'LL JUST CLOSE UP.

ONE WEEK...

...

THANKS FOR STAYING SO LATE, HAYATO. I'LL DRIVE YOU HOME.

Oh boy, it's already tomorrow.

ALL DONE.

OH... ...OKAY.

I'll get the car-- wait here.

HA-YATO...

...I REALLY...

IS IT OKAY?

He even gave me cakes.

...DON'T THINK I'LL COME BY HYUGA TOMORROW.

...

OF COURSE. AND I'D FEEL BETTER IF YOU GOT A RIDE.

MAEZAWA-SAN IS OUR ONLY EMPLOYEE.

HANA...

BUT HE LET ME PURSUE MY SUSHI CHEF DREAM...

I'D BEEN HELPING UNTIL JUST RECENTLY, SO DAD DIDN'T HAVE TO HIRE ANYONE ELSE.

...AND I KNOW HOW TOUGH IT'S BEEN FOR HIM AT THE SHOP.

Extra MV

In the next volume

A new character debuts

Maezawa-san!

He thoroughly recovers...

...from his bout with appendicitis

And look at the time!

An octopus clock

UH-HUH.

I SEE.

YOU'RE RIGHT.

IT'S TIME FOR ME TO HELP HIM NOW.

...NO! YOU NEED TO HELP AT HYUGA, HAYATO.

NO...

I CAN COME HELP TOO.

...THAT'S NOT DOABLE FOR THEM.

LOSING TWO WORKERS AT ONCE...

NOT GOING TO HYUGA...

How boring!

What-- Hana-chan isn't coming?!

IF YOU'RE NOT COMING TO THE SHOP, WE'LL BE GOING HOME IN OPPOSITE DIRECTIONS.

AND SPENDING LESS TIME WITH HAYATO MAKES ME SAD.

Darn it.

Can I still walk you home?

Nope.

A WEDDING CAKE?!

YES.

SEE, MY FRIEND IS GETTING MARRIED TOMORROW.

OH, THAT'S SO NICE OF YOU.

THANK YOU.

AND ALL HER FRIENDS HAVE GOTTEN TOGETHER TO THROW A WEDDING FOR HER.

TO-MORROW, HUH.

BUT JUST TODAY WE LEARNED THAT THERE WAS A MISTAKE IN THE ORDER.

I'VE RUN AROUND TO SHOP AFTER SHOP, BUT I HAVEN'T BEEN ABLE TO FIND ONE WHO CAN HELP ME.

THAT'S REALLY TOUGH.

WE HAVE ORDERS IN FOR TOMORROW. IF ONLY MAEZAWA WERE HERE...

IS IT IMPOSSIBLE?

I GUESS IT'S IMPOSSIBLE.

I CAN HELP!

HUH...

DAD...

...LET'S DO IT!

AND BESIDES, DON'T YOU STILL HAVE AN EXAM TOMORROW?

THAT'S ALL RIGHT. I'M YOUNG. ☆

...BUT HANA...

...I DON'T KNOW HOW LONG THIS WILL TAKE.

《TO BE CONTINUED》

KANKITSU LOVE

I REFUSE TO HAVE A MARRIAGE MEETING!

KAN-SAN, PLEASE DON'T START THAT AGAIN. NOT AFTER WE'VE COME ALL THIS WAY.

THE OTHERS ARE WAITING.

SIXTEEN YEARS AGO...

...BEFORE HANA WAS BORN.

GRR

OH, COME ON! WHAT CENTURY ARE YOU LIVING IN?

YOU AREN'T GETTING ANY YOUNGER, AND IT'S TIME YOU SETTLED DOWN.

LIKE I CARE.

SHE'S A VERY NICE GIRL.

SHWP!

SORRY WE'RE SO LATE.

I DON'T HAVE TIME TO GET MARRIED!

There are still tons of things I want to learn as a pâtissier.

170

FWOO...

I-I'M NOT INTERESTED!

HOW DO YOU DO?

THIS IS...

...YUZU TACHI-BANA.

I WAS GOING TO TURN IT DOWN ANYWAY.

SO IT'S BETTER IF HE'S NOT INTERESTED EITHER.

WHAT A GRUMP!

He doesn't even smile.

WELL, AT LEAST SHE KNOWS HOW TO PRONOUNCE IT.

YOU'RE ...A PÂTIS-SIER?

But, did she know it already? That makes me even less interested.

"PATEE-SHEER"? HAH!

HOW INTERESTING --A "PATEE-SHEER"?!

KAN-SAN IS A YOUNG PATEE... SHEER.

HA HA

URGH

171

Side Dish—End Notes
For those who want to know a little more about the menu.

Page 54, panel 3: Camembert
A soft, creamy cow's milk cheese from the Normandy region of France. It is aged for at least three weeks, and the older it gets, the stronger and more intense its flavor.

Page 56, author notes
Screentone:
Graphic transfer paper that is used to add texture and patterns to manga artwork.
Kibinago:
A kind of round herring that can be deep-fried or sliced and served as sashimi with a miso sauce. It's a specialty of Kagoshima Prefecture.
Ruupara:
The shortened form of *Ruu no Paradaisu* or "Ruu's Paradise," a manga by Sango Tsukishima.

Page 57, panel 3: Nigiri
A kind of sushi in which the rice is hand-molded into oblong mounds and a slice of fish is draped over it. Wasabi (see definition on the following page) is often added between the fish and rice, and sometimes the fish is secured to the rice with a thin band of nori seaweed.

Page 63, author notes: Rain Woman
In Japanese, *ame-onna*, a term often used to describe a woman who seems to bring rain with her wherever she goes.

Page 67, panel 3: Wide-apart eyes
This refers to a scene in *Mixed Vegetables* 4 in which Hanayu mentions that she likes hammerhead sharks, and Hayato takes it to mean she likes guys with wide-set eyes.

Page 75, panel 3: Shari
Sushi term for vinegared rice with *awase-zu*, a seasoning mixture comprised of vinegar, sugar and salt.

Page 76, panel 1: Cutting shari
When making sushi rice, the proper method is to "cut" the shari into the rice with a paddle rather than stirring it. This process keeps the rice grains whole and intact and brings out a sheen on the surface of the rice.

Page 77, panel 3: Tempura
A classic Japanese style of cooking that involves coating seafood and vegetables in a flour-based batter and deep-frying them.

Page 77, panel 4
Sashimi-style:
Raw fish or other food items sliced very thinly and served with a soy dipping sauce and garnishes including shiso or daikon radish.
Bainiku sauce:
A sauce made from pickled plums. The plum seed is removed, and the plum meat is mashed and mixed with vinegar and other ingredients to make a sauce. It is often served with cold tofu as a condiment.

Page 77, panel 5: Shioyaki
Japanese for "salt-grilled," *shioyaki* refers to the traditional practice of coating meat, poultry or fish in salt and grilling it.

Page 80, panel 2:
Gouda
A firm cow's milk cheese from Holland. Gouda has several varieties: young (aged between one to six months), aged (aged up to a year), smoked and Leyden, which is a spiced variety.
Maribo
A semi-hard cow's milk cheese from Denmark that is similar to Gouda. Maribo is sometimes flavored with caraway seeds, and its texture is dry with irregular holes.
Cheddar
A traditional cow's milk cheese from England. The term "cheddar" refers to the cooking process the milk undergoes to make the cheese. Cheddar flavor profiles and consistency range from mild and slightly moist to very sharp and crumbly.
Blue cheese
Blue cheese is a general classification for cheeses made from various milks (goat, cow or sheep) and introduced to Penicillium mold cultures before being aged in caves. The mold cultures bring out the bluish and greenish veins and striations typical for this kind of cheese. Blue cheeses are most frequently described as being strong and stinky, but they can also be sweet, mild or salty.

Feta
A traditional Greek cheese made from either goat or sheep's milk. Feta is cured in a saltwater brine for several months and formed into blocks. Feta can be mild and creamy or salty and crumbly.

Washed rind
A classification of cheeses that have been washed with a brine and aged. The brine can be made up of saltwater, beer, wine, brandy or grape juice. Well-known washed-rind cheeses are Taleggio, Epoissesor or Livarot.

Page 82, author notes: Boss Osawa
Boss Osawa is a professional baseball team manager.

Page 83, panel 3: Okka
A nickname or term of endearment for the name "Okamoto."

Page 88, panel 1: Hana's nosebleed
In manga it's believed that lustful feelings can give one a nosebleed.

Page 95, panel 2
Your drink:
Per the tradition of Japanese sushi establishments, Mr. Okamoto probably has a bottle of liquor labeled with his name that is kept especially for him behind the bar.
Oshibori:
A towel presented to restaurant or bar customers before meals.
Shutou:
Food that pairs well with sake. The name mixes the word for "sake" (rice wine) and "theft," the connotation being that the food is so good, it "steals" the focus from the sake. A variety of salted or highly seasoned fish is a common shutou dish.

Page 100, panel 2: Neta
The ingredient partnered with the sushi rice to make sushi. Egg, fish, octopus, etc. are all considered neta.

Page 106, panel 3: Purin
Purin is a rich, egg-based custard dessert topped with a layer of caramel. Purin is made by coating small dishes—usually high-sided ramekins—with a layer of caramel before filling with the custard mixture. The ramekins are then placed in a water bath and slowly baked. When serving,

the cooled ramekins have to be carefully inverted on a plate to ensure the caramel is on top of the desserts. In French this dessert is known as crème caramel, and in Spanish-speaking countries it is called flan.

Page 120, panel 2: Wasabi
This spicy green paste is made from Japanese horseradish root and is often served with sushi.

Page 123, panel 2:
Nai doufu
A dessert made with milk and agar (a derivative of seaweed). It can look like tofu.
Su mi tang
A Chinese soup made of sweet corn and egg with bits of chicken and/or crab.

Page 124, panel 1: Itadakimasu
A term one utters in Japan before beginning to eat. It literally means "I will partake of it" or "I receive." It's similar to saying "Bon appetit" or saying grace before a meal and expresses gratitude to all involved in preparing the meal.

Page 125, panel 4: Dashi kombu
Dried sea kelp used to make soup stock.

Page 164, panel 3: Croque-em-bouche
Literally translates from the French as "crack in mouth." This dessert is a celebratory cake frequently served at weddings. It is made by piling up profiteroles (choux pastry balls filled with cream) into a tall cone. The profiteroles are secured with caramel, and the entire cake is decorated with delicate golden threads of caramel along with sugared flowers, fruit, chocolate or slivered almonds.

Page 165, panel 1: Choux pastry
The eggy pastry used to make delicate pastries like éclairs, cream puffs, beignets, cheese gougères and profiteroles. The choux paste is piped from a pastry bag into the various shapes and baked or fried.

Page 170, title: Kankitsu Love
This is a play on words based on the Japanese pronunciation/spelling of Hanayu's parents' names. Her father's name is Kan, and the kanji for her mother's surname, Tachibana, can also be read *Kitsu*. In Japanese *Kankitsu* can refer to a type of citrus, as can Hanayu's mother's first name, Yuzu.

Volume 5 has lots of stories that are embarrassing to read over. But I reread them anyway, and I realized how hard I had worked on the drawings and how much I loved them. That's the kind of volume this is.

-Ayumi Komura

Ayumi Komura was born in Kagoshima Prefecture. Her favorite number is 22, and her hobbies include watching baseball. Her previous title is *Hybrid Berry*, about a high school girl who ends up posing as a boy on her school's baseball team.

MIXED VEGETABLES
VOL. 5
The Shojo Beat Manga Edition

STORY AND ART BY
AYUMI KOMURA

English Translation/JN Productions
English Adaptation/Stephanie V.W. Lucianovic
Touch-up Art & Lettering/Jim Keefe
Design/Yukiko Whitley
Editor/Megan Bates

VP, Production/Alvin Lu
VP, Publishing Licensing/Rika Inouye
VP, Sales & Product Marketing/Gonzalo Ferreyra
VP, Creative/Linda Espinosa
Publisher/Hyoe Narita

MIX VEGETABLE © 2005 by Ayumi Komura. All rights reserved.
First published in Japan in 2005 by SHUEISHA Inc., Tokyo.
English translation rights arranged by SHUEISHA Inc.
The stories, characters and incidents mentioned
in this publication are entirely fictional.

Printed in Canada

Published by VIZ Media, LLC
P.O. Box 77010
San Francisco, CA 94107

Shojo Beat Manga Edition
10 9 8 7 6 5 4 3 2 1
First printing, September 2009

www.viz.com

PARENTAL ADVISORY
MIXED VEGETABLES is rated T
for Teen and is recommended
for ages 13 and up.
ratings.viz.com

Full Moon

O Sagashite

By Arina Tanemura

creator of *The Gentlemen's Alliance †*

Mitsuki loves singing, but a malignant throat tumor prevents her from pursuing her passion.

Can two fun-loving Shinigami give her singing career a magical jump-start?

LAND OF *Fantasy*

MIAKA YÛKI IS AN ORDINARY JUNIOR-HIGH STUDENT
WHO IS SUDDENLY WHISKED AWAY INTO THE WORLD OF A
BOOK, *THE UNIVERSE OF THE FOUR GODS*. WILL THE
BEAUTIFUL CELESTIAL BEINGS SHE ENCOUNTERS AND THE
CHANCE TO BECOME A PRIESTESS DIVERT MIAKA FROM
EVER RETURNING HOME?

THREE VOLUMES OF THE
ORIGINAL *FUSHIGI YÛGI*
SERIES COMBINED INTO A
LARGER FORMAT WITH AN
EXCLUSIVE COVER DESIGN
AND BONUS CONTENT

EXPERIENCE
THE BEAUTY OF
FUSHIGI YÛGI WITH
THE HARDCOVER
ART BOOK

ALSO AVAILABLE:
THE *FUSHIGI YÛGI:*
GENBU KAIDEN MANGA,
THE EIGHT VOLUME PREQUEL
TO THIS BEST-SELLING
FANTASY SERIES

TAKE A TRIP TO AN ANCIENT

FUSHIGIYÛGI

FROM THE CREATOR C
ABSOLUTE BOYFRIEND
ALICE 19TH, CERES:
CELESTIAL LEGEND,
AND IMADOKI!

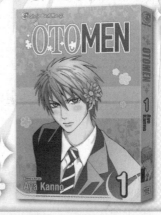

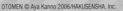